THE DEER KILLERS

THE DEER KILLERS

A Novel

Gunnard Landers

Walker and Company
New York

First published in the United States of America in 1990 by
Walker Publishing Company, Inc.

Published simultaneously in Canada by Thomas Allen & Son
Canada, Limited, Markham, Ontario.

Library of Congress Cataloging-in-Publication Data

Landers, Gunnard.
The deer killers : a novel / Gunnard Landers.
ISBN 0-8027-1134-0
I. Title.
PS3562.A4755D4   1990
813'.54—dc20   90-37346
CIP

Printed in the United States of America

2 4 6 8 10 9 7 5 3 1

THE DEER KILLERS

ONE

Her pain was immediately evident. Special Agent Reed Erickson nodded in his most friendly manner and said, "Hello." With one look he'd been captured by her frail beauty, and just as equally appalled at her prison camp air.

The woman did not reply. Instead, her eyes shifted nervously around the room. Her hands were thin, bony with tapered fingers that trembled as if she needed a drink. She wore a gold wedding ring that she twisted every few minutes with her right hand, as if to insure the simple band of gold was not lost.

Peter Ulysses Waldheim, Director of Special Agents and Reed's boss, jumped to his feet as if the Secretary of the Interior had made a surprise entrance. Peter was in his mid-fifties, a pink-faced man with grey, thinning hair and rimless bifocals. He wore a grey business suit and tie, a sharp contrast to Reed who was wearing brown trousers made of flax, a print flannel shirt, and the worn leather boots of a woodsman.

"This is Marlis Pog, from Louisiana. Marlis, this is Special Agent Reed Erickson. He's one of our best field operatives."

Reed rose and offered his hand. Marlis stared, then reluctantly reached out and touched his fingers. Her skin was cold as snow. "A real woodsman, huh? Just like Wayne." Her voice was an acid, husky mumble.

The spiteful tone puzzled Reed. He half-sat, half-leaned on Peter's window ledge looking out over the grey dirt and grime of Washington DC. Home sweet home. Who would have ever believed he could move this far from the wilds of northern Wisconsin?

The U.S. Fish and Wildlife Service for whom he worked was connected to the Department of the Interior. The Special Operations Branch mission was to initiate long term surveillance and undercover operations against commercial game violators throughout the United States from Alaska to Florida. From enforcement of the Lacey Act, which regulated importation of birds and animals and interstate traffic of game, to the Endangered Species Act, special agents became embroiled in all manner of game trafficking schemes. With more than five billion dollars to be made in world-wide game violations by big-time, sophisticated poachers, the United States saw fit to place two hundred agents in the field. It was, Reed thought sourly, a real contribution toward enforcement of the law. Of course, they did have seven thousand state conservation officers also—to cover the entire United States.

"Marlis has been through a real tragedy," Peter said in his soft whisper of a voice. His tone was such that he might have been whispering national secrets. His diplomas and decorations were framed in glass and hung on the pale yellow walls. A large portrait of Peter, his wife, and three children sat upon his desk. Two original water paintings of Western art added a bit of color. They were gatherings of men on a cattle drive and around a campfire, pictures of a male camaraderie Peter had always desired but never achieved.

"My husband, Wayne, has disappeared." Her voice had taken on a brittle edge. The look in her eyes was possessed, like those of someone trapped too long in a small cell. And yet Reed also saw harsh reason, a woman making judgments on everything she saw, including himself.

"Her husband's a conservation officer for the state of Louisiana," Peter explained. He hovered close like a heron protecting its nest, trying to lend comfort as he awkwardly waved a manicured hand toward the woman and a nearby chair.

"Was," Marlis corrected, with a tone that made the director wince as she sat down. She shifted uncomfortably as if not used to sitting still. "He's dead. They've been chasing his killers for almost a year now." Her eyes fixed on Reed as if challenging him to reveal his stripes. If she seemed insecure on the surface it was not in regard to men. She'd even had an audience with the governor and still no one had done anything.

[2]

Would Reed be any different, her attitude said. "They have some kind of violating ring where 'jacklighters' drive around on certain nights and kill fifty or a hundred deer. They cover a big area, eight or nine thousand square miles, Wayne estimated. He'd been watching these few fields they'd hit once before. One night he went out and didn't come back. The police looked everywhere. Couldn't find him, couldn't find his truck. Some people claim he ran off. I know he didn't. He was killed. By someone who lives right there in Magnolia."

"Ahh, but no witnesses or evidence," Peter said softly, as if to explain for the woman.

"It's a feeling," Marlis snapped. "I know there's no proof. But I also know Wayne's murderer is one of my neighbors. I can feel his eyes. I can smell his guilt. I just don't know who." Her voice rose to a crescendo. She stood and crossed the room, her high heels clicking on the floor. She again sat, picked up her purse, momentarily clutched it to her stomach and then set it on the floor.

Reed held up his hand, palm outward as if instructing a dog to stay, to hold exactly where she was sitting. He concealed an inner turmoil, a rage that erupted with the memory of other conservation wardens he'd known who'd been murdered in some dark and isolated field. Nationwide the enforcement of twentieth century game laws had cost more than one hundred and twenty conservation officers their lives. Out of a force of seven thousand the odds were greater than eighty percent that a conservation warden would be assaulted within the course of his career. If, overall, attitudes toward conservation were improving, in some areas of the country they still lagged far behind. In 1981, a self-styled mountain man named Claude Dallas shot two wildlife officers and then finished them off with a bullet each behind the ear—Idaho citizens saw fit only to find Dallas guilty of manslaughter. Since then five more conservation officers had been murdered. Dozens more had been assaulted. In most cities it was safer to be a street cop. Despite the bile rising in his throat, Reed spoke quietly, as if calming a wild animal. "How long ago did this happen?"

Peter Ulysses, known as P.U. to his subordinates, started to open his mouth. Reed flicked a forefinger in the air. Peter went silent.

"Six months," Marlis said. Tears welled in her eyes. Six months, and this was the first man who could understand. She fought for self control. The big, soft, pink guy, Peter something or other, hovered like a nun over a dying priest. Any second now he was going to pat her on the shoulder and she was going to explode. The other one just sat, his big brown eyes looking in her eyes, informing her he saw and he heard. He was bearded, his face weathered from the outdoors. He wore casual outdoor clothes and boots like a man who preferred comfort over appearance. He was of medium build but gave the impression of being hard, a man in control, a man who would not be rushed, a man who not only knew what he was about but had a world view as well. The presumption made Marlis flush with anger. She knew the self-confident types. Her father had been that way. Even Wayne to a degree. The whole world evolved from their point of view.

"Are you the one that would come?"

Reed tensed at the venom directed in his direction. Why had this become so personal? He looked at P.U. "I haven't been apprised of any operation. Can we get in on this, Peter?"

P.U. waved both hands as if to caution Reed to back away. "Mrs. Pog came here with the idea that one of our agents might go undercover. She, ah, wants someone to move into her home with her."

"Pretend to be my boyfriend," Marlis said. "Wayne worked with an agent several years ago that did undercover work. Everything's changing in Louisiana. But it's still a closed society. If you weren't born there you don't get in. I was born there. Wayne was born there. I can provide a way."

"As I explained, Mrs. Pog, nothing has been decided. We have to establish jurisdiction. We have priorities, manpower restrictions. We'd have to coordinate with state conservation officials."

"If you do that you might as well not even come," Marlis snapped. She stood. She smiled thinly, visibly holding onto her restraint. "I've heard it all before. Everybody's sorry. But there're problems with jurisdiction, manpower, all the excuses in the book. Wayne gave his life. What do I get? A plaque. And with that I'm supposed to get on with my life?"

Reed stepped in front of her as she reached the door. The

lilac scent of her perfume wafted over him. His favorite, a natural scent of the wild. That he felt a measure of attraction along with discomfort, Reed took as a sign of defeat. The woman was in desperate need. He should have at least established some common ground.

"Mrs. Pog," Peter called.

"What?" She challenged him.

Reed deftly moved to the side and opened the door, at least giving her the sense she had complete freedom to escape. "Where are you staying?" he asked. "We're a bureaucracy. Like most bureaucracies we're bigger than the sum of our parts and far removed from those we're supposed to represent. I can't apologize for that because I can't do anything about it. But give us a few hours. No promises. But we'll see what we can do."

Marlis nodded in resignation. There had been others who said they'd see what they could do. No promises. At least this Reed spoke the truth. She took an offered memo pad and wrote down her motel and room number. "I was going back on the morning bus."

"One way or the other, I'll give you a call," Reed said.

Marlis shrugged as if in doubt. "Of course they won't like you, Yankee, federal government, a stranger. Everyone will watch your every move. It's a fishbowl, been that way since Wayne disappeared. You'll stand out even worse."

"Attention's not always bad. Sometimes you have to turn it into something you can use."

"Then you must be good," Marlis said with spite. She turned away.

A familiar nervousness tightened Reed's stomach. Of course she was right, the stranger, the new kid in town. People gave you the eye. Some of them gave you a shot. The hunter and the hunted. Marlis couldn't know, but that's what brought Reed alive.

He watched her pass through the endless rows of desks in the outer room. As always he was drawn to the lure of a pretty woman. Marlis maintained herself and moved with a certain grace, like a dancer upon the stage or a woman of poise and good breeding. But women of class didn't marry game wardens. Wardens were woodsmen, nature nuts, working stiffs as were the poor lonely women they were apt to wed and leave at home. The image did not fit Marlis Pog. She was a class unto herself.

A familiar pain knifed home, the clear image of Pam and his two girls, Stacy and Trish. There'd been a time when they made him whole, a complete family at home in a log cabin in the middle of a northern Wisconsin forest. For all practical purposes, they had lived off the land. For a time it worked. But society intervened. There was an entirely different world outside that log cabin. Pamela wanted part. And of course she hadn't been raised as he had, living alone in a tarpaper shack with his pulp-cutting father. A wizened old Swede, stoop-shouldered, arthritic, a man of few words. Guy never got modern, never sat in a Feller-Buncher, a one-hundred and fifty thousand dollar Tree Harvestor. Guy used a chain saw for cutting and a work horse for skidding. His young son trailed behind. Of course all that was in the past. The boy got his tongue and left home, even went to college and became a naturalist. "The past is past," Pamela reminded Reed more than once. "Why don't you let it be?"

"At least I didn't have television," Reed countered. "That was one salvation, that's for sure."

Reed turned back into the office. How could he, in all justice, remotely compare his loss to that Marlis faced?

"That woman needs help, Peter. That ring is still ongoing. Deer are being slaughtered. Her husband was one of ours and we've just walked away. It's not right. If we have to, we should pull some strings."

"I know," Peter said. He understood her pain, but felt helpless to do anything about it. "I'll make some calls."

"Good," Reed said. "She deserves more than a plaque. We owe her. We owe them both." He patted P.U.'s shoulder. His boss was good that way, Reed understood, a caring man. He just didn't know when or how to be hard.

Reed slowly climbed the steps to his tiny bungalow. It wasn't much, a squat Cape Cod, dirty like the rest of the city around it. At seven-hundred and fifty dollars a month it was all he could afford with Washington-housing prices among the highest in the nation.

Reed rapped on the door and rang the bell. After several

seconds with no answer, he produced a key and, feeling like a first time thief, opened the door.

He stood in the gloom and surveyed the meager belongings of his family. With Pam working as a department manager at Sears, and his job at Fish and Wildlife, they got by. Back in Wisconsin they'd be rich. But now, what with his second apartment and all, the money disappeared before it was made. Too much of it just to keep up appearances, to stay fashionable, he thought and struggled to put the theme aside. It was that as much as anything that had moved him out of the house in the first place. A trial separation, Pam said, not when he was out on assignment, but when he was actually right here in town. To her it was the only separation that made sense, being apart when Reed had time to think.

She had, Reed had come to realize these past weeks, been absolutely right. The long nights alone in his apartment gave him nothing but time to think.

He silently drifted through the house, his ex-house. The knowledge split him like a knife. He'd tried to be considerate, it had been the cornerstone of his life. He frowned in puzzlement like a little boy scolded for something he did not do.

Why, he wondered, at this most critical moment of his life, had he volunteered for a mission that would take him away? Of course even when they'd lived together Pam hadn't minded when he'd gone on a lengthy mission. In later years she'd claimed to enjoy his absences. She'd learned how to get along without him.

The collage of family pictures still hung on the hallway wall; a smiling Trish and Stacy sitting in a canoe with their father, a reminder of ten days on a Canadian river. Even Stacy, although only twelve at the time, had been thrilled and still told stories how their canoe had been charged by a moose. There was the hand-scribed log cabin he and Pam had built by hand. Fresh out of college at Stevens Point, with a major as a naturalist, and he'd taken on a limited term job in the fisheries division of the Wisconsin Department of Natural Resources. Even Pam, who'd been raised in the moderate size town of Eau Claire, had taken to the wilderness. Or at least she'd tried.

But then came Stacy, and two years later Trish. Pam wanted more things. Material things, Reed had kidded. Necessities, Pam had countered, more of what life had to offer. Reed took full time employment as a state game warden. That still wasn't enough. Pam wanted a life of her own, something more . . . fulfilling, she'd said. She wasn't a minimalist like Reed wanted her to be. And they'd moved, leaving the forest behind.

Reed glanced at a family portrait, a year old now, perhaps their last ever. Pam, brown hair cut in a short pixie, stared level-eyed, practical, a woman in control of her emotions and feelings. There'd been a time when passion had been there.

Stacy, her hair frizzed in the wildest manner possible, stared defiantly, as if he was the camera, Reed thought. The more be railed against slaves to fashion, the more fashion-conscious she became. It was her money, Stacy pointed out. At least they'd instilled the work ethic. But now with the separation he could barely get her to talk civilly. It was as if Stacy blamed the separation on him alone.

And Trish; smiling, positive Trish, a swinger of trees, a lover of the outdoors. They had a canoe trip coming up, Reed thought. That'd be cancelled now. Just one more wedge.

A lock turned in the front door. "Pam, it's just me," Reed called. His wife walked in, wearing a properly professional grey business suit with a silk scarf and carrying a bag of groceries. Since the separation she'd lost weight, especially in her hips. Reed thought to take her in his arms. But of course he did not. They made small talk. Eventually Reed got to the point, he had a mission in Louisiana. He didn't know for how long. In order to save the cost of a second apartment he thought might move his things back into the basement.

"You better not," Pam said. Her voice rattled nervously. "I think I'm going to talk to an attorney."

"Couldn't you wait? You said six months."

"Three's long enough. What difference would three more make if you're going to be gone anyhow?"

"Seventeen years is a long time. Three more months might make all the difference in the world." Reed argued. There was no animosity, there'd never been that. It was just a matter of hurt, deep and bitter that never seemed to go away.

"I'm going to talk to an attorney," Pam the decisive declared.

"You don't need an attorney. Why give them our money.

We haven't added to the college fund for the last six months. I'll give you whatever you want, Pam. All I want is time. What do you want? Just tell me."

"Freedom. I just want to be free to live my life my way. Not your's."

Reed stood silently, puzzling at her words. All his life he'd tried to set Pamela free. He'd never wanted any holds. When they'd come upon cub coyotes, they'd nursed them and returned them to the forest. The same with baby raccoons. Reed stared at the family portrait on the wall. He'd have to call the photographer and ask for a second one for himself. Just a year ago; he'd looked younger then, his beard trimmed and his face wide with a smile. Pam and the girls wore dresses and blouses with ruffles. Stacy looked like a Christmas tree, Reed had gently goaded, hanging with earrings, necklaces, bracelets, and rings. He wore his plaid shirt. Pam had been bitter about that, he recalled, but then she'd been bitter about his casual dress the last ten years of their lives.

"This is kind of a rush mission," Reed said. "A woman's husband has disappeared. He's a conservation warden and he was investigating a violating ring. I'm going to jump in and see what it looks like. If things work out I'll stay. Otherwise I'm to bail out and we'll work at them from outside. I'll call you from Louisiana. Maybe later tonight I'll call the kids."

"I wish you would," Pam said. "You're the one who should tell Trish you're cancelling your canoe trip."

"I'll call," Reed said. "Right now that's all I can do." Their eyes locked, a momentary look, a momentary wondering how, after seventeen years, two children, the innumerable intimate couplings, and all that had transpired between them, they'd moved this far apart. Like too many things human, Reed thought, it just didn't make any sense.

[9]

TWO

Reed met his partner, Doug, and state conservation officials in Baton Rouge. The contact supervisor, Gerald Doucet, a dark-haired, red-faced Acadian, admitted they weren't quite sure of the composition of the alleged violating ring. On several occasions they'd received reports of considerable quantities of deer heads, legs, and greasy swirls of grey intestines found near and downstream from bridges. It had been going on for a couple of years. If the violators took up to a hundred deer a night, as they estimated, they'd be getting up to five thousand pounds of potential hamburger meat plus the hides. They could be grossing up to three thousand dollars a night. They'd checked the tanneries; so far they hadn't found anything out of the ordinary. The violators had laid off over the early spring and summer. However, evidence from the previous weekend indicated the violators were back at their gruesome slaughter.

As to Wayne Pog, he hadn't been assigned anywhere that night. He hadn't called in. Gerald took Reed aside and with breath laden with whiskey, whispered, "It was common knowledge Pog and his missus weren't getting along. I think he took off."

Reed kept quiet. He knew the hours most wardens worked. Few accounted for only a small portion of time spent out in the woods. Doucet did not reflect the class of men Reed knew. Obviously Doucet hadn't achieved his supervisor's position by rising through the warden's ranks. Typical state and federal politics, Reed thought sourly. The top positions, the best paying jobs too often were awarded by political patronage.

Other than being a hack for the incumbent party, a person needed no qualifications. Doucet fit the mold.

Reed escaped Doucet as quickly as possible and set up with Doug to search for possible outlets for the venison. For starters Doug would purchase hamburger from likely outlets, package the meat in dry ice, and express mail it to the new Fish and Wildlife forensic laboratory in Ashland, Oregon. The lab would search for any traces of venison mixed in with the beef. Additionally, Doug and two teams of state conservation officers would conduct and be available for search patrols on short notice.

As prearranged, Reed then met Marlis at a local hotel and the two of them drove to the small town of Magnolia, an hour and a half away, in the heart of the French Triangle. They drove through lowland farms, swamps, brown water bayous, and moss-covered forests. The musky smell of decaying matter, brackish water, azaleas and red pine filled the thick humid air. The beauty and the terror, Reed thought. He'd seen too many movies of small Southern towns. Perhaps his sense of reality had been warped. Perhaps he really didn't have much to fear.

Of course that ignored the fact that somewhere Wayne Pog probably lay dead.

"No back-up and out on a limb," big beefy Doug had complained to Reed. "Just like always. And you warn *me* about never approaching these guys alone."

Reed spun the tires like a teenager as he drove into the dusty and pitted dirt parking lot of the Blue Moon tavern and dance hall. "Yeeehah," he whooped through the open window as they rocked to a stop. A mushroom cloud of dust billowed up around Marlis's eight-year-old Ford Escort. "You ready?" Reed said quietly.

Marlis rolled her head around and rested it on the back of the seat. She wore a grey and pink print dress that clung nicely to her slender form. She'd had a permanent and even applied makeup. He'd asked her to pretend to be drunk. "Why pretend?" she'd said.

For a moment Reed thought she might cry. He opened the door and lurched from the car. No telling who could be watching. He strode around the car with the stiff gait of a drunk trying to act sober. He'd only had one beer but the throb of adrenaline made him feel plenty high. For her part Marlis had downed several drinks, including raw whiskey straight from a water glass. She was, she said, beginning to develop a taste for it. Besides, whiskey settled her nerves.

The warm Louisiana night hung heavy with the promise of rain. Cicadas, crickets, and bullfrogs carried on a continuous din from the black sheen of the cypress swamp that lay scant yards behind the bar and it's single blue neon sign. Lights shone through windows high along one wall, but beyond the building and parked cars was a shroud of darkness.

Reed opened Marlis's door. He leaned close. "You have to play the game, Marlis. If you blow my cover, I'm no good. I'm gone. There won't be anyone else. Got it?"

"Well aren't you the tough one," Marlis said, as she struggled to undo her seat belt.

"These aren't just violators we're after here. Someone was willing to kill."

"So you do believe," Marlis said and gracefully rose to her feet.

"I always believe, Marlis. There are dangerous creatures in the night. But they're all two-legged and stand upright. Some people believe they're related to man. I know they're not."

"Oh, they're men," Marlis said as if from a distance. "Ask my father, a Southern gentleman frozen in time without the comfort of a son to carry on the family name. Thank God. Now there's a dangerous creature. Especially if you're a little black girl too frightened to put up a fight."

For a moment Reed stood in embarrassed silence. Family matters were not supposed to be part of his fight.

He gently took Marlis by the hand and, as they weaved across the parking lot, he wrapped his arm around her narrow waist and touched her for the first time. She tensed and he could feel the rows of her ribs, fragile bones that seemingly could shatter under the simple squeeze of his arms.

On first impulse he felt considerable unease, like he was cheating on Pam or caught in the act of violating his own cousin. Marlis was his cover, he reminded himself. She was not a date.

The glowing end of a cigarette gave evidence that a number

of men had gathered at the back of the pickup trucks and cars just outside the entrance. They silently watched as Reed and Marlis passed, trying to figure out in the dark just who in the hell this couple could be.

"Howdy, boys," Reed said. "Smoke 'em if you got 'em."

"I'll smoke 'em up your ass," one man belligerently replied. Reed's heart lurched just a notch, a reminder of the alien soil upon which he tread. When you got into a fight with these Southern boys, you fought until the end. Pain meant nothing compared to humiliation. In the country here you had to beat a man until he could not move. Good ole boys. Louisiana red. "Better watch your lip, Yank," Reed muttered to himself.

The Blue Moon tavern and dance hall was a sagging one-story building filled with cigarette smoke and a yellow gloom. Long fold-up tables were covered with red oil cloth and littered with beer cans, cups, over-laden ash trays, and the ever-present small, individualized brass spittoons for the young tobacco chewing men. The hall was three times as long as it was wide and was clogged with people ranging in age from the early twenties to the seventies, young toughs as well as family types, long-wed couples who liked to dance and have a good time.

"Not exactly the high school prom," Reed said in Marlis's ear. "It looks more family-oriented, like a wedding." The clean lilac scent of her perfume stood out delightfully in contrast to the sour odors of beer, sweat, and cigarette smoke. Involuntarily Reed pulled back.

They found a spot on some folding chairs at the end of one of the tables. A woman rushed up and took both of Marlis's hands in hers. "Marlis, I haven't seen you around for so long." She gave Reed a penetrating glare.

Reed grinned and pursed his lips as if to give the woman a kiss. She recoiled as if violated. Reed forced a laugh. He wasn't here to make friends. He was here to stir the pot.

In the far corner the band struck up a tune. The orchestra consisted of an old accordionist, an old fiddle player, and a skinny, bearded young man with pointed cowboy boots, a low-brimmed cowboy hat, a harmonica, and a triangle or ting-a-ling. In quaint fashion the men bowed as they approached the women and led them to the dance floor to do what Marlis informed Reed was called the Cajun two-step.

[13]

"I'll get us some drinks and we'll give that a go. I love to dance," Reed said, loud enough for Marlis's dark-haired friend to hear. With Marlis on his arm he'd already attracted his share of eyes and brought more than two heads together in whispered conversation.

Reed patted the side of Marlis's buttocks, nodded at the furious glare of her friend, and strutted and weaved down the length of the dance hall toward where the men had gathered back by the bar. It was, he felt, not unlike to newcomer entering hell.

With total lack of timidity he pushed between men much larger than himself and shouldered his way to the bar. Red Jax and Dixie 45 beer signs decorated the back wall just over gallon jars of boiled eggs, beef jerky, and salted pork rinds. "Two Jax beers and a Manhattan," he yelled at the young, squat bartender.

"Manhattan!" the harried barkeep yelped.

"All right, two beers and a rum and coke," Reed said. A half-a-dozen young men had gathered at his shoulder.

"You're not from around here are you?" a man asked. He was eager, aggressive, and broad-shouldered with long, dark, shaggy hair that was badly in need of washing, and an abundance of the loose supple muscles of youth. The man's name was Ross, Reed later learned from Marlis. Ross had dark, mean eyes—the kind that spelled death to every stray cat that wandered within his range.

"Not to my knowledge." Reed gave the man his steady, level-eyed predator stare, holding the gaze just long enough so the youth fully understood, he was not someone to run or be pushed.

He'd learned the predator's stare from the wild. Animals did it all the time, a fixed and silent communication between predator and prey. As often as not a simple stare could communicate whether to attack or not. A weak prey, a nervous prey, would give itself away. If a wolf approached three caribou, two of whom were healthy, it would be the sick one that would rise. The two healthy prey would stare: I can outrun you. I can kick you in the face. They said it with their eyes. It would be the sick one that first would run, as if advertising. I know I'm weak. I know I'm vulnerable. Come, take me. And all on the basis of a stare. Of course, all predators had their eyes to the front, like man.

"Your knowledge?" the man said. He did not avoid Reed's gaze, but he was no wit.

Reed smiled. "Excuse me, fellows." He took his drinks, pushed through, and returned to where half-a-dozen women had gathered around Marlis. He brusquely pushed through them as well. "That's my chair, lady," he said to the dark-haired one. Her lips tightened in a thin line and moved in a silent curse that indicated Marlis had reached into the bottom of the barrel and pulled out one of the dregs.

"Well, we made an entrance," Reed said to Marlis after the women returned to their men. He sat beside Marlis with his arm casually drapped around her shoulders. "If I absolutely had to impress people, this wouldn't be the way."

"You look pretty natural to me," Marlis said.

"Thanks," Reed growled. Then she smiled disarmingly. Once again he was surprised, Marlis had made a joke. One moment she could be so introverted and bitter and the next she was soft and nice. Being around her was like walking on egg shells. Reed couldn't help but wonder if she'd been this way before Wayne's disappearance.

"We'll laugh and have fun," Marlis said. "The ladies didn't exactly say so, but in essence they're embarrassed that I'm with you, a stranger, an outsider. I guess I'm not accepting Wayne's disappearance with the grace, dignity, and silence befitting a Southern woman of breeding."

"Well, we can't please everyone."

For some time they sat in silence. Although Marlis, hunched and hugging herself, could not be still. She constantly shifted in her seat and glanced about and moved her hands as if she could never quite settle on where they belonged. Eventually she spoke, politely, as if trying to show a genuine interest. "How long have you been an agent?"

"Longer than I care to remember. Something like eight years."

"That's not long for a career."

"Well, I worked as a state warden in Wisconsin for some years. I actually made my first arrest when I was fourteen."

"Fourteen!"

"I was hunting. We lived far out in the country. My father used to cut pulp with a chain saw, still does for that matter. And he's seventy years old. This guy was checking deer for horns. Ah, shooting them and then taking a look. He'd shot five does around his stand and then just left them. I walked out to the highway, flagged down a car, and had them call for a warden. I led him back there and he made the arrest."

"My, my, weren't you the little saint."

Reed shrugged, filled with the memory. The scene of wanton destruction remained with him to this day. In spite of his father's lack of education, the old man had an abundance of woods sense. "Never kill something you're not going to use or eat." And always leave seed, he'd said as he ran his trap lines, enough so animals would always remain as part of the scene. He ran his trap lines every single day, no matter how severe the storm. He would not let an animal suffer any longer than he could help it. That was Guy. Only he seldom spoke. And he never touched. It was why, after seventeen years of marriage, exactly the same as Reed's, his mother had finally left. Life was too hard, Harriet said, and she'd moved to town and in with a widowed sister. She'd taken her two daughters with her, leaving her son in the deep forest with Guy. It was what he'd wanted, the boy had said.

Reed stared at the bar, filled with the memory. After the violator had been arrested Reed had, in a sudden fit of righteous fervor, tried to turn in himself and his father as violators. They killed deer out of season, he explained, one in early fall, one or two during season, and occasionally one in January or February. The warden, a tall thin man named Bud, had smiled with grey eyes ringed by lines from squinting into the sun. He'd patted Reed's shoulders. "Laws are made to protect game from excesses like the fellow in the car there, from people who have no understanding and no caring for nature. The people who pass laws are far from infallable. You have to apply common sense. My job is going after the exploiters, Reed. I know your father. He isn't that kind." And the warden had driven away.

Reed shook his head with the memory. It had been a lesson he'd never forgotten.

A blond-haired man with a squared jaw and body built much like a stump stopped after a dance. As blond as the man was, his wife was dark Acadian, her black hair pulled back into a severe bun, her eyes dark and penetrating. Unlike the man, Doyle Monroe, Marlis later explained, his wife Rachel did not even nod hello.

Immediately Doyle locked eyes with Reed, an appraising stare from a man who habitually led the way. Doyle Monroe had never been intimidated in his life. "Are you doing all right, Marlis? We haven't seen you for a few days."

"I'm doing all right," Marlis explained dreamily, she introduced Reed and Doyle.

"Where are you from?" Doyle asked. He wore a colorful red shirt and dark pants. The thickness of his thighs strained at the pant legs and tiny scars around the light colored eyebrows spoke of a man who'd spent time in the ring. His skin was scrubbed clean but his muscled hands were covered with thick callouses.

"Around," Reed said. He briefly debated whether to play this guy hard or friendly. Doyle was older, more mature, not one of the young toughs up there by the bar. He might be a contact he'd need. "Most recently I was in Baton Rouge. That's where I met Marlis here." Reed squeezed Marlis around the waist and was surprised to observe Doyle tense.

"Will we see you in church tomorrow?" Doyle asked Marlis. "You missed last week."

The band struck up another song, drowning further conversation. Marlis shrugged as if unable to respond above the noise.

"What's that guy's position in town?" Reed asked after Doyle and Rachel took their leave.

"Doyle's a good friend," Marlis said into Reed's ear. Her breath was warm as were her fingers touching his shoulder. "Doyle's a community leader. He's lived here all his life. He runs a small grocery store on the square. He's on the town council. Since Wayne's disappeared and they've refused to release his death benefits, Doyle's given me credit at the store. He gets a little funny at times. He's a deacon in my church. He doesn't like to see change. Since they put in the strip mall the square in town is dying and people don't know what to do. As much as anyone, Doyle's helped keep the town together."

"Did you and Doyle ever go out together?"

Marlis recoiled in surprise. "Why would you ever ask that? Years ago, in high school, we went on a couple of dates. It never went anywhere."

Reed nodded as if in understanding. Through the teeming crowd he watched Doyle and Rachel sit down. Doyle drank an RC cola. Rachel had something mixed. They sat silently, not talking and not looking at one another. Even across the room Reed could sense the strain.

He had to move, Reed thought. He turned to Marlis. "Let's dance. I want to try that Cajun two-step."

"Sure," Marlis said. "We'll give them a show."

With pronounced dignity, Reed stood and stiffly bowed. He offered Marlis his hand and then led her onto the floor. Fifty pairs of eyes followed his every move. Reed just looked around, laughed, and took Marlis into his arms.

They danced away the night. Reed, dressed in leather boots and flaxen pants and looking like a weathered mountain man, whirled and stomped and laughed with complete lack of inhibition. On occasion he staggered as if he'd lost his balance. On more than one occasion Marlis actually did and he had to hold on tight as they whirled around and he kept her on her feet. For the most part she maintained a smile, a frozen fixture like a woman smiling over her pain. More than once he caught her staring, her large grey eyes coldly calculating his worth.

In between dances, Reed endured other stares. If Marlis was his into this community, she was not his confidant or friend. In nature he never felt alone. Here, he felt as isolated as a stranger in a city. Occasionally he boldly shouldered his way back through the males in front of the bar. Each time the mean-eyed youth named Ross had a comment.

"Where're you from, buddy?"

"Just about everywhere," Reed said without rancor. As always he gave Ross a level stare, defeating him with his eyes.

In between the dances Reed sat tight at Marlis's side, his arm around her shoulders, his head huddled close like two lovers talking sweet. In actual fact he was conducting business, distracting himself from Marlis's touch by becoming acquainted with the townspeople. He described people by their clothes and then had Marlis give him background on where they lived and worked and what the probabilities were that they were involved in violating. There were a dozen men Wayne had kept his eyes on. But he never specifically identified, nor mentioned to Marlis who he felt was part of the ring.

"Most of these men hunt, I presume?" Reed asked.

"Of course," Marlis said with some spite. "They were born to hunt. They grab a gun as soon as they can grab their dicks. Killing is second nature. What do they care? They'll shoot a game warden as quick as they'd shoot a skunk."

Reed nodded. Not all were like that, he knew. A sense of conservation across the South was actually making some headway. In some cases hunters led the way. But there were still too many from the old school—use what the Lord provided. Man was king. And government got in the way. He'd seen the evolution up north, from backroom bars with a cartoon of a game warden's head upon the wall to organizations committed to hunter education and preservation of habitat. It was like groundwater working through the sand, movement was ever so slow.

Of course these boys hunted. They were as used to killing as a girl or boy raised on a farm. Birth and death were part of life. As beautiful as nature could be, it could also be cruel. It was impossible to separate the two. And of course these boys violated, hunting after hours, shooting from the roads. But who'd become wanton, killing for profit a hundred or more deer a night? And maybe a warden besides?

A gunshot sounded outside the door. With his emotions at fever pitch, Reed started. Marlis laughed. People grumbled. Many began to pick up and depart. "It's from the old days," Marlis explained. "When the band is too tired to continue to play, one of the members fires a pistol into the air to signal the end of the dance." She faced Reed, her hands resting on his knees. "Wayne didn't like to dance."

"I've always liked to move. A pretty lady makes it easier yet. There's no sense making this any more difficult than we have to."

Reed became aware of a group of men crowded up behind them. He knew they'd come. He was surprised they'd taken so long.

One of the boys stepped forward, a large blond man with

pudgy cheeks and fat forming an inner tube around his waist. He wore a blue tee shirt that rode up his burgeoning belly, and blue jeans that sagged beneath. "Are you all right, Marlis? If this guy is bothering you, we can lend a hand." The man spoke politely like a young boy respectfully addressing a school teacher.

"You're bothering me, Billy Bob," Marlis snapped. She rose out of her chair. "All you boys." She glared around the circle of a dozen men. "You guys have nothing to do with my life, nothing at all. Where were you when Wayne was around? Out there with him? Shooting him? Burying the body? Well?" Her voice rose in near hysteria. The men recoiled as if from a mad woman.

"We're just trying to help, Marlis," Ross grumbled. "We want to know who your friend is."

"Name's Reed. I'm a Yankee. Anything else you want to know go to the library." Reed shrugged as if to forgive his own adolescence. It was part of the game. Although the last thing he needed was to get into a fight.

"You've got a big mouth."

"That's been mentioned in my past," Reed said with a neutral tone. The beasts were at bay, he'd have to play this right or there'd be one hell of a price to pay.

"Maybe I ought to stuff it down your throat." Ross was eager, had been thinking on it all evening long.

"A man does what he has to do," Reed said simply.

"What's going on here, Ross?" Doyle Monroe said. "You trying to pick a fight with Marlis's new friend here?"

Immediately Ross and the others moved back. Whatever Doyle Monroe's relationship, the young toughs in this group acted as cowed as dogs about to be whipped by a feared master. Reed was impressed.

"Just finding out who this guy is," Ross said.

"Looking after Marlis," Billy Bob added nervously.

"Marlis can look after herself," Marlis snapped.

"Uh-oh, here comes the black and white," Billy Bob said.

Reed thought they meant a police car. In fact they meant the police—two parish deputies, one black, one white were casually making their way to the point of confrontation. "Do we have a little misunderstanding here?" the black deputy asked. In fact he was caramel-colored, tall, lean and angular with protruding Adam's Apple, lips, moustache, and eyebrows. His name was Hank Jackson. Not Henry, Hank he told people, after the home run king. Although baseball had never been his game. By presence, bearing, and action he immediately established himself as the man in charge.

"We were minding our business. These juveniles came over and tried to start a fight," Marlis said. Her eyes were bitter slits. She weaved unsteadily, leaning against Reed.

Several men yelled in protest. A large circle of people had gathered to watch the proceedings. Hank, the only black man in the Blue Moon, held up his hand to command silence. "It wouldn't be a good idea for any of you boys to be giving us trouble now. In fact it would be just as well if most of you packed it in and started for home." He glanced around the circle and gave them a hint of a smile. "Make sure you have your designated driver there behind the wheel." That brought out a laugh as several men jostled their neighbor and debated who would be the driver.

Tensions ebbed, Deputy Hank, Reed thought, knew what he was about.

"Doyle," Hank said. "If I would have known you were here I would have stayed in the squad. This guy giving you trouble?" He jerked a thumb at Reed.

"No," Doyle said. "But I would like to know who the hell he is."

"Sounds reasonable," Hank said. He turned to Reed. "You're the only guy in this bar that I don't know. Why don't you give me a piece of identification?"

"You want the real thing or the fake?" Reed asked as he extracted his wallet.

"You decide," Hank said with just a trace of irritation that someone would dare to usurp his line. "I can't tell one from the other anyhow. Some of these boys were out to Swamp Creek Bar drinking when they were fifteen and I didn't know the difference." Hank shrugged at the memory. Swamp Creek Bar was just down the road from his house, a dilapidated tavern owned by blacks where bold under-aged white boys came to defy tradition and the law.

"Wisconsin!" Hank said as he examined Reed's driver's license. What are you doing way down here?"

"When all these good ole boys came gathering around me a few minutes ago I asked myself that very question."

"And what did you tell yourself?"

"I travel around. I was in Baton Rouge. I met Marlis." He shrugged, trying to be a bit of a rake. He squeezed Marlis to his side. Her eyes had dulled. Her body sagged. She was on the verge of collapse. Reed nodded. "Maybe I should get her home."

Hank bent forward, trying to see if Marlis could understand. "You want this guy to take you home? Or would you rather Jerry and I did?"

"Reed," Marlis mumbled. "He's the only one who knows. The only one."

Hank frowned in puzzlement. They sat Marlis at the table and he pulled Reed off to one side. "I can't stop you, fella. It looks to me as if you've made yourself some enemies here tonight. I can't stop them either. I can't tell if you're the kind of man who has a conscience. I doubt it. But Marlis has had some tough times. Six months ago her husband disappeared. Run off, killed, no one knows. Her behavior's completely changed. She's vulnerable, easy pickings for any predator that comes along."

Reed hesitated. Hank was not one of those he sought. In fact, although Hank was not yet aware of it, Reed planned to try to make the deputy his number one ally. There was no need to be smart as long as no one else could hear. "Don't worry, deputy. I think you're the kind of man that understands, not everything you see is everything that is."

Hank's eyes flickered with newfound interest. "If you stick around there'll be trouble, bub. But that's your affair. Jerry and I will watch to see you get home."

"Oh, I'll be all right," Reed said.

"I don't care about you," Hank said. "In fact I'd say no one here cares about you. Not even Marlis if you got down to the facts."

Although he could not sleep, Reed waited until late morning before he got up. Marlis had vacated the bed. He gazed around the small bedroom of Marlis's starter–level house, two bedrooms, living room, kitchen, single bathroom. The bedroom was neat with lace curtains, silk embroidery around the bedspread, and a light walnut dresser with an oval mirror ringed with lights. Bright colored wallpaper and original water paintings decorated the walls. It was a small house, but decorated with a touch of class, Reed had observed the night before. Marlis's touch. Like the flower garden out front, azaleas, roses, and hibiscus with huge rocks interspersed. Although this summer they hadn't been touched.

He slipped on a pair of pants and padded down the narrow hallway toward the bathroom. As he passed a small bedroom, Marlis's two children, eleven-year-old Jody and nine-year-old Patty silently watched him pass. He'd met them the day before and now he casually waved as if trying to be friendly. But he did not pause to talk. The kids had enough pain. His presence made it that much worse. The only thing possible was his presence would focus their hate.

When he stepped out of the bathroom, Jody blocked his way. The little boy trembled. His sister peered fearfully from inside their room. "I want you out of my house." The thin voice almost broke.

Reed swallowed. Just standing here caused such pain. This was supposed to be his base of operations, his safe haven where he could come and relax. He spoke in a choked voice. "I'll be leaving, Jody. But not for a few days. I promise."

"No."

"Sorry," Reed touched the boy's thin shoulder and tried to ease past.

Tears streaked down the boy's face. "When my Daddy comes home he's going to thrash you so hard you'll wish you were never born."

Reed's shoulders sagged. The only other time he'd felt this hopeless was when Pam sent him out the door. Your daddy isn't coming home, he thought. But how do you tell that to a little kid?

THREE

Doyle Monroe stood in the dark of his tiny grocery store. He looked out at the thick live oaks and hanging Spanish moss that provided a protecting roof of limbs over the town square. The square was a little park a block across and surrounded by the Magnolia business district, at least those businesses that remained. There had been a time the park had been a gathering place. Politicians stopped to press their cause. Huey Long had once spoke there, gathering just enough of the rural Catholic vote in the South to put him over the top. Entire families came for a picnic and a concert on a Saturday afternoon. Women wore white linen and men wore suits and ties. Children played innocent games such as tag or hide-and-seek. They'd been a community then.

But no more. Now the park was just a place to cross, a few sidewalks, a couple of benches, a water fountain and a cracked and greening bronze statue of Henry Watkins Allen, a man who'd been shot through the cheek at Shiloh and then had his legs mangled in the Battle of Baton Rouge. Allen then went on to become one of the greatest and most caring governors the state of Louisiana ever had. Few kids knew who Governor Henry Watkins Allen was. Even fewer cared.

It all started in 1965, Doyle thought. They'd voted to lift the parishwide prohibition. The next year the parish had its first arrest for drugs. In Baton Rouge they kept adding factories, petrochemicals next to the huge refinery, burning up the earth from the innards torn out from the oil rigs dotting the Gulf. There were so many oil rigs in some areas shrimpers called it Oil City. And everything continued to change.

[24]

Herbicides and mechanical cotton pickers took workers out of the fields. They seeded rice fields with airplanes and fertilized and sprayed them from aloft. Crawfish and catfish grew on farms. Oyster luggers lay rusting while young men broke the traditional line and took to working seven-and-seven, seven days working and seven days off, as roustabouts on oil rigs in the Gulf. Nutrias, imported from South America, were driving out the muskrats and tearing up the marshes. And the Corps of Engineers and the oil companies continued building their canals, controlling the cleansing waters of the Red and Mississippi, while brackish salt brine worked further and further inland destroying breeding grounds and habitat for ducks, oysters, and who knew how many other species of wildlife. All in the name of progress, of getting ahead. That was the joke. Getting ahead.

Nope, the Old South had died. Every time they built a factory, every time they built a mall, they looked a little more just like the North.

Doyle turned back to look down the darkened aisles of his small grocery store. His father had taken over this store during the depression days of the thirties. He'd never refused a customer. The store had never been free of debt. In fifteen minutes he'd open the door. Although it wouldn't make much difference. He could wait an hour and fifteen minutes. He'd miss out on selling a quart of orange juice to old Joe. And Mrs. Adams wouldn't stop by to buy her cans of soup and use up fifteen minutes of his time while he trimmed and set out produce.

Of course he didn't have to set out produce anymore. The turnover had been so slow, spoilage had reached seventy-five percent. Stopping the produce line had cost him customers. But then spoiled produce had cost him customers and money both. The forty thousand square foot supermarket out on the bypass had a produce department as big as his entire store. A produce truck stopped every day.

A supermarket, next to a discount store, buying goods shipped in from Taiwan, Korea, and Japan. And people crowded in. People did not understand. For a few pennies saved they destroyed lives, they destroyed a community, they destroyed all that had gone before. Dan Fowler's hardware store had been closed for three years. Silk Scott had closed his clothing store and moved to Florida. He'd lived in Louisiana fifty years. "Why not," Silk had argued. "All my kids have left the state. Why not me?"

And now the buildings sat empty, like half the buildings around the square. Everything was going to seed.

A fat-tired, four-wheel-drive pickup roared up and stopped crossway over the empty angled parking spots in front of the store. Doyle stepped outside. "Hey, Doyle," Ross called. "We going out his weekend?"

If Ross was broad shouldered with a thick torso, his riding partner, Wyndal, chewing tobacco as normal, was slope shouldered and as thin as a reed. But Wyndal was tough, Doyle knew. Even big guys like Ross left Wyndal alone. Wyndal was quick with a knife and not the least bit hesitant about putting the blade to flesh.

"Friday night," Doyle said softly as he approached the truck. "Born Rebel," the bug shield said on the front. The CB radio crackled with static. Two rifles hung uncased in the window rack behind the seat. That Wyndal and Ross were a dozen years younger than him, Doyle gave not a thought. Besides, he wasn't part of these guys, they were part of him.

"Cutter will be at the Crossroads Wayside at one A.M. I figure we should head out about eleven. Two hours should give everyone time to get a good load. Same sectors as I said the other day. Just remember your security procedures—make some U-turns and double back. Pull off to the side and douse your lights. Drop one guy off and circle a square."

"Did you hear Marlis last night?" Ross said. "She as much as said Wayne disappeared because of us. Can you beat that? I still say the little runt is down in New Orleans shacking up."

On the opposite side of the truck Wyndal pulled out his knife and began whittling on a stick.

"Just kidding," Ross said. He grinned at Doyle, "Good times, boss." He snapped his clutch, stepped on the gas, and roared away down the desolate downtown street.

Yes, good times, Doyle thought. The thought of the hunt stirred him, the planning, the organizing, the camaraderie, the searching through the warm night, the smell of fresh blood, the crackle of the radio, studying maps, sipping hot coffee, and contemplating the night. Nowadays hunting was the only way a man could escape.

Of course he'd always escaped into the forest and the swamps, Doyle thought; now more so than ever. His father, a hard man if there was one, gave him his first .22 at age six. He shot his first deer at eleven. And several hundred more since. It wasn't the killing, Doyle knew. He didn't even think about it anymore. A man got used to killing, at least with deer. But the hunt, just being out there with the guys, no pressure, no demands—the hunt was the thing.

Almost reluctantly Doyle returned to his store. A few minutes later a man wearing a charcoal-grey suit and glasses tapped at the window and cupped his hand to peer into the gloom inside. From three feet away, Doyle stared without moving.

The man called. "Open up, Doyle. We need to talk."

Stan Kendall, loan officer at the Magnolia National Bank. Of course it wasn't the Magnolia National Bank anymore. Not really. Old Carl Harris had died; his heirs had sold out. Some holding company in New Orleans owned the bank. There won't be any changes, they said. Two years later two-thirds of the original employees were gone. Stan was from Baton Rouge, moving around with the corporation, climbing the ladder. He did at least attend church every Sunday, with his wife Mary and three children. They appeared involved, but Doyle could not escape the feeling it was all just for show, like Stan joining the Chamber of Commerce. What the hell did he know or care about Magnolia?

Doyle opened the door.

"Doyle, I've been writing, I've been calling. I sent you the renewal note."

"You almost doubled the payments," Doyle said. He spoke softly, consciously keeping himself under control. Stan was one of those college boy softies, a golfer and a tennis player, not a man who had the nerve to wade out into the depths of a Louisiana swamp. In fact he could see Stan was nervous. Stan liked the safety of his own office where he had his computer and calculator and all his forms, statements, and graphs. He didn't like it out here on the street, standing face to face.

"You're not amortizing principal, Doyle. Your loan hasn't reduced in three years."

Doyle raised his voice, "I've never been late for a payment. I've never missed. Principal! I'm paying every dime I can afford. You're making your profit. What are you doing out here gouging me?"

"We have to turn loans over," Stan tried to explain. "Your store inventory isn't what it used to be. Your equipment's getting old. The building is, well, frankly there are a number of empty ones around."

"In the last two years you've made thirty thousand dollars from me. Thirty thousand! Do you know what I've taken home in that time? Huh? Twenty thousand. For two years."

"It's tough," Stan tried to sympathize.

Doyle exploded. "Tough! What the hell would you know about tough? You're not from Magnolia. You don't know how we've worked, how we've slaved, trying to make this community, trying to keep people together. And then you greed-driven leeches come out here and take over our banks and build your stores and what happens to the people? What happens to the community? You don't care." Doyle's normally ruddy complexion had darkened with rage. "Now we have drugs, here in Magnolia."

Stan shifted uncomfortably. "Perhaps," he began. He'd tried to be tough but Doyle Monroe was not an ordinary man. Stan's voice quavered. "Perhaps you should sell out and quit."

Stan never saw the blow.

That same morning Marlis packed Jody and Patty off to school. Marlis dressed for work. She'd been working at Doctor Pierce's office as a receptionist for four years now, she informed Reed. She'd only gone three years to college. Employment opportunities in Magnolia were limited. Wayne's salary was limited. "The second job helped make ends meet," she said as if in apology that she worked. "It was the only way I could buy clothes. And now that Wayne's gone and his supervisor, some guy named Gerald Doucet, refuses to release his death benefits, it's the only way we can make ends meet."

Reed sat at the formica-topped kitchen table and sipped at a scalding cup of strong, black coffee. He wore a pair of grey warmup pants and nothing else. His upper body was browned, lean, and wiry, without a hint of sag to his stomach even sitting down. Three nights now he'd slept with Marlis. They hadn't touched and already the strain was gone, almost like the final days of his marriage to Pam. "You must have loved Wayne a great deal?"

"No," Marlis said calmly. "I used him." She watched Reed to see how he passed judgment. "I married Wayne to spite my father. Father despised people from Wayne's level. It brought father down. Although once he did ask Wayne if he'd consider changing Jody's last name to Rittenhous. Said he'd pay him ten thousand dollars. Can you imagine offering a man ten thousand dollars to change his son's last name?" Marlis shook her head as if in great mirth. "My father. Then he would probably have willed the house and feed mill to Jody. He would have cut my sister Debra out, even though it's Debra who's run the mill the last ten years. It's Debra who made payments on the farm. And Father doesn't even see."

Reed sipped at his coffee. Family politics were not supposed to be part of his job. "You had Jody and Patty. You stayed with Wayne, what? Twelve years?"

A strange almost savage look twisted Marlis's expression. "Twelve years. And what do I have to show? If I ever get the death benefits I'll move to New Orleans. There's more to do. Maybe there'll be something I like."

The depth of hatred surprised Reed. Once again he sensed there was a lot more going on here than the disappearance of her husband and lack of resolution. "A person never knows when or where they'll find what they like. That's why it's better not to expect or ask for too much. More likely then you'll be satisfied with what you get."

"No wonder your family left. They couldn't take the lecturing. You do it all the time. Do you think everyone should be as righteous as you?"

"I'm not righteous," Reed protested.

"All men are righteous," Marlis said. "They can't conceive of anything else." She stared, the bitterness set on her face as if chiseled out of stone. "Wayne was righteous, but underneath he thought he was good to the children, good to me. I think in the end he knew I didn't really love him. But I didn't hate him either. He was . . . just there. Like you, Reed, sitting in my house, impacting my life."

"But you stayed with him," Reed pointed out. "That's something."

"Maybe I owed him. Maybe I was too frightened to do anthing else. Maybe . . ." Marlis broke off the conversation and reached for her purse.

"Are you going to call that Hank for me?" Reed asked. They'd discussed the matter previously and again the night before. Reed's investigative jurisdiction did not specifically include covering a murder. Plus working into the community was going to take time, and time in this case was limited. He'd asked Marlis if there was one local law enforcement official in whom she had absolute faith and trust, someone who would be willing to assist Reed outside official channels. It was taking a big chance, Reed understood, but that was the nature of the business. If he ever saw any connection between this Hank and the suspected violators he'd just have to turn around and walk.

"Hank Jackson, of course," Marlis had responded. "Hank's the most honest man in this town, except for Doyle Monroe. I've known Hank since we were children. Debra and I used to give him rides to town. He even got beat up for that. Daddy tried to take away our car. His wife Sheila . . ." Marlis paused. Her voice became choked. She trailed off. "Sheila worked for us as a maid."

Marlis dialed. She got Hank out of bed, apologized, and asked him to meet her at ten o'clock in a rest area on the I-10 freeway some twelve miles out of town. After some lying about there being a personal problem, Hank agreed.

"I'll drive you to work then," Reed said. "And you'll call Debra about that part-time job on the loading dock."

"I'll see her for lunch," Marlis said. "I'm sure I can get you into the family business for a few days a week. Minimum wage of course. Debra will be pleased that I've taken up with some- one so ambitious."

"Remember, not one word about my situation here," Reed cautioned. "Let her think I'm the no-account she thinks I am. If people think badly of me, they may not have time to see the truth. I know it hurts you also, but it's the way we have to

[30]

proceed for now. One word to the wrong person and, well, you know what can happen."

"I don't care what people think," Marlis snapped. "I told you that. I have no use for these people. None. They see what they want to see and nothing else." She started for the door. "Are you going to change? I have to get to work."

"It's warm out," Reed said. He carried his cup of coffee and, shirtless and barefoot, followed Marlis out to her car. He casually waved at two neighbors walking down the quiet suburban street. He observed Marlis stiffen at the sour glances in his direction, just one more indication of lies to herself. He knew she was a danger, and considered again lecturing her on maintaining his cover. But she was too much on edge. He'd just have to trust her, have a little faith.

After he returned from dropping Marlis at work, Reed put on a plain cotton, button-up short sleeve shirt, brown flax pants, and his worn leather boots, poured another hot cup of coffee and drove Marlis's Ford Escort out to the rest stop to wait for Hank.

The rest area was located just prior to where the eighteen mile long I-10 bridge rose up and cut a large swathe of civilization across the heart of the one hundred thirty-five mile long Atchafalaya Basin. The bridge was an engineering marvel, Reed thought. A sharp contrast to the Army Corps of Engineers decades-long efforts to follow a mandate from Congress and stop the mighty Mississippi from following its desired course and utilizing the Atchafalaya Basin as a new pathway to the sea. Control nature, the almighty United States Congress had decreed in 1948. Control the mighty Mississippi and force it to continue as a water canal for Baton Rouge and New Orleans. Forget geology and the natural inclination of the mighty river to take a readily available, shorter and steeper, route to the ocean. As Reed hoped and every biologist knew, eventually nature would win and prove its supremacy once again.

For the moment the Corps used the Atchafalaya Basin as a flood control outlet for as much as one-third of the Mississippi, while at the same time they attempted to maintain the natural environment of the Basin and the eight hundred thousand acre Atchafalaya swamp within. The Corps mission was at odds with the various demands of man and certainly at odds with nature. But that did not slow the demands of the competing factions: fishing, oil, timber, landowners, conservationists, sportsmen, and politicians. Each saw their needs as the most important. They could not conceive of themselves within the natural evolution of rivers. Of course he couldn't say evolution in certain areas down South—a fellow might get shot.

Rivers, left in their natural state and over the course of thousands of years, whip back and forth like an untethered fire hose, spreading sediments in an even fan. Except for the five hundred million dollars poured into the Old River Control Structure and the thirty foot levees along the Mississippi, the big river would probably have already taken a new path and left Baton Rouge and New Orleans sinking further and further below sea level on their settling sediment foundations. But man said no.

Reed laughed. It was just a matter of time until the next big flood. With all the water control structures up and down the Mississippi channeling more and more water into the river, it took less and less water up north to produce a flood down south. Already minor floods had eaten holes the size of football stadiums underneath the flood control structure. They'd dumped hundreds of thousands of tons of rocks to fill in the holes. One big flood would wipe it out. Nature, as she was determined to prove with earthquakes and hurricanes, would show herself all powerful. In a cosmic time frame, human beings were but a blip. In that, Reed thought, he could rejoice.

But for now man had the swamp, eight hundred thousand acres. People could drive the I-10 bridge and peer out at the bayous, rivers, islands, and pockets of grey, stark cypress trees rising resiliently out of the black brine. They could see white egrets and flocks of ducks and even an occasional bald eagle. And they could know the waters teemed with bream, bass, catfish, and the famous Louisiana crawfish. And they might read where the islands held deer, foxes, alligators, muskrats, and even an occasional black bear. Of course the muskrats were being pushed out by the fur-bearing nutrias that had been unwisely imported from South America. And amongst all the normal animals there were legends of other swamp creatures, huge, vicious, and hairy creatures that rose up in the night and stole people away without a trace. But it was like television, Reed knew. They could see the surface. They might even imagine they'd been there. But in fact they had no real concept of the life within.

As requested, Hank drove his own car and did not wear his uniform. He pulled in beside Marlis's car and walked over to where Reed sat on a picnic table under several scrub pines. A continuous stream of traffic roared past on the freeway. Hank looked toward the bathrooms. "Is Marlis . . ."

"Marlis is at work," Reed called. "I'm the one who called the meeting. She said you're an honest man, someone with integrity. She said if anyone could be trusted it was Hank Jackson."

Hank flushed at the exaggerated tone of Reed's compliments. He warily rose to the bait. "Why would someone like you care about an honest cop?"

"Appearances can deceive, at least that's what I hope. It's why the fashion industry does so well. If there's one thing I've learned in life it's that the people who dress to look the most hip or the most sophisticated are most often the least. It's why these TV preachers and politicians make out so well. Were you one of the men involved investigating Wayne Pog's death?"

"Death? Disappearance is the way we have it logged. That's the way his own department wanted it. Not that it's any of your business, but the answer's no. One of our detectives asked around. But who knew where to ask. One day he was there and then he was gone." Hank scrutinized Reed as if trying to read his mind. "Why do you say death?"

"Marlis is certain. Wayne was staking out these three different fields over on the east side of the parish. She said the wardens have been after this violating ring in this area for the last year-and-a-half. Violators had killed deer in those fields on previous occasions."

"I heard rumors about the violating ring. I never heard anything about him being near those particular fields on that particular night. Did Marlis tell the detective?"

"She claimed yes. Said he didn't even write it down. The question is, did anyone hear anything out that way on the night Wayne disappeared? The way I understand it, the wardens know the ring was operating that night. They found numerous pieces of deer hair, blood, and pieces of entrails on several bridges that night. They also found deer heads and hooves in the creeks. They figure these guys might take as many as fifty or seventy deer a night."

"You know a lot about this don't you. Who are you?"

Reed backed away. "Marlis knows a lot. Anyhow, if someone with authority asked some questions out around those fields, one just east of Strait's Corner, one over near George Carlson's soybean fields, and another one on what Marlis said was the Walbash Flats, maybe someone would report hearing something."

"Six or seven months is a long time," Hank said. But he was fingering his moustache, contemplating. If a man closed a case like the Wayne Pog disappearance there would be a great deal of publicity. Especially if he did it single-handedly and months after the fact.

"What does it hurt to ask?" Reed said.

"The first thing I'm going to do is ask my computer about you, Mr. Reed Erickson."

"You won't find anything."

"Maybe," Hank said. "If nothing else I might make something up. Cops can do that you know. That way we get to take care of people we just don't like." He and Reed locked eyes. After a few seconds they both smiled.

"I trust you won't tell anyone, your wife, anyone in your department about this."

"Why not?" Hank asked as if innocent.

"It might endanger someone's life."

"I doubt I'd care about that particular life," Hank said.

"Yeah, but I do."

"If word leaks to Sheriff LeBitche I'm conducting an unauthorized investigation it'd be the end of my career," Hank said. "Why would I worry about a leak?"

"If word of who or what I am leaks to the wrong people and I get into the wrong circumstances, I'll be the one dead." Reed continued the amused, exaggerated charade of each man looking out only for himself. "All you'll have to do is investigate a homicide."

"It'd probably be the same men who killed Wayne . . . if Wayne is dead," Hank said. Reed shrugged as if to acknowledge

[34]

the uncertainty. "Are you going to show me ID and tell me the agency or do I have to guess?"

"U.S. Fish and Wildlife, Special Operations Division. If you need ID stop by Marlis's sometime after dark. I don't carry it around. We do have peace officer status in most states, but primarily we're here on the violations aspect. That's why I need you for the murder side, unofficially of course."

"Of course." Hank stared at the passing traffic and frowned. "Unofficially, if Sheila knew about this, knew I was risking my job and our future, she'd skin me alive. But the Rittenhous girls have been good to me, Marlis, Debra. These last six months for Marlis must have been a living hell."

Reed nimbly jumped to his feet. "If I get out of line, go ahead and roust me. No special treatment. And let's try to keep our contacts discreet. I want to see if I can get these boys to jump."

"Good luck," Hank said. "As bad as some of these boys hate blacks, that's nothing as to how they hate Yankees, and one who works for the federal government besides . . . whoooeee." Hank jerked his head toward a nearby swamp. "They get you out there in the dark where no one can see and they'll kill you in a minute."

"That's what happened to Wayne," Reed said soberly. "And he was hometown."

FOUR

Reed's life settled into some resemblance of a routine. Week mornings Jody and Patty went off to school. Marlis went to her receptionist's job at Doctor Pierce's office out by the new strip mall. Three days a week Reed drove into work at the Rittenhous Mill where Marlis had induced her sister, Debra, to take him on as a day laborer on the loading dock. Debra, a big-boned woman in contrast to Marlis, had been cordial, too cordial, Reed thought and worried on how much Marlis had revealed of his identity. Marlis did have her pride.

Although they were, he sometimes thought, just like a real family. But of course that was just an illusion, a feeling when they were all seated for dinner. The family feeling had been exactly that way with Pam, Stacy, and Trish. But after all was said and done Pam and the girls had left and the family, the togetherness, became just a memory, a part of his past and a part of his daily life he could never forget.

In truth there were too many strains living with Marlis and her children. Jody resented his presence at every turn and absolutely refused Reed's efforts to make contact. Patty of course followed her big brother. There were even times Marlis acted as if he did not exist. She would casually disrobe in front of him as she changed into her nightgown. They could have been a long-time married couple, although once he and Pam were on the outs he'd never seen her naked again. After seventeen years Pam had become self-conscious.

Reed could never quite decipher if Marlis was unstable, playing games, or was simply erratic because of the trauma she'd faced. One night the four of them would eat a big supper.

The next evening Jody and Patty would have to fend for themselves and Marlis would not eat at all. When Reed tried to cook for everyone Jody refused to eat. Naturally Patty copied her brother's lead. And Marlis was not hungry. Marlis was never hungry.

"You need flesh on those bones," Reed once said, risking the indelicate for what needed to be said.

"My body is not part of your concern," Marlis snapped. "You're supposed to locate Wayne's killer and you haven't located a damn thing. Seems to me you're just about like all the rest."

Reed smiled. Marlis did know her cuts. "It takes time. I've told you that. It's only been a week. There have been a couple of tidbits, a word here and there."

"What?"

He was a fool, Reed thought. Now she had him concerned about his ego, for crissake. "Nothing substantial, just hints."

"Well, what are the hints?" Marlis demanded. She read the look on Reed's face. "You sonofabitch! I bring you in here and then you cut me out."

Yes, Reed thought, life had settled down.

Most evenings he showed his face down at the Blue Moon, keeping up appearances. The plus from working at the mill was rubbing shoulders with Billy Bob. It didn't take long to realize Billy Bob, the big, insecure little baby who lived at home with his aged and impoverished mother, was in with the local boys. Billy Bob looked like a bully and acted like a sissy. For all his size Billy Bob would not be a man to bear up under pain. But most important, at the bottom line, Billy Bob was braggart number one.

From his first day on the job Reed talked guns and hunting, two subjects few rural Southern boys could leave alone. He'd worked in Louisiana once before, in the fall, going after the legendary Louisiana outlaw duck hunters who frequented the vast marshes near the Gulf. At one point the liberalized Louisiana duck hunting regulations permitted hunters to kill over one million ducks a year, more than the entire Atlantic flyway. Some conservation officers estimated hunters took another four million birds illegally.

It was the way men were raised. Hunters took their boys

out with cases of shells, sneaking along dikes and standing up a dozen strong and ground swatting thick flocks of ducks and geese. On the marsh a good day was a hundred ducks, enough to sink a pirogue. Only belatedly did some hunters see the error of their excesses. Spurred by drought, industrialization, and the demands of commerce and agriculture, millions of acres of habitat had been lost. Some hunters aided in the destruction. Only in recent years had some long-time outlaws become born-again conservationists. But not enough, Reed knew. There were too many left like Billy Bob who lacked any kind of concern for other creatures and who could not see wider than or beyond the parameters of his gunsight. Of course Billy Bob wasn't vicious, Reed understood. He was simply dumb.

In good part Billy Bob's lack of vision proved to be Reed's boon. It didn't take many days at all and Billy Bob was singing his song and talking guns and hunting every minute of the day. And when he saw Billy Bob down at the Blue Moon, naturally Reed sat nearby, working into the group in spite of the dour looks from Ross. He knew Ross was looking for an excuse, anything to make him put up his dukes and give him a chance to expand his reputation and mash in some Yankee's face. And of course as much as he tried, Ross simply did not have the wit.

Most evenings Reed played pool, most often with Billy Bob. The others were still suspicious, or perhaps they didn't care for his appearance, Reed thought charitably.

They played for beers. Because he was on the expense tab anyhow, Reed carefully lost two out of three games. And, at least at first, he carried the conversation load, talking about hunting, guns, people, his travels. He'd been just about everywhere, although not exactly in the fashion Billy Bob imagined. And of course he traveled alone. Just like his father, living in the deep forest. A man lived in the forest in order to exist in harmony with nature. The man was never alone. But a man lived in the city in order to live with other men. A man alone in the city was as lonely as a man could get.

"Where did you work? Get the money to travel around?" Billy Bob asked. He wore blue jeans and an army olive drab tee shirt that was still white with grain dust from the mill.

"You name it, I've done it. Shoveling coal on the docks, cooking in a mining camp, cutting pulp, driving cabs, driving trucks." As usual, working undercover Reed stuck as close to the truth as possible. It was easier than recalling a bunch of lies. "Some rich guy's always looking for a strong back. He'll wear yours out by the time you're forty and then toss you in the gutter and look for someone younger and more fit." Reed shrugged. "It's the way the world works."

"Tell me about it," Billy Bob complained. "I once thought of going to trade school to become a medical technician. You know, work in a nice clean hospital. I even enrolled."

"But you didn't go." Reed cut a ball a little too sharp. "Damn, I'm off on my angles today."

"I get like that," Billy Bob said.

"I like the South," Reed continued. Chuck, Wyndal, and Ross watched him from the bar. He was getting a feeling about this group of young Turks. "There's a hell of a diversity of people down here. If you don't mind my saying, you people cover the extremes quite well. And nowadays you're starting to get a wad there in between."

"The middle class," Billy Bob said as if pleased with his recognition of what Reed meant. "That's why we're getting to be such a bore, Doyle says. He says television is the worst thing that was ever invented. It's making us all the same."

Doyle? Doyle Monroe, Reed wondered. Billy Bob surely was an innocent boy. "Yeah, I sure miss the hunting in Wisconsin. Won't be long now the leaves would be changing. Time to get out, grouse, ducks, deer." He leaned close as if to confide a secret. "One year when I was working for this lumber camp. This was a number of years ago, of course. They used to have me drive the back roads and shoot deer for the camp. I shot fifty-six one year. Fifty-six."

Billy Bob slammed home the eight ball. He glanced at the others sitting at the bar. A thin sheen of sweat had gathered at his temples. His big stomach hung out under his shirt. His blue eyes were eager with anticipation. "I shot twenty deer in one night."

"Twenty!" Reed said purposely loud. Billy Bob grimaced in panic. "Twenty?" Reed contained his anger in clenched teeth. Billy Bob was one of those who simply killed. He did not know.

He did not comprehend what it was he did. Reed took on a note of incredulity. "How the hell could you shoot twenty? What would you do with twenty? You couldn't possibly process them."

Billy Bob glanced at his friends sitting along the bar. He stiffened as if suddenly realizing his transgression. "Oh, there are ways. It was a long time ago. There's not as many deer around as there used to be."

"I wonder why that is?" Reed asked, as if sincere.

Doyle said grace. They passed the dishes clockwise. They ate in near silence, Doyle, his wife Rachel, his daughter Lisa, and of course his eighty-four year old mother who sat hunched-back and nibbled at her food. From time to time Rachel reached over with a napkin and wiped the drool off her mother-in-law's chin.

Rachel glanced at Doyle. He was in one of his trance moods, serene he called it, absorbed by the clatter of forks on the blue porcelain plates and the inner workings of his mind. What went on in there Rachel no longer knew. Some where, some time, perhaps after business at the store had started to decline, Doyle had left her behind. She was his wife. Fix supper, clean house, take care of his mother who could not even control her bowels.

Rachel tucked a stray hair back into place. She wore her coal black hair in a bun, her look severe, like her life. She wore more makeup than necessary, but there were lines she should not have and besides, it had been her one battle with Doyle ever since they had wed. Doyle didn't like makeup, thus Rachel wore it all the time. He no longer said anything to her, it was Lisa who took the brunt.

Poor Lisa. After David had escaped to Atlanta, Lisa was all Doyle had left. "May I please be excused, Father?" Lisa asked. She was sixteen, a tall girl with angular lines and a pouty French mouth men found attractive.

"Not until everyone finishes their main course."

Lisa looked around. "Everyone is finished."

"Not your grandmother."

Lisa beseeched her mother for assistance. Grandmother never finished her meal.

[40]

Rachel shuddered and turned her head. For what Doyle did to Lisa, she always took the blame.

"A few minutes with your family is not going to hurt," Doyle lectured. "Dinner is a time of sharing, of communing together in silence. It's part of the continuity of being home in your own house. The world is a whole, we do not walk alone. I tried to make your brother see that." Doyle's eyes seemed to glaze at the mention of his son, David, who'd abandoned his family and his state and moved to Atlanta where he worked as a stockbroker. "But he had bigger ideas."

Abruptly Doyle raised his eyes. "If you can't stand to be with your family, with your mother, father, and grandmother, then go. Go!"

Lisa sat meekly in her chair. In a minute or so Rachel stood and took her mother-in-law's plate. "I think that's enough, Eunice. Lisa, you may go."

Doyle sat silently while Rachel cleared the table around him and his mother. "I took in four hundred dollars today at the store. Four hundred dollars gross." Doyle shook his head from side to side. "If I was a drinking man, I'd have a drink, Rachel. As it is, I just wonder where it's all going to end."

Rachel stood at the kitchen sink and rinsed dishes before loading them into the dishwasher. A lump clogged her throat. Tears blurred her vision. If she could only talk to Doyle she would have told him that she did not care where it all ended. She just wanted it to end.

Immediately after supper, Hank Jackson left home. He had unfinished business, he informed Sheila. He could not tell her what it was. Sheila had absolutely no use for the Rittenhous family. None of them, even though as a young girl she'd worked there as a maid. She hated sweet little Marlis worst of all, although she'd been adamant in her refusal to discuss the matter. "It doesn't concern you," she'd said in that imperious tone that said he was trespassing. Well, he had secrets of his own. A little mystery about your mate kept life interesting.

Hank drove north down the parish road toward Strait's Corner. He'd tripled his chances of detection by wearing his uniform and taking the squad car. But no parish officers were scheduled for this section and he wanted the image of official authority. People might be more likely to respond. Or else they wouldn't tell him a thing. He'd never quite figured which way was best.

As usual driving the country road brought back a wave of nostalgia. The times he'd walked this road. It hadn't been paved back then, and it wasn't near as straight. How many kids were there like him, a black mama and no papa? His father had gone north to Chicago looking for work. At first he wrote. A few times he sent money. And then they heard no more. If he saw the man he'd kill him, Hank had said. And there wouldn't be a shred of guilt.

He passed the Rittenhous place, a redbrick house covered over with ivy and set back on the side of a hill overlooking the valley. They'd had cotton fields at one time. Now it was nothing but scrub. The cement water fountain in the front was grey and cracked. No one trimmed the shrubs or tended to the flower garden. In summertime when the flowers were in bloom this had been one of the prettiest little corners in all of Louisiana. Now weeks would pass before someone mowed the grass.

There'd been a time Blaine Rittenhous fancied himself as an aristocrat, Hank knew. Maybe he still did. Few people related to the old man these days. He'd turned his own daughters against him, first Debra and then Marlis. Although Debra had returned.

"And the world goes around," Hank said aloud. A man looks around and finds he hasn't moved at all.

He rattled over a bridge with wooden planks and paused to gaze at the deep, muddy waters of the Krotz River, one of the feeder tributaries into the Atchafalaya. Come springtime the waters could chew up tree stumps all the way down from Wisconsin. Men and boats had been sucked into two hundred foot deep eddies and never a trace had been found. One report had it they'd found traces of deer hair and entrails on this bridge. If a group wanted to dispose of guts and heads of deer this would be the place. Or even a game warden and his truck.

He wondered if anyone had searched the banks six months previously, and knew they hadn't. He could ask to drag the river and they'd laugh in his face.

Hank drove on, passing through rich, river-bottom farmland. Even with all the levees and dams and channels built by the Army Corps of Engineers the bottoms were subject to periodic floods. People were washed out and then they moved back in. It was a way of life.

Hank opened his window to the rich humus of good soil and the musty scent of cypress coated with Spanish moss. He smiled contentedly, like a man long gone who'd just entered home.

Strait's Corner wasn't much, but it had once been home. He stopped at the tiny, unpainted grocery store first. Even though the squad car wasn't in need of gas he topped off the tank and bought an orange soda out of the cooler. He nodded his hellos. Fifteen years gone, there weren't many of the old timers left.

There were six shacks in the town, if you chose to call it that. They were all small and none were freshly painted. A couple were covered with brown asphalt shingles and covered over with tin roofs that thundered like the coming of death under a driving rain. The yards were dirt, rooted up by pigs, a few scrawny cattle, and even one decrepit horse. Patchwork fences constructed from planks, tires, milk crates, and rusted wire provided some separation for the homes.

There were four men and a woman seated around the store. Hank knew their names and they knew him. But only the owner, Old Sidney, had known him as a boy. The others viewed him as a cop. The car had been a mistake. And the uniform had been a mistake. Or maybe his simple presence would have been just as bad. These people didn't owe him the time of day. If he asked Sidney, it would be all right. Sidney understood where Hank Jackson stood. If he asked the others they wouldn't answer him straight and then word would get around.

Hank made small talk, guzzled his soda and paid his tab. "Blyden still walk the roads at night?"

"Day and night," Sidney said. He was a thick man with thick skin and thick jowls that were poxed and black. His fingers were thick like sausages and scarred from years shucking oysters. "He's got the arthritis bad now. It don't let him sleep. There's times he's been talking about taking a swim."

In the river, Hank understood. He remembered twenty

years ago when old Joe Wiezner did the same. The main thing was to make sure you drowned before the alligators came along.

Hank nodded his goodbyes. It struck him as sad that the blacks were no longer a community as they'd once been in the past. Of course, as Sheila proclaimed, "That's good. It means we all aren't on the bottom of the heap." Hank smiled. He might one day run for sheriff, but for certain Sheila was no diplomat. He'd have to do as he'd threatened more than once—bring out the adhesive tape.

"Door's open," Blyden Jackson called when Hank tapped on the door. A hard rap would break the thin pane.

Hank pushed open the door and stepped into the gloom. "It's Hank," he said in case Blyden couldn't see. As far as anyone knew, Blyden was a distant relative, but no one knew just how. Blyden didn't even know the day or year when he was born. "Don't get any older that way," he'd say with a laugh.

The house was built so that if you fired a rifle the bullet would pass through every room. His home had been the same, the front room had been filled with four beds and two wooden chairs. Each child kept his clothes in a paper bag under the bed. There were holes in the floor and the walls and a plywood board nailed over one window. A wood space-heater provided heat and was mama's cooking stove as well. They used an old galvanized tub to store their wood. In the summer, when the heat built and the lowland swamp humidity rose, a child could scarcely breathe. For twelve years these shacks had been his life.

Hank sat down on a bed and wondered if there were any lice. His lips compressed with anger at himself. A person born to dirt and poverty doesn't give it a second thought, at least not until he sees the other side. A person used to cleanliness cannot abide filth. And it was all just part of the mind.

He passed the time of day. How were the crawfish this year?

"Good," Blyden said. He was keen-eyed, wizened with his arms, legs, and hips bowed like a bent willow taking on the wind. The knuckles of his hands were swollen and gnarled from the ravages of arthritis. "It was a dry summer last year, a wet fall, and then a fairly mild winter. The crawfish did well. Although the market was down. What with the farms and all."

"Yeah," Hank laughed. "Can you beat it, growing crawfish in the same fields with organic rice."

Hank continued to circle around. Finally Blyden moved him along. "You didn't come to visit an old man, Hank. Not in that fancy uniform."

"No," Hank admitted. He went into his story, going back six months to the time the game warden Wayne Pog had disappeared. Word was there had been some violating that night, some of it out this way. Possibly Pog had come along.

"Oh, I remember that," Blyden said. He shuffled outside to the porch and settled back in a wicker rocker that was pulling apart at the seams. "I was sitting right here most of the night. That was a few days before I heard the warden disappeared. But it might have been the same day."

"You wouldn't know what day."

"The next day it stormed. It was a cold rain, straight out of the north. Temperature never got over fifty-five."

"That's good enough," Hank said.

"Earlier that night a truck stopped down the road there, quarter-mile or so. Someone fired a shot. Violator I figured. Then they drove on past."

"I don't suppose you'd recognize the truck?"

"Headlights and dark," Blyden said as if Hank were stupid. He cut off a wad of tobacco with a jackknife and slowly worked it in against his cheek and gum.

Hank waited. He gazed out toward the highway a hundred feet away. He'd questioned at least twenty people and this was the best he had, an unidentifiable truck and one shot.

"Two hours later the truck came back. It was followed by another. They turned down there on Strait's Levee. Must've been gone an hour or more when one of them came back. The other one's still out there."

Hank stood unmoved. That his palms were sweaty and his heart beat fast, no one could tell. His dark eyes blinked with excitement and it took every fiber of will to keep himself from offending Blyden and asking him if he was sure.

"This is still the only entrance onto and off of Strait's Levee, if I recall?"

"People die, people go, the earth remains the same," Blyden said. But his eyes were glazed over. For even he understood that was no longer the truth.

Hank met Reed out on the interstate rest stop.

"This is good," Reed said as Hank approached him at the same picnic table as the previous meeting. "You have a local place here where mostly outsiders tread. It's a good place to hide, the national arteries of the freeways and the byways. No one knows anyone. It's part of the reason our national psyche is badly in need of repair."

"You must have been waiting here a long time," Hank said. He sat his long, lanky form on the table beside Reed so they could both watch the passing traffic and any cars driving into the rest area.

"Got some coffee here." Reed indicated a metal thermos at his side.

"Sure," Hank said. "Never trust a cop who doesn't drink coffee. I'll take mine black."

"That's what I like about stakeouts; drinking coffee and holding your bladder. There've been cases I spent days on end doing that. What do you have?"

"A firm lead," Hank said. He could not resist a grin at his rapid success. "Old fellow I know saw two trucks drive down Strait's Levee the night Wayne disappeared. Only one truck came back."

"Guy must have one hell of a memory to pinpoint something like that to the day."

"Oh, he didn't know which day. He wouldn't know what day of the week today was. But the next day a cold rain front dropped down out of Yankee land, exactly as the newspaper said the day after Wayne disappeared."

Reed whistled. "Nothing we can use in court, but it sounds as reliable as we'll get."

'I've got a fellow, Choctaw Indian named Story Diver, he lives just down the road a piece in a cabin set on stilts. He traps muskrat and nutria and fishes the swamp. He's going to check the shoreline, do some poling along side the levee in his pirogue. I gave him a few bucks. If you've got a budget I could give him a few more."

[46]

Reed handed Hank fifty dollars. "No telling what a man might stick."

"Of course then I'll have to take it to the Sheriff. If I hold out on The Bitch he'll have my butt."

"And we'll probably lose our case. The Sheriff will take credit and you'll never get to run for his office."

"Who said I'm running for sheriff," Hank protested loudly.

Reed smiled as if to rest his case. "I've got movement of my own. I've been working with Billy Bob down at the mill and shooting pool at the Blue Moon. As you well know, Billy Bob likes to talk. Every group has a couple. A lot of violators are the same. What good is killing something if you can't tell people what you've done? It's the number one reason people hunt in this country. Not to kill. Not to hunt. To get something and then tell people they did it. Billy Bob's at the head of the game. I tell Billy Bob I've killed a bunch of deer and he tells me he's killed more. All this in less than two weeks. I don't know if he's blowing smoke or if he's part of the same group we're seeking or not. But he did seem awful proud and I did talk my way into going along on a gator hunt. Some guy's willing to pay a couple of thousand dollars for the full-size carcass of a ten to twelve foot bull. I told Billy Bob I've never killed a gator and that I'd love to kill one of those."

It was Hank's turn to purse his lips. He gazed out at the nearby backwaters of the Atchafalaya Swamp. The fingered roots of huge cypress trees covered with thick whiskers of hanging moss reached into black and green algae covered waters. Hank motioned. "You'll be going out there. All alone. Who the hell are you going with besides Billy Bob?"

"I don't know," Reed said in his laconic, dry drawl. He could have been a cowboy talking about the weather. "I would presume it would be some of his cronies from the bar. I can't conceive of why, but they haven't taken a liking to me yet. Besides, I don't think they know I'm coming. I sort of invited myself. Billy Bob was too frightened to tell me no. And I don't think he had the nerve to tell them I was coming along."

"And of course you have no idea where you're going."

"No idea," Reed said casually.

Hank sighed and shook his head. "It doesn't sound too smart, Yankee."

"That's what Doug would say." Reed handed Hank a piece of paper. "That's my partner and where he's staying in Baton Rouge. He's searching for outlets for the meat on that end as well as coordinating things with the state. If I'm not back in a couple days give him a call."

"I shouldn't tell you your job, but I think you're nuts. Guys down here don't care much for the federal government. A game warden's even worse."

"That's true, Hank. But I have to take the shot here. Normally we can be on an operation several months before we get an invite like this. Besides, we don't even know that these are the right guys. And they'll understand that other people know I'm going out with them. And as you know, hunting a particular deer is a hundred times more difficult than hunting just any old deer in general. The same's true when your quarry is a particular man. You have to find a way to get close."

"Sure," Hank said as if talking from a distance. He even moved a step away, putting distance between himself and a form of behavior he could not understand. "I guess that makes me a generalist. If I see a crime, I'll try to stop it. But I wouldn't tie myself out as bait. It's not worth the risk."

Reed looked Hank in the eyes. "You have family, Hank. I don't. They left. Or at least they're leaving. Mostly my fault . . . I guess. Maybe it was the way I was raised. The way I live. You try to pare life down, live with less, stay with the necessities. But it's hard to fight television and peer groups. When my girls were young they believed as I believed. Now . . . they believe what they hear in music or see on television" Reed lapsed into silence and contemplated the green Bermuda grass and sand burrs growing under the table. He rubbed at his thin beard. "That was a long time ago. I don't know. Maybe I quit paying attention. Things got away. Maybe I got wrapped up in myself, my job. Like everyone else. I just don't know. Music, television are there every minute of the day. The rest of us get on with our lives."

Hank looked away as if embarrassed by Reed's frank talk.

"People use and use and they never give back," Reed continued. "Like these violators. Deer are a managed commodity in this country. From a few hundred thousand at the turn of the century to twenty million today, they're under the control of man, like cattle. If we let deer go unchecked, in three years time the herd doubles. Disease would spread. Farmers are howling now about damage. The anti-hunters resolutely refuse to look at the entire picture, to even look beyond the life of a single animal. Man increased the food supply for deer and made the herd what it is. Deer are one of our few successes. Hunters serve as our control. But these violators corrupt those controls. They'll take what's abundant, but they're also the kind who'd take the last of an endangered species just to claim the kill. And they kill a man over a deer? What does Marlis have? No, someone has to pay." Reed spoke softly, still contemplating. "Besides, once you've hunted man in the wild, it's hard to go back to anything else."

Reed kneaded the knuckles of one hand in the palm of the other. In truth, if Pam went through with the divorce the hunt would be all he'd have. But he could not tell Hank. He gazed into Hank's dark eyes and then he understood, Hank already knew.

Reed sighed. "Enough lecture. Back to work." Reed contemplated the ground and thickets of sand burrs. "No, I lost my family. Just like Marlis has lost hers." Reed shrugged. He spoke softly. "Someone has to pay."

FIVE

Doyle's first impulse was to put a bullet into Billy Bob's jiggly, lard stomach. Let the fat boy writhe and squirm for a while before he put one through his brain, assuming Billy Bob had a brain.

Doyle's open palm cracked the side of Billy Bob's face, one side and then the other. Billy Bob recoiled in terror. What Marine boot camp couldn't do with this tub of lard, Doyle thought with disgust. And to think his life, his future hung in the balance with the caliber of a man such as this. It surely made a man stop and think.

Reed stood silently and watched the show. The hair-trigger and vehemence of Doyle's attack initiated an abrupt shot of adrenaline. He'd understood the base intelligence and reactions of the other young men. He hadn't expected a Doyle Monroe.

He'd bummed a ride with Billy Bob to the rendezvous at Wyndal's shanty of a country home. The rectangular stucco house had once, many years previous, been painted turquoise blue. Thigh-high patches of long weeds at the edges of the dirt yard partially concealed several vehicles that had long ago died and were gradually being stripped for parts. Four four-wheel drive pickup trucks clogged the balance of the junk yard.

"Who told you to bring him?" Doyle jerked a thumb at Reed. This was, Reed understood, one man you did not move through intimidation.

Billy Bob's face bunched up like that of a young boy verging on tears. "He works at the mill. He . . . he likes to hunt, Doyle. I . . ."

Reed interrupted, looking to save Billy Bob from additional

distress. "I thought we were just going out to get a big gator. I've never killed a gator. I sort of invited myself along. What's the big deal?"

Doyle's red, square-jawed face pinched up as if he'd bitten into a sour lemon. He barely held back from slamming his fist through that bearded face. That the Yankee revealed no sign of intimidation was just one more irritation heaped on top of all the rest. Doyle spoke with an accent made thicker by his rage. "You're not one of us. You're not from this town or even this state. What we do is none of your business. Billy Bob should know that. We don't want or need outsiders. The best thing you could do is walk right out of here."

"It's four or five miles back to town," Reed said simply. His skin tingled nervously as he took a provocative tact. "Why the hell would I leave? Because an asshole like you says so? Who are you?" The words were magical. Everyone ceased to talk. All eyes focused on him. The bodies were spread, six men covering him from every side.

Reed stood easy, legs shoulder width, balance on the balls of his feet. He quietly drew in more breath, building oxygen reserves in his lungs and trying to control the nervous vibrations of his hands. Doyle's deep blue eyes focused on him with all the intensity of a prison guard picking out a mark. Doyle's presence on the illicit gator hunt represented but a moderate surprise. Community leaders, businessmen, politicians, policemen, over the years Reed had arrested violators of every socio-economic stripe.

"There is no need to swear," Doyle said. "Blasphemy is the refuge of the unclean. Who are you? What are you doing in our town and messing with our women? Marlis doesn't belong with the likes of you."

Why would Doyle mention Marlis? Reed wondered in passing. "Are we going hunting gators or not? Or do you guys just stand around and talk like a bunch of bully boys. I came to hunt, not blow steam." Behind his words Reed tensed as everyone except Billy Bob moved in. They all, he could sense, waited on Doyle to give the word. Ross of course was the closest, the most eager-looking.

Doyle gave the slightest nod of his head. Reed stepped sideways toward Ross and ducked into his attacker as a haymaker swooshed air over his head. The blubber of Ross's stomach slammed Reed's head and shoulder and the two of them were forced back into the others. They quickly had him pinned, but in the close quarters he managed to avoid any major blows. They forced him to the ground. Ross knelt with his knee in the small of Reed's back while they took his wallet.

"There's nothing here," Wyndal said. "Wisconsin driver's license, two twenties, a picture of some dame and two kids and, look at this, a library card. L.E. Phillips. Where the hell is that?" He kept one of the twenties and handed the spoils to Doyle.

Doyle held his hand out for the money. "We don't steal." He carefully examined the wallet for any hidden compartment. He instructed the men to take Reed's boots off.

"Nothing here," Chuck said when the task was complete.

"Who are you?" Doyle again asked in a steady, controlled voice. Something here was not right. He knew drunks. Before he'd been saved, he'd been one himself; and he knew men who'd leech off women. Cowards—everyone. If they were surrounded like this guy, Reed, they'd be pleading for mercy.

Mercy, that was God's prerogative. It was not his. Not with a man who moved in with Marlis Rittenhous.

Ross gripped Reed's hair and jerked his head back while kneeling harder in the small of Reed's back. Reed grunted, "Just one of you guys face me like a man. Just one."

"Let him up," Doyle said.

Ross looked up to protest, thought better of it and abruptly let Reed's head snap forward. With slow deliberation Reed climbed to his feet and brushed himself off. He looked Ross in the eyes and smiled. If he ever got Ross off by himself . . .

"So are we going after that gator or what?" Reed asked. "That's if you big brave boys are done with your fun."

"You want to get out with us awfully bad," Doyle observed. His eyes narrowed. "Well, let's go. We're heading out into the deep of the swamp."

"Good," Reed said. "What do you take for guns?"

"We don't take guns," Doyle said. "They make noise. We lasso a big bull gator in his den. Then we take him with our hands."

"Sounds exciting," Reed said. He felt as though he'd just put a cocked pistol to his head.

They crept along the levee, one truck behind the other. Bright spotlights shone across the black sheen of water to a tangled shore ten feet away. On several occasions red alligator eyes gleamed, low, squat, smaller animals two to three feet long. Once they spotted a four to five footer and Doyle coasted to a stop.

"Take him with the Hornet?" Ross asked. He sat on the rider's side while Doyle drove. They'd wedged Reed in between them where his knees were jammed over by the gearshift.

Doyle considered.

"Our newby here could wade across and get him," Ross suggested.

"Sure, why not," Reed said before Doyle had the chance. "Plug him good so he doesn't crawl away to where I have to thrash around in the brush with my knife."

Without a word Doyle slowly eased the clutch and they moved ahead. Ross blew air in disappointment but he did not argue. No one argued with Doyle Monroe, Reed had observed. These boys might be tough with strangers and each other, but they were straight line legionaires when Doyle spoke.

"We'll get the big one first and then see how time sits," Doyle said.

"I just want to kill one," Reed said just to keep up some conversation. "Just to say I did it."

"You ever eat gator?" Ross asked.

"Once in Florida. It wasn't bad, a bit chewy and just a little fishy tasting. But it could have been the restaurant."

"The best way is grilled," Ross said. "They're paying five and six dollars a pound wholesale for gator meat."

"Legal gator meat," Doyle added. "Twenty-plus dollars a foot for the hide, legal hide. The government's controlling everything. First they said it was endangered and wouldn't let us hunt for twenty years. They killed the open market. Now there are just a couple of major outlets. And now the biologists tell us they weren't endangered at all, we just didn't know where they were hiding. Now you can hunt, but the government has the controls."

The length and passion of the speech surprised Reed. This Doyle was no fool. Some biologists had contended exactly that. One Louisiana fisheries man estimated there were one hundred and fifty thousand alligators in the state in 1970 and the population had increased to more than a half a million. Hunting wasn't the threat as much as the loss of habitat. Each year Louisiana lost more than twenty-five thousand acres of freshwater marsh to enroaching seawater because of canals for the oil and gas industry. Alligators, ducks, heron, egrets, muskrats, crayfish, and countless other creatures were summarily shunted aside so unseeing and unknowing city dwellers could have their material comforts. Hell, the Fast Food restaurants used beef raised on destroyed rain forests. They didn't understand the connection, Reed thought, but it was the demands of city folks that destroyed the countryside. Violators were just a small part, but they were his part.

"The government gets into everything a man does," Reed said as if in agreement. The young boys he understood. He could hunt and kill and drink and laugh and curse and play their game. Hell, they just killed for fun. But Doyle . . .

"The Bible tells us, 'Be fruitful and multiply.' Genesis, one-twenty-eight. 'And fill the earth and subdue it, and have dominion over the fish of the sea and over the birds of the air and over every living thing that moves upon the earth.' The government and their rules corrupt the Bible."

Reed looked away so Doyle could not see his face. Overpopulation was the world's number one environmental problem; two billion over the first four million years of human growth, two more billion over the next forty-six years and then only twenty-two years to add two billion more. And all the while unrenewable resources were being depleted. But how do you tell that to a Doyle Monroe.

"Lookee there," Ross said and focused the spotlight on a piece of white bobbing in the water.

"Bob-tail," Doyle grunted, talking of an alligator that had been shot and then had the tail cut off for steaks. "Looks a day or so old."

"Probably some locals getting a meal," Reed said.

"Niggers," Ross grunted.

"Coloreds don't come out this way too much," Doyle said

as if in normal conversation. They moved ahead. The moss-draped foliage across the canal widened out into a grassy marsh mostly coated with thick bog between slivers of black water. "Over there," Doyle said. He stopped the truck. Ross manipulated the spotlight. "To your left," Doyle snapped like a coach chastising one of his players. Ross swung too far. Reed reached up and steadied Ross's hand so the light fell upon a dark trail across the bog and the scattered remains of fish and feathers from waterfowl.

"Look at that track," Ross said with a touch of nervousness. "You think he's under the bank here?"

"He ate on the bog, he's under the bog," Doyle said impatiently. "Let's get out there. If he's not in his den maybe we can stick the Yankee's leg here in the water, slice off a little piece and lure him out."

"I wouldn't appreciate that," Reed said as if trying to joke. "Next time I might not come along."

Doyle leaned across the seat so his face was six inches away. Reed could smell the pinch of tobacco Doyle'd tucked under his lower lip. "Next time you won't. Guaranteed."

He should push him, Reed thought, call him on his authority. But it just did not seem like the time nor place.

They unloaded the trucks and picked up an axe, shovel, machete, lanterns, and two twenty foot poles, one with an iron hook under the end. Billy Bob carried a rifle.

"Put that away," Doyle said softly. His young charges stared in wonderment.

"Just in case," Billy Bob said.

"Just in case means you messed up," Doyle said. "Then you get your leg bit off. Maybe go down for a swim and a death roll. No, we give the animal a chance, take him on with your hands like man."

Billy Bob slowly replaced the rifle in the rack in the back window. The night grew quiet. A warm, moist breeze blew up out of the Gulf a hundred miles to the south. The young men stared at one another and then at Reed. The fun times had been erased. Doyle was in a bad mood, all because of Reed. As they trekked single file down across the dirt levee, Ross angrily dug an elbow into Billy Bob's ribs.

With Doyle in the lead, they found a spot where the bog

almost touched the steep levee bank. They stepped out on the bog and began wading across the spongy surface. Almost immediately the bigger men, Billy Bob and Ross began breaking through, falling into the thin film of water on top and floundering as they, in near panic, sought to jerk their legs up from dangling beneath the surface.

"Settle down," Doyle hissed at their wallowing and heavy breathing. "You sound like a bunch of sissies."

Doyle had the knack for walking on bog, Reed observed. He walked bent-kneed and whenever one foot started to break through he fell forward on the knee to spread his weight. In a smooth motion his opposite foot moved ahead and he seemed to hop ahead and rise up on his feet.

They struggled out across the bog, aiming for the muddy trail of clawed prints and the remains of fish and waterfowl. The musky odor of a bull alligator filled the muggy night. Lightning flashed in the distance toward the Gulf. Doyle took one of the twenty foot poles and began probing beneath the bog. The others stood in a circle, waiting expectantly, once again looking to test their manhood in front of their peers, Reed thought. Except for Doyle, these guys weren't regular alligator poachers, not like some of the old, wizened gator hunters he'd met down in Florida in the days poachers took twenty to thirty thousand gators a year. Alligator Bill, just a little wizened, tobacco-chewing fellow about five foot five, had calmly informed Reed he'd never shot an alligator in his life. But he'd killed thousands with his pocketknife. Alligator Bill had, Reed felt then and now, been speaking the truth.

"Up, I felt him move," Doyle said. "Billy Bob, Ross, get in here with those shovels and peel away this bog."

The two big men moved forward, their white faces shiny and grim under the glare from the propane lantern light. They dug a trench down into the bog. Once Billy Bob broke through and he scrambled backward. A whine escaped his lips. Before Doyle could speak Reed picked up the shovel and took Billy Bob's spot.

"Don't fall in the hole," Ross said from across the trench. Sweat streamed down his face and dripped off the end of his nose.

"I never rode an alligator," Reed said with a laugh. "Can't

be much worse than riding a Brahma bull. Unless a man doesn't like to swim."

"You think you're a tough bastard don't you?" Ross muttered.

Doyle reached forward with the iron hook and hooked one end of the bog they'd cut and peeled it back as if it were a rug. He moved up alongside the bog. "Get ready boys. And watch out for that tail." He carefully probed down with the pole and the hook. "Let me see if he's still down here and I can figure out which end is his head."

A powerful force swirled under the black sheen of water. "He's there," Doyle said. For the first time a touch of excitement entered his voice. He grinned as if in anticipation. He moved the pole ahead and then suddenly gave a powerful jerk upward. A tremendous fury erupted.

With deft quickness Reed slipped away from the pressure at his shoulder. Ross almost tumbled forward into the hole.

"Give me a hand," Doyle grunted.

While others floundered around, Reed leapt across the hole and seized the pole with Doyle. They heaved and the huge head of a twelve foot alligator erupted out of the hole. Powerful jaws with more than a ton of force per square inch, snapped at the air. Stout legs clawed and a serpentine tail slammed back and forth throwing water and ripping apart the bog. Except for Reed and Doyle grimly hanging onto the pole, everyone scrambled backward.

"Get in here you cowards," Doyle bellowed. "Get him across the neck."

Wyndal tried first, machete in hand, approaching too far from the rear. But the thrashing tail slammed him in the legs and he clawed frantically for safety. The others circled uselessly, trying to be a part but unwilling to make the move all the way into the center of the fray.

"Damn cowards," Doyle hissed to Reed. For the instant the two of them were companions, fighting for a common cause. "I told them, just past the outer storm and aim for the gator's back, like the eye of a hurricane."

"Ross, grab the pole," Reed grunted. His arms felt half jerked from their sockets as he and Doyle fought to keep the gator on top of the bog though just out of reach. If the hook came loose and they dropped through the bog the alligator would cover the three feet separating them in a flash.

As soon as Ross moved in, Reed scrambled sideways and seized the axe from Chuck. In a rapid, crabbing motion Reed moved toward the alligator, carefully watching the thrashing head and tail. He feinted once and the tail whiplashed in his direction. Almost immediately Reed launched himself through the air, his legs clamping around the powerful torso. The alligator clawed at his legs. With an arcing, overhead swing the axe flashed through the air finding its mark in the scaly flesh across the back of the alligator's neck. The creature arched from head to tail then quivered as if electrocuted, finally lying still.

A collective sigh escaped the men. Billy Bob and Ross dropped to their sides in the wet water on top of the bog. Even Doyle sank to his knees. When Doyle spoke it was with a hint of both admiration and suspicion. "That was one hell of a shot. Half the time these guys have to cut a head half off before the thing quits thrashing. You hit the nerve right on the button."

"You said behind the neck. I like a good clean kill. I cut pulp in Wisconsin. I'm not a stranger to an axe."

"I told you he could do it," Billy Bob said as if taking credit. He'd tentatively moved in beside the alligator. "That's twelve feet if it's an inch. We've never gotten one that big before. We should get a bonus from Sam. . . ."

Doyle swung the twenty foot pole so it caught Billy Bob across the shins. Billy Bob fell backward, howling and writhing in the water. Doyle towered over him. "I told you, Billy Bob, you've got to muzzle that mouth. Reed there did all right. Maybe too good. But he's still a stranger, and strangers are a danger. Isn't that right?" Doyle asked Reed.

"Sometimes," Reed said. "Sometimes not. I like to hunt and fish. I wanted to kill an alligator. Thanks for the chance. If you get something bigger than this give me a call." Reed stood from the back of the alligator. "Well, are we going to horse this thing up to the trucks or what?"

"Wyndal has a winch," Ross said.

"If I can walk," Wyndal moaned. "The way that thing caught me now I have an alligator knee."

"Look at this," Ross pointed at Reed's trembling hands. "He's shaking like a leaf."

"I didn't see you in there," Doyle snapped.

Ross ducked his head.

Reed nodded his thanks but Doyle had simply turned away. Reed stared at the huge alligator and the stream of blood drying on the back of its head. For more than two decades it lived out there in the swamp, a part of nature, a part of the whole. And along come some good old boys looking to make some bucks. Looking for excitement. Or just looking to kill. A deep sadness seized Reed. Of course man was part of nature also. He was not, like some city slickers and anti-hunters liked to think, above the fray. Man was part. Still it was sad. The good ole boys were mindlessly whooping it up with joy. But Reed knew better. A part of nature had been destroyed. He'd been the instrument of the big creature's death.

They collected their tools and struggled back up to the levee. "Solid ground never felt so good," Billy Bob said. In spite of Doyle's blow to the stomach he was in good spirits over the successful hunt.

"What's with Doyle?" Reed asked.

"Oh, Doyle's funny about certain things. It takes him a long time to accept new people. Even from town. You just have to give him time. He doesn't hunt with us all the time."

What about when you're after deer, Reed wanted to ask. But Billy Bob had moved away so as not to appear too buddy-buddy. Reed's back, shoulders, neck, and arms ached from the strain of the fight. He'd moved closer to young guys, even impressed them some. But the more he saw of Doyle, the more Reed was certain Doyle Monroe was the key to this whole thing.

SIX

Reed had hoped the illegal alligator hunt would bring him in as a solid member of the group. In a sense he'd succeeded. Even Ross, who harbored an obvious dislike, had conceded Reed's bravery at jumping onto the back of the thrashing alligator. When he showed up at the Blue Moon he could drink and laugh and play a little pool with the young toughs. But with Doyle he could not get close. Any direct attempts at friendliness would simply fuel further suspicions. As the boys said, Doyle did not curse, drink, or frequent bars. At best Reed could stop by Doyle's store to purchase a gallon of milk. And in the morning he could stop at the Magnolia Cafe and sit alone at the counter while Doyle and seven or eight local businessmen talked and laughed and shook dice to see who would buy coffee and rolls. Reed would nod and say hello and maybe receive a nod or grunt in return. But he could get no further than that.

And contrary to his hopes, life with Marlis Pog and family did not become easier with time. Jody openly resented him at every turn. And Patty would not look at him or let him get close. On several occasions he and Marlis went out drinking or dancing, holding hands, and acting like lovers. That the smooth velvet of her skin burned with unusual warmth served to stir Reed to excitement. At ninety-five pounds Marlis had not one ounce of fat. Publicly she'd press into him with her body and then gaze at him with eyes as flat and cold as a grey, frozen pond. In private they did not touch.

And of course Marlis did not pretend to drink. She drank. And then she could become loud, argumentative, obnoxious, especially when Reed tried to calm her down or point out the importance of maintaining his cover.

"Why," Marlis would breathe. "You haven't done anything. You haven't discovered anything. What did you come down here for, to try to get a poke?" Reed jerked forward and hissed in Marlis's face. "We've slept together in the same bed for almost a month. And have I touched you once?"

Marlis moved her hands forward on Reed's thigh. Her red lips pushed out in a pretend kiss six inches from his. Other patrons in the Blue Moon glanced away as if embarrassed at their brazen display of public affection. She wore too much makeup, Reed thought, but then he'd thought that of Pam and then Stacy. But the combination on Marlis was exquisite, a magnet combining with the scent of her perfume to draw him forward against his will. At the last second Marlis pulled back. She laughed at the easy success of her demonstration. "You men are all alike. Are you going to call your wife again tonight?"

Reed, red-faced over his weakness, turned away. Maybe he was simply horny. The young toughs he could handle. Marlis was out of his league.

One day Marlis even invited him to her family house. As much out of curiosity as anything, Reed went along, one more mistake.

The Rittenhous estate had reached an advanced state of decay. The blacktop driveway was crumpling like a jigsaw puzzle. Large cracks zig-zagged up the sides of the ivy-covered redbrick walls. A scum-covered pool of rain water bred mosquitoes in the bottom of a grey fountain in the front yard. At one time it might have been country gentility, Reed thought, colored in the cotton fields down in the valley, men in white suits and fair ladies in elaborate gowns sipping mint julips on the porch. But now the only thing of true quality remaining were the gigantic, gnarled three-hundred-year-old oaks draped with Spanish moss.

Reed climbed the cracked cement steps. Parts of the screen were rusting and had holes. Dirt gathered in corners of the porch and the grey floor and white wicker furniture were badly in need of paint. He held the screen door for Marlis who'd gone as taut as a drumhead with strain.

"When Debra and I were young we used to call this 'The Dungeon.' Mother and Father called it home."

The inside, with dark paneling, pulled drapes, and feeble lighting, was indeed dark as a dungeon. "What in hell are you doing bringing that scum in here," were the first words out of Blaine Rittenhous. Like his silent wife, April, and his youngest daughter, Marlis, he had a starvation-thin frame and white parched skin. Of the entire family it seemed only Debra was capable of carrying flesh, Reed thought, and of course the way Debra talked she carried too much.

"And a good day to you, Mr. Rittenhous," Reed had replied to the tiny, grey and watery eyes.

Marlis laughed. "Reed's the no-account drunk that moved in with me and the children," she told her father as if bragging on the fact.

Of course, Reed understood, Marlis had come here just to provoke a fight, he was just the means. He could see it in her eyes, a loathing toward her father that made her body as rigid as a steel rod. Her eyes were fixed, twisted with vehemence just as the old man's were defiant and withdrawn with hurt. April, using the defense of one traumatized beyond her limits, simply blocked the vision from her mind.

Debra entered. As usual she wore her dusty mill clothes of black jeans and a light blue cotton blouse. Her black hair was tied back with a red handkerchief folded into a band. She closed her eyes as if momentarily embarrassed. If anyone in this household saw reality, Reed thought, Debra was the one. "Lemonade?" she asked Reed.

Reed nodded.

"Bourbon or sugar?"

"Better give me a little of each," Reed said pointedly. Debra laughed, but the sound was out of place.

Blaine pointed his thin, palsied fingers at Marlis. "You did this on purpose. I know. You bring this scum into your home in front of your children. You spend nights in public drunkenness down at the Blue Moon. People talk, smear our name. As a mother you're unfit."

"As a human being you're unfit," Marlis yelled with a

passion that made her wide, grey eyes tiny slits. "What do you call sipping bourbon on the front porch every day of your life?"

"Jody and Patty need a stable home environment. I'm going to see Judge Stone." The rush of Blaine's words were incoherent and spittle flew as he yelled.

"You do that and I'll see Hank Jackson," Marlis screamed. "He doesn't know about Sheila. He'll set some things right."

"What does Hank or Sheila have to do with anything?" Debra demanded.

"Out! You get out. You're not any daughter of mine." Blaine turned to push Reed but Reed easily stepped aside. Like a blind man set alone in a strange room, Blaine staggered to catch his balance.

"I'll be outside," Reed growled at Marlis.

"Sure. Whatever," Marlis said and dismissed him with a wave of her hand. He'd served his purpose. She'd made her point.

That night Reed called Pam. Trish answered the telephone. "Hi Daddy," she said brightly when she heard his voice.

"Trish, gal, how are things going?" Reed smiled at the pure joy of his youngest daughter's voice. Unconditional love, what better reason to have children. But of course he was absent, long distance as he'd been too much of his life. Living his job. What good was knowing you're selfish if you don't change?

He talked to Trish several minutes and then requested Pam. As soon as Pam started talking Reed noticed the strain. How was the job, his and hers? Had he found out anything? How was it living in Louisiana? And oh, by the way, she'd gone ahead and had an attorney file papers for a no-fault divorce.

For a moment Reed was silent, trying to catch his breath after a sharp blow to the solar plexus. He would not whine. He would not beg. He cleared his throat and blinked at tears brimming in his eyes. "Then that's it? No further reconsideration?"

"We've been through this so many times," Pam said. She became markedly calm, her determined state, Reed knew. She'd made up her mind. "You've said yourself people seldom make real changes. I have the strength to do this now . . . and that's it. I'm sorry."

A brief surge of anger coursed through Reed's veins. "You're sorry," he spat. He struggled for control. "You're sorry. Seventeen years and you're sorry. That helps a lot," he snarled and hung up the telephone before he said any more. He'd tried to change, become modern as Pam claimed to desire. But it all went against everything he believed.

Reed sensed a presence and looked up. Marlis casually leaned in the bedroom doorway. As always she appeared uniquely feminine with a light touch of makeup, perfume, and wearing a dress. She stood poised with her slender calves crossed as were her arms. Her grey eyes were direct and, for one of the few times since he'd met her, they were neutral, even sympathetic.

"Well, I guess I'll go make my nightly appearance down at the Moon," Reed said. In truth he looked forward to his nights down at the Blue Moon. The less time he spent cooped up in the house with Marlis, Jody, and Patty, the less strain there was for everyone involved. Besides, it was what he desired, have a beer or two, escape, rot his guts, erase his mind.

"You could stay," Marlis said. "I wouldn't mind the company."

Reed hesitated. Almost a month living together and he did not understand her at all. Did she mean just to talk or did she mean more? Was she being genuinely friendly for the first time? Was this a breakthrough? Or just pity?

Reed waved a hand as if in dismissal. "Thanks. I ah, want to touch base with the boys. I won't stay long."

A brief anger flickered behind Marlis's direct gaze. She'd made an overture and been slammed in the face. She'd not make that mistake again. "Who cares? We're not married, you know."

And then she was gone, just like Pam. Reed closed his eyes as if in deep pain at his stupidity—and still he wondered why.

Naturally he got drunk. On the night of the final breakup of a seventeen-year marriage it seemed like the thing to do. Few people at the bar thought much of his drinking. None of them knew this time it wasn't an act. He did hear a story about some guys up the road taking a twelve-foot alligator and that some guy jumped on the gator's back and finished it with an axe. Billy Bob, Reed thought, a story such as that was too good to be left untold.

Of course he did stay long. When he returned home it was after midnight. He washed, brushed his teeth, and then quietly crawled into bed and lay facing the curved outline of Marlis's back. She could have been Pam. How many times during those final months had they lain just like this and never reached out to touch? It was a national crisis. Roles were no longer predetermined. With everyone so busy finding their own identity it was surprising couples ever did connect. Pam, as she put it, had moved on. Changed, Red thought, while he had not.

Marlis stirred. She turned and took Reed's head and pulled it to her warm, naked chest. He went along, like a little boy going into his mother's arms. Poor little Reed Erickson, injured and all alone. Her mouth sought his, warm, passionate. Her body burned with desire. The silk of her skin flowed under the gentle touch of his hand. It had been so long, for her and for him. This was wrong, Reed thought, but he'd already moved beyond the boundaries of control.

Afterwards, lying in each other's arms, concealed by the veil of the night, he could feel Marlis wanted to talk. But he'd drunk too much, used too much of his emotional reserves. He held her close and quickly fell asleep.

He awoke to sunlight, and an empty bed and an empty house. When he saw Marlis that evening nothing had changed. The animosity she bore toward the world in general had not been erased. Once again they made love. Although this time Marlis was not inclined to talk.

Reed was. "I just want us to be clear on what we're doing here," Reed said into the dark of Marlis's back.

"I think that's self-evident," Marlis snapped.

"I mean . . . I don't want anyone to get hurt."

"Why do you men think everything a woman does is because of some emotional need. Maybe it's physical. Did you ever think of that? I know it's unlikely, but when it comes to sex women can be just as frivolous as men."

Reed went silent. He lay behind Marlis with his arms wrapped around her from behind, the smooth, lean silk of her body bonded like cupped spoons into his. He'd swear that in the midst of their love-making she was as passionately involved as any women he'd ever met. Certainly more so than Pam had ever been. But afterwards she'd be so cold, as if they'd never touched or like a prostitute who'd been paid. But Reed was certain, the passion was no act.

Besides, he knew what he felt. In seventeen years he hadn't cheated on Pamela once. And now he was a free man.

Doyle parked in the limestone rock driveway as if it was his own. He checked under the doormat, over the door ledge, and under a flowerpot nearby where he located a spare key. He opened the door and walked inside. Marlis was at work. Jody and Patty were in school. Reed was at the mill.

Something about Reed hadn't rung true from day one. The guy was just a little too aware, a little too self-assured to be some simple, no-account drunk Marlis picked up in Baton Rouge. Of course Marlis had gone to hell since Wayne disappeared. He'd tried to help, Doyle thought. Given her credit, tried to talk, tried to get her back to church. All to no avail.

Doyle whistled and then called, "Anyone home?" The small house stood dark and empty, quite a step down from the mansion where Marlis had been raised. Wayne Pog was, or at least had been, as close to white trash as a man could get, even if he did go to college. That Marlis would run off and marry a little runt like Pog had taken everyone by complete surprise. What the hell had she thought, Wayne would end up rich? A man who worked for the conservation department?

Doyle walked down the hallway to the back bedroom. In one bottom drawer he found Reed's things. One drawer. Pants, shirts, socks, and nothing else, not even underwear. Other than a toothbrush and a razor blade the man didn't even have any toiletries. Nothing. Not even in the long closet. That had mostly Marlis's things. There were thirty dresses if there was one. Some were evening wear a woman could never wear in Magnolia. Where did she wear expensive dresses like that? It was almost as bad as Rachel, although Rachel only dressed up for church.

He searched the entire house for more of Reed's things but found nothing, a fact in itself he found more than strange. If the guy was a road bum he must have an accumulated something. Life couldn't be as simple as one dresser drawer of clothes.

In what served as a tiny storage room he came across Wayne's glass-fronted gun case. It was locked, a precaution because of the children, although the keys were easily located in a drawer in Marlis's dresser. Doyle unlocked the case. Wayne wasn't a collector. Everything there was for use: shotguns, rifles, a .22 and even one muzzle loader. There was a nice Browning twelve gauge, Wayne's trap gun. When it came to trap Wayne had been one of the best, almost as good as Doyle Monroe.

Doyle checked the heft of the gun then replaced it in the rack. He opened the lower drawer. His heart beat slowed. A nice flat little nine millimeter Beretta. Government issue? Did Wayne have one of those? Doyle copied the serial numbers. Maybe he'd put the touch on Hank and see if he could run a check.

The front door opened. "Doyle," Marlis called. "Are you in here? I see your truck out front."

She was frightened, Doyle thought. Of him. He grinned. That was good. He moved his solid two hundred pound frame out into the hallway. Marlis flinched and then held her ground. "What are you doing in my house?"

"Just looking around, Marlis. Don't worry. I'm a little curious about your boyfriend, Reed. Something about him doesn't ring true."

"This is wrong," Marlis said. "You're breaking and entering."

"I didn't break anything and I'm not taking anything," Doyle said angrily. "You know me better than that." He gazed into Marlis's eyes. She was a beauty. The old flame surged, a time when he was young and strong and a girl like Marlis was sweet and as tender as the petals of a rose. The thought struck him that Marlis had been the first to batter his dreams, turning him aside and then humiliating him by taking up with a twerp like Wayne Pog. And then in a brief, uncontrolled moment of lust Rachel got pregnant and dreams of college were torn to shreds. His father got sick and he took over the family store. Yes, Doyle did his duty. It had been the same in the Marines. People expected nothing less.

"What do you want?" Marlis demanded.

Doyle's lips curled as if in a sneer. Schooled in the land of gentry, it seemed she'd forgotten her way. It was surprising she'd stand up to him like this. "This guy you're living with. Like I said, I want to know who he is."

"That's none of your business. I told you that before. This is my life."

"I don't mean because he's living with you." Doyle's voice sounded strangely hollow, distant even to himself. "I'm not passing judgment on that. That's up to God. But we have a responsibility here, a responsibility to this town just as you have a responsibility to your children. This guy asks questions. He horns-in on people's business. He hangs around with guys much younger than himself. He's after something. I want to know what."

"I'm sorry, Doyle. I know things have been hard for you. You've been so good to me and the children. But I have my own life, things only I can resolve. I don't want interference." Marlis gently rested her fingertips on Doyle's arm as if in sympathy.

The electricity of her touch vibrated more intense than the one time they'd kissed as adolescents. But she'd touched him, Doyle thought. The recognition clicked; Marlis picked her men. She'd always picked her men. She'd picked Wayne. She'd approached this Reed; he hadn't approached her. It suddenly became clear, like the lifting of the fog on the river. Marlis was the whore, the Philistine in their midst, Mary Magadalen lapping at Christ's toes, an abomination of all that was good and clean. Just like Rachel, only his wife's price had been his life.

Doyle jerked back from Marlis's touch. She'd rejected him. All these years and he'd been as blind as a sinner.

"Are you all right?" Marlis asked.

Marlis pretending concern. His mother had been the same with his father, and in the end she let him die.

"I'm going to find out about this guy. People should know."

"Just stay out of this, Doyle. This is my life. If you interfere you'll just mess things up. I beg you."

"You beg me? You beg me!" Doyle shouted. "There was a time I begged you. You just threw me aside. Like I was dirt, not

[68]

good enough for the Rittenhous tramp. And then you took Wayne. And now you've got another one. Does he whore for the government also? Are you going to suck the blood from him as well?"

"What are you talking about? You and I went out on one date. That was over fifteen years ago."

"Did you think I'd forget?"

"Leave. Get out of here." Marlis angrily pushed at Doyle's chest.

Abruptly Doyle seized her in a bear hug, pulling her close, forcing her lips toward his. Marlis bucked and clawed but Doyle was a force she could not move. "Doyle! Don't! You'll be sorry the rest of your life." But the force did not hear. It could not hear, Marlis realized. A panic brought the bitter taste of bile into her throat. She'd never seen a man so possessed.

Something smacked the side of Doyle's leg. Jody, just home from school, tears streaming down his cheeks, pounded at Doyle with tiny fists. Doyle released Marlis. She staggered back against the wall and Jody rushed to her side. She cradled him in her arms. He was Wayne's boy all right, as feisty as they come no matter what the odds.

Doyle gasped for air. His eyes locked with Marlis's. The glazed look of a moment before had been replaced with a wildness that made her skin crawl. He spoke solemnly as if with absolute control. "The day of reckoning is near. I can feel it in the air. It aches within my bones. Be prepared. You cannot hide behind your children forever. Sins of the flesh poison the blood of your kin. I know."

"You know shit, Doyle. Get the hell out of here," Marlis commanded past her fear.

"Sure," Doyle said. "For now." He turned on his heel. But for the presence of the boy he would have informed her she was simply a common whore.

Doyle strode down the front walk. He felt at peace. The fresh scent of blossoming flowers filled his nostrils. The sun shone on the thickets of city greenery. He climbed into his truck. He shook his head with regret. He should have called her a whore. The boy had a right to know.

SEVEN

It was Friday night and the Blue Moon was hopping. As Reed crossed the parking lot he dropped his key ring. As he bent to pick up the keys he casually slipped a small magnetic tracking device inside the bumper on Ross's truck. Not even Marlis noticed his surreptitious move.

They entered the crowded tavern. The three-piece band played and people danced. Marlis sat at a table with Reed, her knees between his thighs, her hands on his hips. From time to time she leaned forward and brazenly kissed him on the mouth. Dark glances carried from women at nearby tables. Marlis gulped at her rum and coke then smiled dreamily and leaned forward again, hungrily wrapping her tongue with Reed's. The judgmental cows turned away in disgust. Marlis laughed.

"We're having a good time now," Reed said loudly. His lean, strong hands rested gently on her twenty inch waist. His nerves tingled. Like a schoolboy in heat, he thought. What the hell could Marlis expect coming onto him like this in public? Who said old men shriveled in the clutch?

To the considerable discomfort of those sitting nearby, Marlis lapped Reed's face and then breathed in his ear. "You're the best lover I've ever had."

"Good lovin' takes two," Reed said. But when he looked into Marlis's eyes they were void of any emotion.

"Of course you're the only lover I've ever had."

Reed roared with laughter, further offending those nearby. "Marlis made a joke. Let me log that," Reed said and looked into her grey eyes. Nothing, nothing at all.

Marlis looked away. For a long time they were silent, a strained silence like a long-time married couple no longer comfortable with each other.

How could he explain. Any deep undercover operation wore on a man. There were times that his life here and his past with Pam, Stacy, and Trish merged as one big blur, a confused paranoia as to who he was and exactly who were these men he sought. And whatever it was that made it impossible for Marlis to relate to people, made it just that much worse for Reed to maintain his perspective. If he could just establish some sense of normalcy with Marlis, some common ground beyond their nocturnal coupling.

"So what was life like growing up at the Rittenhous estate?" Reed asked into the din.

"What do you care?"

"I don't," Reed snarled. "Jesus, I'm just trying to make conversation. Can't you at least humor me? We have to live together. Let's just pass the time."

"When I was a little girl, I saw with little girl eyes. Life was a joy. But then I saw differently. Life was a hypocrisy. It's been one ever since."

The vehemence touched Reed like a dark cloud. "What happened?"

Reed looked away. Billy Bob was circling the far side of the dance floor and then went out the front door. Chuck followed behind. The quick way out was right past his table, Reed thought. Why would Billy Bob slip around? The lack of certainty was irritating. Reed looked back to Marlis. She'd noted his attention had been diverted. The thread of conversation had been lost. He'd been listening to her, but using his eyes elsewhere. But of course she did not understand what he faced, just as Pam did not understand.

"I think I've got most people around here buffaloed," Reed said after a spell. "These young guys don't see too well. Of course I'm still not positive they're part of the deer violating group. If they are I'd bet Doyle's leading this entire show. But with him I can't get close. I don't know if that's his nature, if he's suspicious of me or even if he's the right man."

"Wayne mentioned Doyle once. But then he thought that was too far-fetched. Doyle's too much of a community leader, he said. Wayne should have asked me. He didn't know Doyle like I do."

"You didn't volunteer the information?" Reed asked.

"Why should I?" Marlis demanded.

Reed backed away, staying with a neutral tone. "Does Doyle ever ask you questions about me? Do you think he could be part of the deer violating ring? Do you think he's suspicious?"

Marlis stared Reed directly in the eyes. "Ask him. I can tell he doesn't like you because you're an outsider and not exactly an upstanding citizen."

Once again Reed glanced away, down one side of the bar and then the other. The uneasy sensation stirring his stomach would not abate. Ross and Wyndal passed along the edge of the crowded dance floor, their backs pointedly toward Reed. They appeared sober. They glanced around once, lads guilty to the core, and then they went out the front door.

"We have to go," Reed said.

"Oh, no," Marlis said, she jerked back. People turned to watch the argument. "You don't run my life. No one runs my life."

Reed gripped her shoulders and hissed in her ear. "I'm not running your life. Something is going on. The boys have been leaving one by one. I have to get to a telephone and alert Doug."

"You mean . . . "

"Shhh," Reed hissed angrily.

Marlis scowled, a murderous, defiant look.

Reed stood. Marlis followed. She smirked at those watching her every move. She took Reed's hands and followed him past gyrating bodies and out into the black night.

While Marlis distracted the babysitter into the kitchen, Reed called Doug from the living room. Doug, patrolling with a state game warden answered over the cellular telephone and agreed to meet Reed at a nearby wayside.

"I'm coming," Marlis insisted after Reed hung up.

"No you're not," Reed said. "It's against the rules."

"Well damn you. Damn all of you. What do I have to do, resolve all this myself?"

"No. We're trying to help, got it?" Reed said angrily. "Don't you understand that everytime I go out there I might not come back? Or don't you even care?" The babysitter peeked in from the hallway.

"I guess I really don't care," Marlis said. She looked away. Her face twisted as if verging on tears. Marlis Pog, verging on tears. "Maybe that's the problem." She beseeched Reed for help. "I can't care. How can I. I . . . " She turned and walked to her bedroom.

Reed hung his head in shame at his lack of understanding. After a time he turned. "C'mon," he said to the teenage babysitter. "I'll give you a ride home."

The girl nodded. She was frightened as well.

Reed and Doug patrolled back country roads north and east of Magnolia. Twenty miles west a truck with Louisiana State conservation officers patrolled a second area. Both trucks were equipped with U.S. Fish and Wildlife owned transponders and directional antennas for picking up the tracking device Reed had placed on the inside of Ross's bumper. In two hours time they'd cruised a hundred miles and hadn't closed within the ten mile range necessary to pick up the tracker.

"He's shacking up somewhere and we're just spinning our wheels," Doug asserted for the third time.

"All I know is he left town headed northeast," Reed said. "After that they could have gone in any direction. Let's head farther east."

"I had a midnight meet," Doug spoke of a cancelled rendezvous with a woman at a tavern in Baton Rouge. "And here I am cruising the sticks with you."

"Life's a hard time," Reed said.

"Don't I wish," Doug said and laughed. He worked the four-wheel drive easily, his thick, meaty hands encasing half the wheel. Doug was a mover, a laugher, forever pursuing rawboned women who enjoyed physical contact as much as he did. Doug had a macho ego and the size to back it up. But he could be counted on in a crisis, Reed knew. And Doug enjoyed life. It was why he and Reed were friends. Best friends, Doug would say. But Reed knew better. Men like Doug didn't really have best friends, at least not those to whom they'd open up their personal lives.

[73]

"Those boys were acting different tonight. None of them were drinking much. Some just stuck to soda. Ross just had a couple of beers and when he left he was chewing down mints."

"There, shows he was meeting a woman."

"Man like Ross meets a woman stone drunk and smelling like a sewer. No. He was meeting someone he was frightened of or for whom he had more than ordinary respect. Someone like me." Reed grinned in the dim glow of the dash lights.

Doug looked to the sky as if for assistance. "It's getting deep."

"And they all left in ones and twos. That's not the way they normally work. No, they're out jacklighting. I can feel it in my bones. These guys are heavy drinkers. But when they do something with Doyle, they aren't allowed to drink or curse."

"That Doyle sounds like a rich one," Doug said. "Jimmy Swaggert in drag or what?"

They rounded a corner and passed a semi-tractor and trailor. "What's a guy doing out on a backwoods road like this at one o'clock in the morning?"

"Probably some independent who's been out hauling all week and is headed home," Reed said. "Those guys drive eighty hours a week just to break even and pay for their rig. Hell, I remember . . . " A faint beep made Reed pause and bend forward. He turned the nob on the roof mounted directional antenna.

"Got something?" Doug asked. For the first time that evening excitement entered his tone.

"I'm not sure. There was something and then it quit. Head south at the next junction."

Doug accelerated and grinned as he spun tires into the next turn. "The only people out on the roads on Saturday morning at one-thirty are drunks and violators."

"And a few adulterers. A few bums. A couple of game wardens, and teenagers. All individuals of a type."

"You're just jealous."

"I've got them," Reed interrupted, in a voice as dry as sage. But his heart sang. Contact. And he was not alone, not isolated in a situation where he could disappear and never be seen. Not like Wayne Pog.

"Hot damn," Doug said, and slammed the dash. "It's been

too long since you and I last got our hands on one of these scum."

"These aren't simple rednecks leading this thing. Oh, these guys we're trailing are as dumb as a horse. And some of them are as mean as a new gelding. But whoever is leading this thing has some basic smarts. He can organize and he can lead young thugs and command their respect. And he can justify killing a human being rather than pay a few thousand dollars in fines. Either he doesn't give a damn about human life, or he's a man skating on the edge of a different plane."

"That covers just about everyone we meet," Doug said.

"Just trying to narrow it down, partner." Reed bent forward listening to the intensity of the beeps. "Quick, stop here, turn off the motor."

They pulled to the side of the narrow blacktop road. Thick foliage hung over the roadside. They stepped out and listened to the night calls of crickets, bullfrogs, and buzzing mosquitoes. A faint crack carried from a considerable distance. Reed sucked air between his teeth. Somewhere nearby a deer had died. "Bastards," he said with heartfelt intensity. "And some of these guys call themselves sportsmen." Reed shook his head. "They're as dumb as rocks. They don't have the foggiest notion what they're doing. Let's get going. The trick tonight is to find their outlet and not get spotted. Then we can go from there."

"So this is as close as we get?" Doug said. "At least until they make their stop. And then?"

"We play it as it lies. But we won't be moving in tonight. We have to have leverage on the other end."

They drove on, stopping when the truck stopped, listening for a shot. Some stops were longer than others, either watching their back trail or rendezvousing with someone else, Reed surmised. He surprised himself by thinking of Marlis. There had been an opening there tonight. But he was too preoccupied with his own life, his own problems. He'd let it slip away. . . . Or maybe he was just scared. Somehow it seemed that when he faced Marlis it was too much like facing himself.

Time dragged. How could he explain life in the field, being hot on the track of his foe, operating side by side with his partner, Doug, feeling the camaraderie, feeling as if he was accomplishing something worthwhile? Life had purpose at such times.

Reed closed his eyes and rubbed at the soft growth of his beard. A man could thrill to the world. Then there were the days he just wanted to sit, smell the lilacs, and lie warm in the arms of a woman. When he told that to Doug, his partner didn't know how to respond.

"They're stopping," Reed said, breaking the silence between them.

Doug coasted to a stop. Both men got out and stood on the blacktop, listening to the night. A panorama of stars filled the sky. A warm night breeze, carrying the humus scent of swamp and rich river bottom, caressed their skins.

"Damn long stop," Doug said. "Think they're up to something?"

"Could be. Uh oh." Reed glanced down the road behind them. The glow of headlights carried from around the bend. "Let's fly. We might have to drive past and play it straight."

They jumped into the truck and drove on. Fortunately they passed one corner before the trailing truck drove into view. "Our number one's moving," Reed said. "But we're close. I hope he doesn't see our lights."

"Should I douse them?"

"No, that'd really make the guy behind suspicious if he spots us. What's this?" Reed pointed off to one side.

"I'll bet that's the same eighteen wheeler," Doug said as they drove past a semi parked on a side dirt road.

"That was twenty miles back, but I'll bet your next expense check you're right. As soon as you get around the next corner, slow down, no brakes. Give me one to two hours. I'll meet you at the next road to the right."

"Ross could drive out of tracking range," Doug pointed out.

"Chance we have to take," Reed said. "I want to stay with the semi for now." He rapidly checked his gear, a flashlight, his pistol, while watching front and back for any lights. The truck coasted. He opened the door.

"Watch your ass, partner," Doug said.

At fifteen miles an hour Reed hit the road running as fast as he could. He made three steps, slowing his momentum

[76]

before he tumbled, doing a clean front somersault and ending up on his feet. Doug gently gave the four-wheel drive gas and continued out of sight. Reed turned back. The vehicle that had forced them to move should be close behind. But there were no lights. The only possible turn was where the semi sat. Reed started back down the road at a run.

He rounded the bend and slowed. A hundred yards or so from the semi he slowed to a walk, rolling his feet heel to toe so they did not make a sound. But he was covered, he knew, not by the sounds of night as much as by the whine of a compressor. The dim glow of lights shone through the foliage. If he continued down the road and someone was watching they'd spot him clean. And they had to see the truck pass. That alone would raise their suspicions a notch.

But if he took to the foliage in the pure black of night it would take an hour to creep up without making a sound. Reed paused, alone in the middle of a warm Louisiana night, miles from the nearest town, miles from prying eyes, thinking about approaching armed men. Wardens did this all the time, wardens like Wayne Pog.

Did anyone give a damn? The question surprised him. He'd asked it before and then laughed. He didn't care if anyone else gave a damn, he did. But now the question had meaning, as if he had doubts on the course of his life. Pam, Marlis, age— perhaps he'd reached a turning point.

Resolve tightened like banjo strings across the muscled lines of Reed's flat stomach. He was a professional. Act like it, he told himself. Concentrate on the job at hand.

He moved across the road to place the road between himself and any watching eyes. As usual on a night operation he'd worn dark clothes. He kept the roadside foliage tight to his back, trying to eliminate any silhouette. He drifted forward, crouching, gliding as quietly as a panther.

He neared the corner. The compressor hummed. Muffled voices carried from the back of the semi where he could see a pickup truck had backed. Probably off-loading the deer, he surmised. He should get closer, pick out faces and names. If he'd only brought a tracking device so they could follow the semi.

So many options, and all fraught with risk. Mosquitoes

homed in, attracted by his perspiration. Reed ignored their bites. He moved one step forward in order to get a better view of the back of the truck. And then he saw the dim shadow of the man standing beside the front fender of the old semi-tractor. Reed froze. The man held something in his arms. A rifle? He raised it and pointed in Reed's direction.

Reed did not move. If he ran he'd give them the alarm. If the man fired he was dead. Mosquitoes buzzed louder as if attracted by his fear. What good could he be lying cold and dead?

Time stood as still as did Reed. He understood the man's indecision. It happened all the time in the jungles of Vietnam. Was that a bush or was that a man? If he even twitched the man would squeeze the trigger.

A motor coughed to life. The pickup was making a U-turn and coming out to the road. When the driver hit his headlights Reed would be caught in a spotlight. The truck, with only its parking lights lit, crept down alongside the semi. The man lowered the rifle and turned his head.

Reed dropped to his knees and slid backwards under the thick overhang of roadside brush. The headlights clicked on full. Reed, his head lowered to conceal the gleam of his face, did not move. Someone spoke. Were those the footsteps of a man walking across the road? Discipline, Reed thought. He did not move.

The truck pulled onto the road, stopped, backed up and then stopped again. Now what the hell? Reed wondered. Bugs gnawed at his flesh. The tractor's diesel roared into life and the big rig pulled out onto the highway, the front bumper brushing the foliage just over Reed's head. He seized the roaring cover to move five feet farther back into the brush. The semi left and the pickup followed.

Reed silently crept to the edge of the road. Was it possible they had left a man behind, hiding on the opposite side? He had not the time to wait. He sprang from the brush and sprinted down the road. If someone was waiting to shoot, they'd have a damn tough target to hit. But no one fired.

He had to get to Doug. They had to get after that truck. He dropped back to a steady eight-mile-an-hour pace, a pace he could handle for hours on end.

Headlights gleamed around the corner. Reed ducked down into the brush. The truck lights blinked, hi-low, hi-low. Reed stepped out onto the road. Doug stopped and Reed climbed in. "Where have you been?" Doug said to his panting partner. He squealed the truck around in a tight three-point turn. "I was well back off the road. I saw the two trucks pass. I figured you'd be lolligagging up the road here." Doug glanced over at his sweating partner. "You look like you just left a Southern whorehouse in the middle of July." Doug sniffed the air. "Smell about the same too."

"They're loading the deer into the semi," Reed said. He guzzled from a canteen. "The damn thing is refrigerated for crissakes."

"These guys are sweet. They've got it figured all the way around. Only two things they didn't figure on."

Reed willingly took the bait. "What's that?"

"You and me."

"I just hope that's enough," Reed said. "Don't forget this is their country down here. We're the foreigners, just like in the Nam. People like to handle their own affairs of state."

They raced on. Twice Doug braked and backed up to inspect tire tracks on dirt roads that intersected with the town blacktop road. They reached a T-junction with a state highway. "Left or right?" Doug asked.

Reed jumped out and briefly inspected the corner. "Dual wheels cutting to the right when he swung the corner with the trailer. That'd be the smart way to try."

Doug started to the left then abruptly wheeled back to the right. Reed buckled his seat belt. "Better start dousing your lights going around the corners. Keep one eye closed and try to develop some night vision."

"Yeah, and what do I have for depth perception?"

"Oh, I'll do the same, Douglas. We'll each have one eye. You can't get wider binocular vision than that."

In reply Doug snapped his own seat harness. "Why don't you try radioing those state wardens on the CB. See if they're in range. Let them know what we've got."

"In case we're eliminated?" Reed asked.

"In case you're eliminated," Doug said. The four-wheel-drive truck crept up toward the one-hundred-mile-per-hour mark. Doug chuckled. "This is the way the job is supposed to be, hell for leather chasing the bad guys."

"Just like the job description said. Only when you snap off your lights to go around a corner you might think about slowing down to eighty. These roadside canals and ditches have a lot of alligators. Solunar tables say three A.M. is a major feeding period for gators."

"Sorry," Doug said. As they approached a corner he backed off slightly on the gas. "I hadn't consulted the tables, myself." He reached down and snapped off the lights. If they rounded the corner onto a long straight stretch and the lights of the semi were in view, the hope was that without telltale headlights they would not be seen.

"A little right," Reed yelled. They squealed tires as Doug fought for control. "It's clear ahead, turn on your lights," Reed yelled. He clamped a hand over one eye. "Why the hell didn't you bring night goggles?"

"Because I didn't know I'd be driving without lights," Doug snapped. He straightened the truck and accelerated. He laughed in relief. "The first one's always a little tough, especially when you're coming out of the lights."

Three darkened corners later they saw the red taillights of the semi. They slowed to less than fifty miles per hour, maintaining position, driving without headlights less than a quarter-mile behind the truck.

"He's going the wrong way to get back to Baton Rouge," Doug said. With his eyes accustomed to the dark and the truck lights as a guide, the driving was easier.

"Maybe he has another pickup," Reed said. "They might make two or three a night. Four or five pickups out knocking off deer, off-loading onto the semi. It's quite an operation. I just wonder who's the brains. And which one of these guys killed Wayne Pog. Maybe the others don't know."

"Then again maybe they do," Doug said. "I swear, I go to some of those cracker bars near the refinery and some of those boys are still fighting the civil war."

"Yeah, but just those who have heard about it."

They drove on in companionable silence, concentrating on the road and the dim glow of taillights four hundred yards ahead. This was the life, Reed thought, utilizing your senses, feeling the throb and urgency of blood pumping through your veins.

"It appears to me you're following the same old routine and getting overly involved with that Marlis," Doug said as if reading Reed's silence. "You get so involved there you lose perspective. You forget, she's the victim here."

"Well, Douglas, you've only one example of that in your life. But you got jealous. Possessive would be the word. And then you turned and ran."

Doug sped up so he could see the truck lights as they rounded a sharp corner. "I walked before she walked on me."

"But she wouldn't have. She loved you just as much as you loved her. All you remember is the distress. That's part of the game. You forget the good times. A man feels as alive as a man can be when he's in love. The entire world is shiny and sweet. Bad things become minor irritations. But you have it all wrong here, Marlis and I are as far from a number as two people could get."

"And you still sleep in the same bed. C'mon, Reed. This is your bud you're talking to."

"Lookout!" Reed called. At the same instant lights flashed high and bright and a pickup truck pulled onto the highway from the left side. Doug slammed the brakes and pulled to the side. Too late. The truck slammed them on the left front side. Thunder clapped. Debris flew in the cab of the truck. Foliage raked the cab and a tree limb slammed across the windshield as they bore down into the ditch. The world stopped and then was filled with hissing steam and the odor of burnt rubber and gasoline.

Reed gasped for breath. "You okay?"

"Yeah," Doug grunted through clenched teeth. "Banged my knee. Got my ribs. Left arm is sore. Movable."

Reed glanced over his shoulder. The other truck had stopped on the highway. One light had been shattered but the other gleamed in the night, providing illumination down the road.

Reed rolled down the window. Limbs of ditch brush reached into the cab. He braced himself against the crazy tilt. "I'll lay odds that's one of their group. I can't let them see me and blow my cover. Get on the radio and call the police. Keep your gun handy. I'll be nearby in the brush in case they try anything."

"How are you getting back?" Doug was already switching radio bands. He grunted with pain as he braced to keep from falling down into Reed.

Reed again glanced back. The black silhouette of a man emerged from the pickup. "Just watch yourself." He tunnelled out the window, kicking back as Doug pushed at his feet. He slid out into the limbs like a snake. He gasped at the pain stabbing through one shoulder and ribs on his right side. But he could not make a sound.

Abruptly one of the limbs gave way and Reed crashed through the brush and into a small stream of ditch water that ran knee deep. He gasped at the pain.

"You all right in there?" A heavily accented voice asked from the road.

Reed froze, crouched in the dark just beside the truck. If it went any farther and flipped on its side he would be crushed.

"You alone in there?"

"Yeah, one second," Doug said. "Roger, we're on Highway ninety-three, about ten miles east of Arnaudville."

"What the hell's that?" the southern drawl asked.

"A CB radio," Doug said. "I just called the police. They're on the way."

"What the hell were you doing driving without your lights, buddy?" A second voice, Reed realized. This one was as belligerent as could be. Doug could handle himself, but if they pulled down on his partner, he was in no position to assist. And he could not move without making considerable noise.

"What do you mean without my lights?" Doug asked. Abruptly the truck lights flashed down into the thick green foliage. Reed smiled. "How come you boys pulled out into me like that?" Doug said.

"You bastard," one of the men swore.

The truck door slammed. Doug must have crawled out onto the highway. The angry voices became muffled as if they had moved out onto the highway in front of the second truck. Reed squatted in the foul smelling water and, gritting his teeth against the pain, slowly duckwalked down the tiny tunnel washed out by the stream. The voices on the highway became increasingly vocal. Reed thought of cutting up to the road but then sirens wailed in the distance. If the men were going to make any further moves, they'd waited too long.

Reed continued down the ditch. Leeches would be sucking at his calves. The first mosquitoes homed in. His ribs burned. His shoulder ached. If these guys were part of the violating operation, and of that Reed had few doubts, then they'd discover Doug's identity. And they knew they'd been followed earlier from when they passed the semi. They'd blown it, Reed thought. The ring had been alerted. If they had half a brain they'd close it down.

Reed paused. It was twenty-five miles back to Magnolia. What would he tell Marlis? He moved his right shoulder as if to aggravate the pain in his ribs and his arm. She was already angered at the lack of progress. What would she say if he told her they'd blown the case?

One squad car pulled up. A few minutes later two others arrived. Reed glimpsed the distant figures of Doug and the two men, both of whom were gesturing wildly, talking to the police. The third squad car pulled down near Reed and a man got out to set roadside flares in case late night traffic wandered past. As the man passed in front of his own headlights, Reed grinned. Hank Jackson. Now if that wasn't at least one stroke of luck.

After Hank ignited the flares he strolled back to the scene of the wreck. Reed, sopping wet and smelling of swamp, crawled out of the brush and into the back of Hank's squad car. He lay back and rested his eyes. He hadn't seen Hank for two days. He was certain the deputy would be pleased.

EIGHT

Reed lay in the back seat of Hank Jackson's squad car and napped while the officers investigated the wreck and radioed for two wreckers. Doug and the two others each departed with the wreckers towing their respective vehicles. And then the four cops on the scene stood around on the road at four-thirty in the morning and talked. Again Reed lay back. The sharp pain in his shoulder and ribs had settled into a dull throb. One thing for certain, it would be damn hard to move come the dawn.

Footsteps cruched on gravel. Reed could not suppress a grin. The dome light glared in his eyes. Hank settled into the car without looking into the back. He radioed dispatch he was clearing the wreck and then started the car. The angular protrusions of his eyebrows, nose, moustache, lips, and Adam's Apple showed in brief profile against the gleam of headlights on thick roadside foliage. He sniffed the air as if for a foul odor and then drove away. The tires hummed their roadway song. Hank hummed one of his own, a soft rock, a man at ease with himself.

And unsuspecting, Reed thought and barely suppressed a chuckle. "A good cop always makes sure he knows who's riding in his back seat."

"Wha . . ." Hank swerved the car and slammed on the brakes.

"Easy Hank, it's just Reed."

"Uh, you Yankee sonofabitch!" Hank lowered his pistol and snapped on the dome light. He blinked and glared at Reed. "None of those boy's stories rang true. And now I can see why." He stopped the squad and waited until Reed got out to climb into the front seat. As soon as Reed was outside he hit the automatic locks and drove down the road several feet. Reed walked after. After two go arounds Hank unlocked the door and Reed climbed into the front seat. "Looks like you have a little pain there. Good," Hank said. "In addition to which you stink like swamp."

"You should smell the back seat," Reed said brightly. "Your ditches along here are mighty scummy. They should get patrolmen out cleaning things up."

"If we still had chain gangs I'd put you on," Hank growled.

"Easy now, Hank. Just because you got suckered. Did you issue any tickets?"

"How could we? Wyndal and Chuck testified the big guy was going down the road without his headlights. The big guy, Douglas LaRue . . . as you well know of course, said he had his lights on and had the right-of-way. The driver's license gave his address as Washington. Said he was on his way to Baton Rouge and got lost. That was real rich. Is that the best you can lie? The other two said they'd been to a party. But they hadn't been drinking. When those guys go to a party they get blind stone drunk. And here you show up, just down the road and sore as hell. What'd you do, crawl out the window like some snake?"

"That's it. Has Mr. Story Diver been having any luck in his search?"

"I usually don't like to tell people my story until I've heard theirs." Hank slowed as two deer crossed the road under the glare of his headlights.

"That's how they get 'em. Easy as slipping up behind a Southern sheriff."

"I could still let you walk," Hank growled.

Reed laughed. "They must have three or four trucks going. Every once in a while they meet with a big refrigerated semi-trailer and off-load their deer. I don't think it's beyond them to take seventy-five or a hundred deer a night."

"And they make money?"

"With the wholesale price of venison and hides I'd venture they gross two to three thousand dollars a night. You give the young drivers a hundred dollars or so and they're happy as a

[85]

pig in slop. They get money and get to drive around and shoot deer besides."

"I never hunted," Hank said. "We couldn't afford a rifle for one. Secondly, back then it wasn't a good idea for a black man to be walking around in the same forest with a bunch of gun-toting Southern white boys."

"But officer, he looked like a bear to me," Reed kidded with a fake drawl.

"Yeah, right. So why is it most conservation officers aren't opposed to hunting per se?"

"Most of them used to hunt themselves. Once they become wardens they don't have much time. Most of us were born to the outdoors and were looking for a job that would keep us there. Now we hunt men."

"You don't think hunting is wrong?"

"It could be if left uncontrolled. There's always someone who wants to be the one to kill the last of anything. The more rare a species the more valuable it becomes. We see that out west with Bighorn Sheep. Guys will pay twenty-five to thirty grand for a full curl ram. People have to remember, man's a predator also. As soon as you start thinking people are above nature rather than a part you're in trouble. Truth is, we're just not that smart. At the turn of the century there were a few hundred thousand deer in all of the United States. Winters were hard. Deer didn't have the food supplies. The timber was mature. Now we have more than twenty million. Because of farming and lumbering the carrying capacity of the habitat has expanded many times over what it used to be. Man has knocked off natural predators like the wolf. Now it's a managed hunt to control the population. Louisiana game managers have increased the Louisiana herd from less than one-hundred thousand in nineteen-sixty to more than five-hundred thousand today. Some anti-hunters say we should quit. But if man bowed out, he should also quit farming and lumbering because those are the two factors that had the biggest impact on the herd; they improved the habitat so the deer herd could expand. So now we try to control the herd through hunting. It's cruel, but that's the way all of nature is. Pestilence or starvation are not good ways to die either."

"Quite a deal," Hank acknowledged. "Tell me this: with

twenty million deer, why are you risking your life trying to stop these guys from taking a few extra?"

"It's the principle, Hank. People have to recognize and be responsible for their impact on nature. You stop the excesses now, otherwise it becomes too late. Besides, you're forgetting about Wayne."

"Maybe not." Hank drove on in silence as if collecting his own thoughts. He then related his own news. Story Diver, the Choctaw Indian who lived in a house on stilts on the edge of the swamp, had found something that felt like a truck under the black water beside the levee.

"Well, that's a start. After tonight I was getting the feeling we'd been blown out of the water. These guys will know Doug's from Washington so they may just crawl in a hole. Ross and those guys aren't too smart. But if Doyle's part of this, he . . . "

"Doyle Monroe?"

"Yeah, I haven't had time to tell you he was heading up that gator hunt. Doyle runs the show with these guys, no drinking, no cursing."

Hank spoke in a strained whisper. "Doyle's been good to me. He gave me my first job when no one else would. He helped get me on the police force."

"Let's hope I'm wrong," Reed said sympathetically.

"Doyle has a cousin," Hank continued grimly. "Name's Cutter. He lives in Baton Rouge now. He used to drive a semi. For the last ten or twelve years he's been a butcher. Cutter and I never saw eye to eye. He used to be a lineman when Doyle was a fullback. Monroe followed Monroe. Both All-Conference. Cutter's a tough, mean sonofabitch. He could head up an operation like this. Doyle would just go along."

"Thanks," Reed said softly. "We don't have hard evidence on anyone right now. We'll start checking this Cutter out. After our mishap tonight, we have to move fast. I want to get down and look at that truck tomorrow morning if I can. Can you locate some scuba gear without alerting anyone?"

"You can't see in that water."

"I've done black water diving before. Once you get past the vertigo it's not too bad. I feel for the license plate number, I can feel inside the cab. If you have a light and press your face mask right up against something, you can see even in swamp water."

"Technically I have to figure a cover story and report this to the Sheriff," Hank said.

"Then he gets all the credit," Reed said. "And you get a reprimand for not following procedure. No, we can't jump the gun. If you don't bang the drum at just the right moment the rabbit will freeze in his hole and we may never get him out."

"What the hell are you now, a philosopher? What about my job? Any way you cut it the Sheriff's going to be standing with his size twelve boondockers right on the middle of my neck."

"Oh, Hank, you're a service veteran. You could always get a job carrying mail."

"Everyone says you're a sonofabitch. I come to think that's true. I'm glad you got a little dinged back there. It probably serves you right."

Reed slapped Hank on the shoulder. "I knew we'd be friends."

Rather than pull in front of Marlis's house, Reed had Hank drop him off in the deserted town square at four o'clock in the morning. As soon as Hank disappeared, a truck drove into the square and circled over toward Reed. Reed tensed, trapped on the cracked sidewalks in front of a wall of empty stores. The truck slowed. A man peered out of the dark. Reed walked on. The truck continued down the square and stopped on the opposite side. It was a black three-quarter ton, four-wheel drive. It could have been Doyle, but he could not tell for certain.

Reed walked the empty streets the three blocks to Marlis's house. The old time nervousness was starting to take its toll. How much did they know? How much did they suspect? He hadn't paid it that much attention before, but there was more foliage along these town streets than he'd thought possible. The lush and green of day had turned black and sinister. Since the first deer wardens in 1739 in Massachusetts, how many wardens had surrendered their lives?

Reed reached the house without incident and quietly opened the front door, then locked it behind him. He could take the living room sofa, but Jody and Patty would be getting up and watching cartoons in a few hours. He heard a vehicle and peered outside as a truck passed on the street. His mouth went dry. Could Marlis and the children be in danger? Perhaps it was time to pull the ripcord. Cut and run. And what would Marlis have?

He padded to the bathroom and closed the door. He'd removed his shirt and was inspecting the puffed red and purple scrape down his right rib cage when the door swung in behind him. A shot of adrenaline coursed his veins before he realized it was Marlis.

"You're hurt," Marlis said softly. She closed the door behind her. She wore a pale blue silk and nylon nightgown with white lace decorating the slight, but firm rise of her breasts. She exuded trapped heat from being under the covers and smelled of sleep. Her fingers gently touched his shoulder and traced down his arm and around the outside of his wound.

For a moment Reed felt like a little boy.

"We were close."

"They got away?"

"We weren't trying to make an arrest," Reed mumbled. His head bobbed. A great weariness almost made his knees buckle. He blinked as if to stay awake. Marlis took him in her arms like a mother lending comfort to her child. It was amazing. He'd felt strong out there in the night. But now, with someone close by to lend comfort it was as if he'd been shorn of strength.

"I guess this isn't like your normal undercover," Marlis said sympathetically.

"None of them are normal. But yes, this is different than most," Reed mumbled into the white silk of her shoulder.

"I'm sorry. I haven't been as helpful as I could." Marlis caressed his wound as if in empathy.

"Don't. It hasn't been easy for you. You've lost Wayne. I'm having the thing with Pamela. It's . . ." Reed trailed off. They stood silently, holding one another in the still of the night. "We found something out on a levee. There's a remote possibility it could be Wayne's truck. I'm going out tomorrow and take a look."

Marlis stiffened. "I'd like to come along."

"Sure," Reed said. "I guess that's your right. Things may

be breaking anyhow. We have to protect Hank, of course. He's not exactly following police procedure. The thing is, how much will these guys tie back to me. Chuck and Wyndal are the only guys we know for certain, although I'm positive Ross and Billy Bob were there. They aren't too sharp. Doyle's the question. Is he part of the violating ring? Does he know anything about Wayne? Does he link that accident tonight back to me?"

"What if he did?" Marlis asked.

"It means he doesn't buy my cover. I'd have to get out. It's one of the rules."

"And then what?"

"I don't know, Marlis. We'd still try to work it from outside. You just have to be aware of the dangers. It isn't beyond the realm of possibility you and your children could be in danger just for bringing me in here."

Marlis looked Reed in the face as if inspecting his honesty. She kissed him lightly on the lips and turned and went to bed. Reed washed up and followed, lying on his left side and staring at the dark curve of Marlis's back. He thought of Pam alone in her bed and wondered if Marlis or Pam felt as lonely as he did. For one of the first times ever he and Marlis had talked without animosity. Perhaps honesty did pay. It was as if, in those few minutes in the bathroom, she'd seen evidence of his efforts. They were victims of broken dreams and therefore bonded, friends from this day forward. At least so he hoped.

In the morning they packed the children off to school and then Marlis called in sick. Reed drove west to the strip mall just outside of town and then turned back east, carefully eyeing the rearview mirror to insure they were not trailed. His shoulder felt better. His ribs still throbbed. He badly needed a full night's sleep.

As they passed the Rittenhous estate Marlis became visibly depressed. "Hank's going to meet us out there," Reed said as if to interrupt her thoughts. "He's trying to get some scuba gear without anyone knowing."

"Hank's wife, Sheila, used to work for us as a maid," Marlis said. She spoke as if from a great distance. "Sheila was my age, fourteen. My father raped her." Marlis spoke simply, in a voice completely void of emotion. "I saw him. I closed the door and walked away."

A deep alarm buzzed at the back of Reed's head. A bitter taste coated his mouth. A heavy weight bore down upon his shoulders. There were instances in nature that turned a man sick with disgust. A starving wolf could consume her deceased young. A boar bear could kill a cub. A wild mare might refuse her foal a chance to nurse. And human beings, supposedly superior to all, could commit the most unspeakable acts upon their own young. How then did people cope?

"You were young," Reed explained as if in Marlis's defense. "Did you ever talk to anyone?"

Marlis shook her head. "He's still free, sipping his bourbon on that dirty old porch with his cronies. Do you think I'm free? Do you think Sheila is free? I married Wayne just to spite my father." Marlis looked as if into the distance. "And now Wayne's dead. If I don't find out who killed him . . ."

"We'll find out," Reed said. He thought to touch Marlis's hands but she kept them on her lap. "I promise."

Hank Jackson was dismayed when he saw Marlis. "Possibly that's her husband down there. I thought she had the right," Reed said as if reading Hank's despair. Reed glanced away. Hank, of course, was right. Marlis shouldn't be here. But Hank didn't know what Marlis faced. He understood, in her mind finding Wayne's killer was Marlis's way of resolving her past and perhaps getting her life back on track. At least it was a good first step.

"Hello, Hank," Marlis said with an easy smile.

"Miss Marlis," Hank said with a wide smile. "That's Story Diver over there. He found the object under the water." Hank indicated the Choctaw Indian down the levee and near the water. Story was a slight, lean man with smooth, high cheekbones, a complexion darker than Hank's and coal black hair that was combed straight back and hung down on his shoulders. His dark eyes surveyed Marlis and then quickly turned away.

"Where did you get this diving equipment, Davy Jones's locker?" Reed asked as he surveyed the gear in Hank's trunk. "The hose is rotten. The neoprene on the mask is cracked. The tank hasn't been hydrostatic tested for ten years. They probably filled the tank next to some motor and there's a concentration of carbon monoxide."

"You said you didn't want anyone to know," Hank said and shot a knowing glance at Marlis. "Truthfully, I borrowed it from Rodney, my brother-in-law. He was going to be a bigtime, rich commercial diver down on the oil rigs on the Gulf."

"With this!"

"You don't know Rodney. He buys the equipment because he got a deal. Then checks on the school and never attends. It's on to the next idea."

"Yeah, well," Reed grumbled.

"Besides, if you drown then I'll have good reason to call the department out here and conduct a proper full-scale search," Hank said with a straight face.

"Did you ever think about joining Fish and Wildlife?"

"What, and walk up to men with loaded guns in the middle of the night out in the middle of nowhere and say, hey, Jack you're under arrest." Hank started to laugh when he saw Reed roll his eyes toward Marlis standing twenty feet down the dike staring into the thickets of the swamp and the black sheen of water beside the levee.

"Did you want a safety line?" Hank asked seriously.

"No, it would just get tangled. But you can stand by with a coiled rope on shore and keep your feet out of your mouth in case I need you."

Reed stripped down to shorts and tee shirt and Hank helped him don the tank and old double hose regulator. The two carefully picked their way down the steep dirt and limestone of the levee wall. Reed balanced on Hank's shoulder while he slipped on his fins.

"Where's it at, Story?"

Story, push-pole in hand, stood easily in the hollowed dugout of his pirogue. "I'll show you the back. You can guide down along my pole. The water's twelve feet deep. The top of the truck is five." Story spoke in the clipped tones of a man who seldom talked. He pushed once from shore and easily glided out twenty feet.

Reed assessed the water. The swamp here was like a lake newly formed in the forest of cypress trees. Thickets of reeds and cane grew in islands and spread outward into the black swamp water that was further overgrown with lush green duckweed and lilypads. Alligators and water moccasins swam these waters. But with the commotion of the dive they wouldn't be a problem, Reed thought. The big thing was to stay out of the tangle of weeds. A guy could get tangled up and drown.

Reed glanced back at Marlis, a small and forlorn figure, huddled with her arms clutching her ribs standing at the top of the dike waiting to see if they found her husband down below. Reed gave a small wave. Marlis did not respond. Last night he'd decided to trust her with his life. Today, in the broad light of day he just didn't know.

"It drops right off," Hank said, as Reed lowered his mask and sucked air through the regulator. Despite the age the equipment seemed functional.

Reed stepped into the water and immediately began sliding away. The best thing would be to stride forward and get right in. Immediately the old mask began to fill with water. He drew air and also a small bit of water that seeped into his lungs. He coughed and drew air more carefully. One of the seals on the regulator leaked. When the water in the mask reached his nose he pressed the top of the mask against his forehead and blew air through his nose to clear the mask. It immediately began to refill. Black water diving with water in his mask and water in his regulator. Of late it was the way life had been going.

Reed swam the few feet over to Story's pirogue pole. The last thing he saw was the black of Story's eyes before he sank down, guiding on the pole that was forked on the bottom so it wouldn't stick in the mud when Story pushed.

He kept the pole less than a foot from his face. At least he had one point of reference in the dark brown of the water. Water filled the mask to his nose and again he blew it clear. He touched a bottom of muck and sticks. Suddenly, as if trying to get out of his way, Story drew the pole away. A cloud of silt turned the water from dark brown to pure black. A dizzy sensation whirled in Reed's brain, the onset of vertigo, the loss of points of reference. He paused, orienting himself to the bottom. After a few seconds of concentrated thought, the sensation cleared. He knew up and he knew down. He held his hand to his mask then moved it out and away. Within eight inches he could not even see the outline of his hand.

Reed probed ahead, feeling in the direction the pole had been located. His hand bumped the hard metal of the back of a pickup truck. Moving slowly so as not to stir the muck, he traced the back of the truck until he touched the handle to the camper shell. He slowly bent, his mask three inches from the brown of the truck, tracing down to the bumper. He felt with his hand and then bent forward to read the license plate. The certainty had been confirmed, the truck belonged to Wayne Pog.

A heaviness sat in Reed's chest. Hank was right, he never should have let Marlis come along. No matter how insistent she'd been.

Again Reed cleared his mask. He rose up. Was the body here, inside the cab, inside the back? He opened the camper door and then the tailgate. He slowly probed inside, feeling ahead into the black with one hand and guiding himself with the other. Each time he found an object he'd pull ahead until it pressed up against the glass of his mask. But other than a tool box and a piece of canvas, he found nothing of interest.

Reed slowly backed from the truck, closed the tailgate and door and felt his way along one side toward the cab that sat even further down the steep slope. He worked his jaw and swallowed to clear his ears against the increased pressure. Twice he cleared the mask and once spit water from the regulator. He felt the door. Naturally he could not look inside, he could only feel.

The window was rolled down, probably to ensure the truck would sink faster. He carefully opened the door and probed inside. Something fluttered past, a fish, a turtle, a gator. Whatever, it was gone. He felt across the cab, the gearshift lever, all the way to the opposite side. There was no body.

Down in the corner he found a jacket and felt the sharp edges of a badge. He held it to his face. Wayne's number all right. As he backed from the cab he brought the jacket with him. The heaviness in his chest became a burden, a true pain.

With his remaining minutes of air, Reed probed the muck adjacent to the truck, stirring up silt until it totally erased any sense of light. Would the body be here? Would there be much of anything left? A game warden down. Who would kill a man just to avoid a few thousand dollars in fines?

Too many men, he knew. Far too many to make him feel at ease. His jaw clenched, the girding of strength just before a fight. These boys imagined they liked to hunt—well he'd give the bastards a hunt.

He worked to the back of the truck. What the area needed was a widespread search, teams of divers, boats, grappling hooks, the works.

Later, Reed thought. Later. Almost reluctantly he pushed off away from this isolated world of murky brown water and slowly kicked to the surface to warm sunlight, to where Marlis waited.

"It's about time," Hank called. "Long time between those bubbles from down there."

Reed exchanged glances with Story who waited silently and patiently in his pirogue. Reed nodded in the affirmative, all Story needed to know the truck was Wayne's. "No body," Reed said quietly. "Either it floated off or they dumped it somewhere else."

"Then it's gone," Story said in his naturally low voice.

Reed back-kicked to shore. Hank braced against a rock and helped Reed up the steep slope and onto the shore at the base of the levee. The sunshine and the warm air felt good, a contrast from the wet and darkness of being below. Normally Reed savored the moment, the contrast that made life so worthwhile. But Marlis stood on top of the levee. It was as if she'd never moved. And he could not look at her without thinking of Pam and the girls and all that he had lost. He cleared the caked spittle from his dry mouth and spit hard and bitterly to one side.

"It's Wayne's truck," Reed said across the twenty feet that separated him and Marlis.

"Is Wayne inside?" Marlis asked in a small voice.

"There's no sign. He could have . . ." Reed gestured helplessly at the swamp.

Marlis nodded as if in grave understanding. Her eyes locked with Reed as though once again judging his honesty. She slowly turned and disappeared down the levee.

"Damnit," Reed muttered. Either she found out now or she found out later. There simply was not an easy way.

"We should drag this entire area," Hank said.

"I know. But I'd rather keep the truck hush-hush for now. We have to try to get someone to break or at least flush the killer, make him break so we can see who he is. If you go with widespread publicity on this, they all get together and then sit tight."

"If I sit on this I'm going to get hung. Not reporting my suspicions are one thing. Sitting on hard evidence is something else."

"If we catch the killer you'll be all right."

"If?" Hank said. "You want me to base my career on one big if."

"That's part of the fun of life."

"I hate you, Erickson."

Reed wrapped his wet arm around Hank's shoulders. "No you don't."

Hank howled and pulled away. "It's too bad some gator didn't come and bite off your lips."

"Speaking of which, I'm telling you straight now. What I saw down there was an old junk car. That's all, an old junker. What choice do you have but to believe me. You're just a dumb Southern deputy and I work for the federal government. What do you know."

"I know you and me are going to have a tussle one of these days."

"Tell Story that's all we found. I'll talk to Marlis. If worse comes to worse we'll make a strategic leak that something is in the works."

Reed dragged the scuba gear up the slope and set it in the back of Hank's trunk. He toweled off, said his good-byes and then drove down the levee toward Marlis who had walked a half mile away. She readily climbed into the car. Her eyes brimmed with tears. Reed patted her shoulders and she fell across the seat and into his arms.

"It's a start, Marlis. You have to look at it as progress. I know it confirms your worst fears, but . . ."

"It doesn't confirm anything," Marlis sobbed. She lay her head on Reed's lap and curled into a tiny ball. Reed patted her side as if to comfort her. "What do I have? I don't have anything at all. I have Wayne's truck. People could say he put it there and ran off. That's what they'll say. I know. They always think the worst."

For a moment Reed was silent. Maybe he misunderstood.

"The main thing for now is to keep this quiet," Reed eventually continued. "We have to break this so Hank gets credit and we don't ruin his career. But mainly we want to hold off going after the violating ring until we can get a fix on the guilty party. At least finding the truck gives us a little leverage."

"Then you won't arrest them and find out who killed Wayne? Your boss said you have no jurisdiction over the murder case."

"You've been worried about that? No. Absolutely not. He meant officially. That's why I brought in Hank. The murder takes priority, Marlis. I promise." Marlis settled further into his lap. Reed gently stroked her silky hair, washed, conditioned, it was a dream. He'd been too rigid, he thought. He hadn't adapted to the life Pam and the girls wanted. They were just going along with society, with fashion. Who the hell was he to say no?

He looked down at Marlis. Her eyes were closed, like a little girl going to sleep. The scent of her perfume wafted into his nostrils. Certainly her jewelry, makeup, and perfume made her an appealing woman. He could not deny that. Even more than if she simply went natural. Perhaps he was just an idealist, or a hypocrite. He could adapt. He was sure he could adapt. He'd have to talk to Pam.

NINE

Reed confronted Doyle in the street out in front of the Magnolia Cafe. It was ten in the morning. Doyle, wearing black pants and a white shirt and tie, was on his way to the cafe for coffee and rolls with the regulars.

Perhaps confrontation wasn't the best tactic, Reed thought, but who knew. Every situation was different. If it wasn't for Doyle he'd have already worked inside the group. He hailed his adversary. "Hey, Doyle. Just a word."

Doyle paused with his hand on the cafe door. "Why would I want a word with you? You do nothing for this town."

"I'm not here about that," Reed dismissed the argument and saw Doyle stiffen with anger. "I was scheduled to go dove hunting with Billy Bob and the boys Saturday. Now Billy Bob informs me I'd better not go along. It seems Doyle wants to go. What the hell seems to be your problem?"

Given the nature of the man Reed had anticipated a strong reaction, a good confrontation that either settled the air or made his inclusion in the group an impossibility. He had not anticipated an instant fight.

But if Doyle was powerful, Reed was quick. He almost slipped the blur of the fist, taking a glancing blow to the jaw that knocked him back on his heels. A follow-up blow caught him on the side of the stomach. But as Doyle stepped forward to finish it, Reed exploded upward with a furious series of jabs into Doyle's face.

A line of blood drained from Doyle's nose. He grinned and dropped into his fighter's crouch, pleased with the knowledge this was no street fighter he faced. "I keep forgetting that what you pretend to be and who you are, are two different things," Doyle said.

Reed realized with regret he should have taken the first punch full and stayed on his back. But pride said fight. It was one reason wardens got killed. Their ego wouldn't let them take the precautions they should. Machismo, just like in war. As Pam had said, women should be in charge of the country. They didn't think with their testosterone.

A half-dozen men flooded from the cafe and gingerly circled the combatants. "Get him, Doyle," several called. For the most part they were older, businessmen, not much of a threat, Reed thought when he was suddenly seized from behind.

Doyle straightened. "What are you doing, Jakes?" he asked the tall, scrawny man who'd grabbed Reed from behind. "The good Lord hates a coward? You'd fight two on one? You should know me better than that. I fight fair. One on one like a man's supposed to."

The man let go. Reed turned. Jakes had a long, homely face and close cropped hair. He shot Doyle a hateful glance.

"They're out of it," Doyle said. Eagerly, as if looking forward to this moment for a long time, he moved into the fray.

It was the eagerness, the lack of normal discipline, that gave Reed his hope. Too often Doyle swung from his heels, going for the knockout, giving Reed a split second in which to feint and slip the blows. Nevertheless, more than enough blows found their mark. One smacked Reed in his bruised ribs and he gasped with pain.

"How'd you hurt your ribs?" Doyle grunted. Like Reed he was already gasping for air. "Have an accident?"

"The only accident around here is you, trying to be a dictator to those young men."

"Boys need leadership. I provide a way," Doyle said and the two moved in, toe to toe, trading shot for shot. It was, Reed knew in the midst of the flurry, the kind of fight he could not win. But as much as he hated to fight, detested the swollen knuckles, the puffed eyes, the painful throbbing, he could not back away. It was like a duty to the memory of Guy, his father, a tough old Swede who never started a fight in his life. But also a man who never turned his back, who never walked away a loser, who never quit.

In desperation Reed clinched, head to head, holding Doyle's arms to restrict their range. Sweat and blood streamed down their faces as the two men gasped for air. "A man fights and he fights and what does he get?" Doyle gasped into Reed's shoulder. He sounded close to tears. The surrounding audience, a dozen strong now, looked at one another in embarrassment. There had been a time Doyle had been one of their best. They looked at one another and shook their heads. No more. Their small town grocer had become mired in the past, unable to grow, unable to change. It was why his wife and daughter had left home. It was why the bank was taking his store.

Slowly, as if without strength, Doyle sank to his knees. Reed held his shoulders, maintaining a grip as if hanging on to a drowning man. He could see the crowd back away. He could sense the change in attitude. A surge of anger made Reed glare. Not one of these people could match Doyle's commitment to the community nor his strength. And now as Doyle fell, they turned their backs in disdain.

A siren wailed, one low squawk as Hank pulled over and jumped from the squad car. Reed stepped back. Doyle climbed to his feet, face red with embarrassment. The momentary lapse was past. He spoke with force and without a hint of friendliness. "You can leave, Hank. This is man to man. The government has no business here."

Hank winced at the tone—Doyle, his childhood mentor, his friend. He tried to play it light. "It looks to me like you've wacked each other enough. Who started it?"

"He did," old man Shervey said and pointed a thin, palsied finger at Reed.

"Maybe I ought to run you in," Hank said to Reed.

"Please, we don't need the show," Doyle snarled. "You don't think people know what's going on here?"

Reed's blood slowed as if laced with ice. Did Doyle suspect him or did he truly know? Then it had to be Doyle who saw Hank drop him in the square the other night. But did that mean Doyle was a threat? Was Doyle part of the ring? Did he even know who killed Wayne?

"It was a good fight," Reed said, diverting attention away

from Hank. He held out his hand to Doyle and looked his adversary in the eye with as much sincerity as he could muster. "I don't know who or what you think I am, Doyle. But I'm not your problem. I can tell you that."

Doyle shook. He even smiled. "Maybe it doesn't matter who you are." He fingered his jaw. "At least I know what you are. Most men can't say that about themselves. Certainly none of these guys here. They're just marking time."

Doyle turned to depart but then turned back and thrust a meaty finger in Jake's long horse face. "If you ever interfere in one of my fights again I'll rip that head of yours right off your shoulders." And then Doyle pushed through and returned to his store. The bank was coming to repossess his fixtures and inventory. The sheriff, the banker, and a truck were scheduled to show up at noon. Doyle was supposed to stand quietly and watch them take his life.

Hank glanced at Reed and shook his head. Sheriff LeBitche had ordered Hank to serve the papers because he knew Doyle was a friend. "Maybe he won't act up if you're there," LeBitche had said, and gave Hank his tight little smile. And to think the sheriff hadn't even learned about Wayne's truck yet.

Reed gave Hank a sympathetic nod and went inside the cafe for his morning coffee and roll. Hank came in also and took a seat at the opposite end of the counter. They had decided that, at least for the time being, they'd keep their knowledge of the whereabouts of the truck a secret, sort of their ace in the hole until they had an exact target. Of course the truck was only step one, they knew. What they really needed was a body, if there was still one around.

Reed took supper with Marlis, Jody, and Patty. Marlis cooked a complete meal, a shrimp gumbo, some of which she even ate herself. If anything, since they'd located Wayne's truck, her spirits had picked up. It was as if, at long last, she had some movement in her life, some sense that things indeed could change, that problems could be resolved.

But if Marlis's spirits were looking up, Reed's spirits were dropping. He'd called home. Trish and Pam had been out. Stacy answered. "Oh, Dad, it's you. Mother and Trish are out. I'm expecting an important call."

"Isn't a call from your father important?"

And Stacy had just sat there, absolutely refusing to answer. What was a man to say? He quietly hung up and prepared to take his leave.

"Going out tonight?" Marlis asked into Reed's silence.

The hint of resentment surprised Reed. Was that a proprietary note? "I have to try to get something going," Reed said. He looked at Jody. The boy watched his every move, listened to his every word. Another one making judgments. It happened everywhere he turned.

At Reed's insistence he stayed long enough to clean the table and wash dishes. And then, feeling not unlike a father abandoning his wife and children, he took his evening trek down to the Blue Moon.

As usual Billy Bob, Ross, Chuck, and Wyndal were down drinking beer and playing their games. Reed bought a round and glumly settled in at the bar. His ribs ached and a small purple knot pushed out over his right eye. Billy Bob looked pleased to see him, as if for the first time he felt like they were truly friends.

"I heard you fought Doyle to a draw. I don't think anyone has ever done that." Billy Bob spoke proudly, as if he were somehow part of Reed's team. "Doyle used to box in the Marines, never lost a fight."

"Doyle's getting old," Ross said as if in defense. But the thick-shouldered lad gazed on Reed with suspicion, one more hint of the self-doubt that had developed ever since Reed jumped onto the back of the alligator.

"We're going hunting late Saturday," Billy Bob said. He leaned close and whispered secretively, "Deer hunting. Doyle said to ask you along."

"Sure," Reed said without a hint of hesitation. He'd played poker. When you ran a bluff you went straight and firm, without a hint of doubt. His blood raced. His hands tingled. He might just as well have volunteered to stand before a firing squad. Doyle all but told him to his face he knew he was an agent of some kind. And then to invite him on a hunt? No. Hank, Doug, they'd know enough to get out. It was standard procedure if you thought you'd been made, you got out. Make the arrest another day, another way.

"What about the dove hunt in the afternoon," Reed asked. The chubby cheeks of Billy Bob's twenty-two-year-old face turned bright red. He stammered, "I, I don't know. Ah, Doyle didn't say anything." "What the hell do you mean Doyle didn't say anything. Who gives a damn what Doyle says or doesn't say. What are you, his damn slave? You can't stand up and make decisions on your own? You assholes call yourselves men? You're like a bunch of damn little boys." Reed's argumentative tone called attention from everyone in the tavern. He challenged the men one by one. Billy Bob turned away. Ross met his gaze and considered his chances. But he did not move. Wyndal sneered and checked to see his switch-blade was handy. Chuck just shrugged.

Reed guzzled his beer and took his leave. Perhaps he'd worked an out. But he'd also left an opening, if he wanted to take the risk.

The question was what did Doyle want? And if Reed didn't go on the hunt, what did he have? What had he accomplished?

"The guy was a fed, Washington DC. It said so on his license," Cutter complained. He sat in the dark of his living room. As usual, even in mid-afternoon, the shades were drawn placing the dimly lit room in deep gloom. The small window air conditioner whirred helplessly against the heavy humidity. Cutter shifted his bulk on the brown bedspread Bonnie had covering the new sofa. He pointedly guzzled at a beer. There'd been a time, before he married Rachel, Doyle would have a beer with the guys. Now you couldn't even drink or curse.

"Well, we know they're on to us. I told you that," Doyle said. He sat on a sheet covering the matching easy chair. "We'll just have to look at it as a bigger challenge."

Cutter snorted. "What are you, nuts? We'll just have to close 'er down for a while. They'll be watching for that semi. Hell, they could pick that up from the air."

"No. We don't close down," Doyle snarled.

Cutter stilled his reply while his wife, Bonnie, entered the room with a tray of snacks, sandwiches, pickled pigs feet, and cookies. She was a big woman, close to Cutter's weight and wore a loose-fitting, flowered dress. Her hair hung long and curled around her thick face. She glanced at Cutter and he nodded toward the outer room. This was man-talk. Bonnie offered Cutter a sandwich then set the tray in front of Doyle. "More lemonade?"

"I'm fine. The hospitality is fine," Doyle said.

As Bonnie turned to leave, Cutter patted her affectionately on the thigh. He clinked his beer can, a quiet signal for a refill. Bonnie brought another can and then quickly took her leave.

While Bonnie brought him his beer, Cutter sat quietly and considered. Doyle was kin, his first cousin. In high school Doyle had been the fullback, while Cutter played left tackle. Whenever they needed an extra yard, Monroe followed Monroe. They'd both made All-Conference, the only two players from the team. The operation was as much his as Doyle's. They were a team. Cutter could not recall a time when they'd disagreed—until now.

"I don't think we have a choice here, Doyle. We're not exactly equipped to take on the federal government."

Doyle stared with growing irritation at Cutter's large screen Japanese television set. The New Orleans Saints and Green Bay Packers were running strings of inept rookies and free agents onto the field during the middle stages of a pre-season contest that had as much relevance and importance as a weekend game of golf. Cutter lay like a beached walrus, sprawled in his Lazy-Boy. Gravity spread his stomach to cover the chair side to side. His jowls sagged beneath the stiff bristles of his crew cut. The television remote lay cradled in the thick fingers of his left hand.

Television. Why the Lord allowed that abomination Doyle could not understand. It ruined the country, ruined the area. Television made everyone the same. Like Cutter there; it was as if his mind had been taken away.

Doyle turned his head in disgust. There'd been a time Cutter had been as tough as any of them. Back during Doyle's drinking days, before he'd been saved, they'd had a few memorable tussles. One night over at Jackson he and Cutter had stood back to back between two pool tables and taken out a half-dozen Jackson toughs. Big talking beer drinkers who never put on a set of pads. Those boys didn't know what tough was about. But no more. Cutter had gone to fat. Gone soft. These days he couldn't cross the room without starting to wheeze.

"If there's an agent living in Magnolia as you claim, and they almost had us the other night, then now is the time to lie low," Cutter continued his side of the argument. "To go out now in the face of that would be pure stupidity." Cutter did not mince his words. He'd worn out reason with Doyle. The only choice here was to get tough.

Doyle slowly rose to his feet. "Turn that damn thing off." Cutter glared. No one gave him orders.

"What do I have to do, kick out the screen?" Doyle spoke softly, a voice of promise.

In compromise, Cutter thumbed the sound to mute. His small eyes never left Doyle. If Doyle so much as made a move toward that television there'd be a war.

Doyle smiled. "You wouldn't last two minutes, Cutter. If you don't understand that then you don't understand how far you've dropped. The glory days are past. Me, I've been running. Lifting weights. I'm in better shape now than when I was in the Marines." Doyle thumped his flat stomach for emphasis. "During the old days when there was a fight you'd be there. Hell, most of the time you led the way. Now we have a bit of a challenge and you sit there wheezing on that broken-down fat man's chair."

Cutter rocked forward and heaved to his feet. His face was mottled and purple with rage. "That's enough, Doyle. This is my house. You were a guest, now you can leave. You don't know when to quit do you? That's why you're losing your store. That's why Rachel left. You're not always right. In fact lately you've never been right. Even I know better than to take on the federal government when it's breathing down my neck. That's my truck. I put the outlets together. Sixty cents a pound for lean venison for hamburger and never a question asked. I say we lie low. Wait until they go away." Sweat formed on Cutter's temples. His chest heaved with the exertion of his anger. He might be just a little short on wind, but he hadn't lost his strength. Doyle had just better be aware of that.

"You know what your problem is?" Doyle asked.

"No. What's my problem?" Cutter was as sarcastic as he could be.

Doyle waved his hand around the cluttered living room with its new and covered furniture, the giant screen television and VCR where Cutter watched football all weekend long. "You have too many things. It makes a man think he has too much to lose. Man like that becomes a coward and doesn't even know it. Me, I've been set free. The bank took the store. Rachel and the kids have left. I don't have anything to lose." Doyle bent close. His lips were curled in a disdainful sneer. His eyes glittered like laser beams. "Nothing at all."

"That's your failure, not mine," Cutter replied angrily.

"You just don't have the guts to make a stand. I'm not talking about being foolish. I'm not talking about taking chances. I'm talking about taking precautions, of knowing they're out there and then standing up and showing them we can't be tamed, we can't be trampled into the dirt like insects. We're men. Men stand on two legs. They don't turn and run. Cowards do that. They cower and hide. We thumb our noses. We live our lives. And nothing can change that. Nothing. Not even the federal government."

"We lie low," Cutter declared. "It's my truck. It's not leaving the barn."

"Friday night, Cutter. We're going. If it looks all right, the next night I might even bring a special guest. I've already informed the boys about Friday. They're ready, one and all. Not one of them hesitated. They all thought it would be great fun."

"That's because they're too block-headed to understand what's going on. Besides, they don't have anything to lose."

"That's exactly the point," Doyle said. "That's why you've gone soft, Cousin. Once you get scared of getting hurt, you've already lost the fight. The man who loses in combat is the man who's afraid to die."

"That's bullshit. The man who loses in combat is the man who is stupid enough to stand up when bullets are whizzing through the air."

"I'd rather die on my feet like a man than die groveling in a hole."

"Ah," Cutter waved a hand in dismissal. He glanced at the television set where some quarterback named Wright had just completed six in a row and was still booed for taking the field.

"Friday night," Doyle said as he made to depart. "We'll show them what Louisiana men are made of."

"Nope. Not me," Cutter said casily. "Not until things cool down."

"Fine," Doyle said with deadly calm. "The rest of us are going out. You can come or you can stay. If we have to we'll dump the carcasses on your front yard. It'll be more driving, but if we're lucky we can get a hundred or more. You can take care of them come the dawn."

Cutter flushed. His thick hands tingled as if the circulation had been stopped and they'd fallen asleep. If he rushed Doyle now they'd break up the house. Everything. Besides, he stared at Doyle's squat, solid frame. He hadn't really noticed previously, but the man *was* in shape, just like a block of granite. And Doyle was fast, he'd always been fast. He could stick and move as good as any nigger fighter Cutter had ever seen. The only choice would be to wrap him in his arms. If he could get him in his arms.

Something inside Cutter clicked, an image of him wallowing around the room, his face bloodied, the living room in shambles, shards of glass lying in front of the television set. And Doyle wouldn't be touched. If he hit him he'd kill him. All the guys knew that. When Cutter Monroe gave an order everyone jumped. But Doyle . . . Cutter's hands trembled. They actually trembled. He closed his eyes as if about to cry. He was frightened, him, Cutter Monroe.

When he opened his eyes Cutter saw Doyle and understood his cousin knew. His shoulders sagged and he settled back onto his Lazy-Boy, belly up like a bitch hound dog who has finally submitted. He growled, seeking salvation by sounding tough. "All right, Doyle. I'll play stupid with you. What time do you want to head out?"

"I knew I could count on you. Eleven o'clock. We'll hit Avoyelles Parish. That's a good area. We've got the roads down pat. We can watch each other's tails." Doyle grinned. His eyes crinkled tight with genuine mirth. "We'll have some fun, Cousin. Like in the old days before everything went to hell. We'll give those feds a run they'll never forget."

Cutter barely nodded. His head was lowered, eyes heavily lidded while he watched the game. He could not bring himself to reply.

TEN

Reed hadn't realized they were going to war. The meeting room in the Federal Office Building at One America Place in Baton Rouge was crowded with state conservation officers and U.S. Marshals. They'd moved in wholesale with banks of telephones and even a complete radio base connected coaxially to an antenna on the roof. Most of the state wardens wore uniforms. The U.S. Marshals were dressed more casually and wore dark blue jackets with bright yellow lettering across the back. Even Doug had improved his garb and wore a brown corduroy sport coat, albeit without tie.

Doug had called him on a late Friday afternoon. They'd had Cutter Monroe under surveillance. They'd observed a visit from one Doyle Monroe. And later in the afternoon Cutter had pulled his semi-tractor out of the pole building and gassed it up. "We think they're going out tonight," Doug had said. "Get your ass over here. I haven't been able to reach you all afternoon. Doucet's been talking to his higher ups and they've been talking to our higher ups and now they think they want to make a big ass public show of this and close it all down."

"No," Reed exploded. "We'll lose the murder case. I'm set up to go out with these guys tomorrow night."

"You know better than that," Doug growled. "If they have suspicions that's out. Maybe they were trying to misdirect."

"Don't move until I get there," Reed snapped. He slammed the telephone on its cradle. Marlis stared from across the room, watching his every move. "I need your car. It's an emergency."

"What is it?" Marlis asked suspiciously. If yesterday there

had been trust, now there was none as each of them kept their own counsel, their own secrets.

"Maybe nothing, if I can put a stop to it," Reed said. He took her keys and started to take his leave.

"You promised," Marlis yelled with the certainty of one who knew she was being deceived. "You promised. Wayne comes first. Remember? Do you think I can't see? You're playing games with me again. Just like all the others. Pursuing your own agenda." She was shrill, certain in her indignation.

Somehow Reed had escaped. But the words rang in his ears, a sad reminder of how events moved beyond his control.

He drove ninety miles an hour all the way to Baton Rouge. Reed hurriedly flashed his badge and ID to a young U.S. Marshal at the doorway then brushed past. "What the hell is going on here?" Reed demanded from Doug. "I didn't order all this."

Doug shrugged in apology. "It's past us, partner. Like I told you on the telephone. The state boys here wanted to make the arrests out in the field. We don't have solid evidence against some of these guys. And then I talked to P.U., er, Peter. The operation is still in our jurisdiction, however, he talked to the state mucky-mucks down in Lafayette and they concurred that a nice public arrest, with joint publicity of course, might be the best for both agencies. Loosening up purse strings and all that." Doug could barely contain his mirth. His thick jowls and thick torso shook with laughter. He knew how Reed detested it whenever politics took over an operation. It was as bad as chasing drug traffickers, politics and publicity was never for the best.

"Well if that isn't a sonofabitch then I don't know what is," Reed snapped. He glared at a nearby warden, a tall rangy man with coal black hair, pure blue eyes and a sun-reddened complexion. Captain Gerald Doucet. His initial liaison. Wayne's supervisor. The man who'd never been in the field and who still refused to declare Wayne dead.

"I'm the case agent on this, Doucet. You knew that. What the hell do you think you're doing initiating all this behind my back?"

"We couldn't contact you. So I was in touch with your superiors. They concurred," Doucet said mildly.

Reed spoke with a profound and natural disdain for authority. "You realize that you're being damn premature on this. We'll probably lose some of the bastards. But more important, we might have had something going on your officer that was murdered out in these parts. The one you guys made a brief search for and then abandoned." Every state warden in the room had focused their attention on Reed. "Now because of the big publicity show here you can kiss any movement in that direction good-bye."

"Wayne Pog," Gerald Doucet said with the solemn voice of authority. "We could never determine if he got killed or just ran off and left his wife, the one you're shacking up with."

"The woman that got me inside the community. You know that. Or do you always get taken in by appearances? How the hell do you think we came up with all this information? What do you think undercover entails?"

Doucet's complexion turned flaming red. For a heartbeat he considered swinging. "Mr. Waldheim claimed you were a professional," Gerald said with equal disdain. He referred to Reed's boss, Peter Ulysses Waldheim. "What I would like to do is get on with the operation here. The semi has been out on the road for an hour and a half. Doug insisted we wait for you. So we did. And all you want to do is scream and call names. I'd like to get out and make some arrests. Stop this slaughter of Louisiana game." Gerald spoke calmly, with deep resonance, a man born to authority in bearing and in temperament. His cold blue eyes spoke eons. He'd not get down and grovel and call names with Reed Erickson. He'd been surprised. Professionals conducted themselves with a certain bearing and class, with respect for order and authority. But not this Reed. At every opportunity Gerald Doucet would put out the word, this federal agent, this Reed Erickson, was one piece of dirt.

"What about the slaughter of Louisiana wardens?" Reed asked.

"You don't know and we don't know Wayne Pog is dead."

"He's dead. In any case this is our show. You can ride. When I give the word we move in, not before. You can get the glory. You can smile and talk to the press. Until then, Mr. Doucet, you stay the hell out of my way. Two quarterbacks on the same field of play simply does not work. I call the shots.

When you decide to tattle to my superiors, I'd appreciate it if you could wait until later, when the bad guys are out of the way."

Doucet swept the room with his eyes. Every warden there met his gaze. He did not have a friend in the place, not even his own men. For a moment his jaw sagged in surprise. Who the hell was this Reed? He looked like some thick-headed logger. But then Doucet caught himself. Apparently he was the only leader with class. He stepped back, his bearing precisely erect. He spoke with an exact degree of spite, "It's your operation, Mr. Erickson. We're just here to lend a hand, as your boss requested."

Reed turned his back. His anger was as directed at himself as it was Doucet. He should stop this, he knew. Just say no. Take the consequences. He closed his eyes as if in pain. Like a man alone in the forest he was just a tiny part of the whole. The operation had become a flood. It couldn't be stopped. Not any more. The best he could hope for was to go along and try to control the flow. A tiny part of the whole. It was the reason for his pain.

"What do you have, Doug? What's the situation in the field?"

Doug led Reed over to a blowup of a section map of Louisiana roads. "Compliments of the state," he said with a smile. "You're a little hot tonight partner. Either you haven't been getting any lately or you've geen getting too much. P.U.'s going to fry your nuts. And you'll spend the next six months attending seminars on public and interpersonal relations."

"The guy reminds me of Westmoreland in Vietnam," Reed hissed in a low voice. "He looks like a general. He talks like a general. But his head's made out of wood."

Doug picked up a pointer and snapped it at the map with the precision of a man giving a military briefing. At least it made Reed smile. "I've got an M-six tracking device on the semi, sir. And we have a pursuit vehicle tracking from two miles back. Said vehicle contains two state wardens and one federal marshal. The word is a pickup truck dropped in a mile behind the semi, apparently thinking they'd cover his tail and make sure no one was following. We, of course, are well out of sight in back of the protective rear guard."

"We've got them wired," a young rosy-cheeked man at the radio counsel said. "We're scanning now to try to pick up any CB talk. We can cover every channel there is right here. Every vehicle has cellular telephone connections in addition to the radio. There isn't anyplace in the area that's outside the range of a base station. We could track these guys by satellite if we wanted to." He grinned, a man enthralled with his job. "Technologically they're overwhelmed. Taking on the old U.S. of A. Strictly third world."

"Vietnam was third world," Reed said. "I saw a lot of you technology boys there with ground antipersonnel radar, people sniffers, and the works. How'd you boys do?"

The young man turned bright red. He faced his equipment. Reed clapped his shoulder as if in affection. "The technology is fine, son. It helps. But what really counts is when you're standing out there in the dark, alone and facing a man with a gun. Just like Wayne Pog."

Reed and Doug rode together in a four-wheel-drive jeep. A second jeep followed, filled with two state wardens and three federal marshals. In addition to the vehicle already trailing the semi, two additional vehicles worked parallel roads six to ten miles on either flank. The base scanner as well as vehicular mounted scanners worked the airways to pick out any CB broadcasts that might be connected to their quarry.

"The lab boys have documented venison in the hamburger in two outlets in the city," Doug said. "So we've got some solid evidence on that end. If we tie this up tonight we'll hit the outlet people tomorrow morning. They should still have more venison left in stock."

"This is going to kill the murder investigation," Reed said.

"I told P.U., but he said we don't have any evidence and that it isn't part of our jurisdiction. Maybe if we told him about finding the pickup."

"Can't. That'd leave Hank out to dry."

"Well, after Mr. Doucet there gets done complaining to his boss and so on up the line you won't be getting any consideration from anyone for some time. Let's just hope everything tonight goes real smooth. That's the only mitigating factor you've got. I still don't see why you got so hot. It isn't like you."

Reed shrugged in the dim green glow from the dash lights. "Doucet was the guy pushing to make this a show. I knew that from the start. He was also the first guy to give up searching for Wayne. He's the same guy who suggested Wayne ran off and left his kids. No downstream loyalty at all. P.U. may be a bureaucrat, but he sticks by his men."

"That's why he's as high as he'll ever go."

"Ain't that the truth."

The low hiss of the CB broke. "Base to ten. Try twenty-five point niner. We've got coded traffic. Break, also nine reports the refrigerator has stopped at location thirty-three on your map."

"Ten here, right, thanks." Reed quickly spun the dials on their radio and then dialed the base station on the cellular telephone.

For some seconds the radio hissed with an empty airway. And then someone broke squelch. "Muskrat, clear. Six in the bin."

"Boss One. Looks clear. Rebel One, go."

"Rebel One inbound."

And then silence.

"Sounds like a military operation," Doug remarked.

"That's Doyle," Reed said. "He's Marine, strake troop. He keeps his boys straight. They're frightened of him but they respect him. In truth, they probably like playing soldier. Although I'm sure not as much as Doyle."

"He the one that gave you that bump on your head?" Doug kidded. "What happened to the guy who doesn't like to fight?"

"I gave him lip and he swung first. I didn't have a choice. He thought I was pretty good. Too good for a drunk."

"You should have taken a fall." Doug shrugged. He knew the way these operations went. You never knew how a man would respond. "How are we going to take these guys?" Doug asked. "I can't believe they won't give us a chase. We don't have them all bugged. It could get hairy, especially when you consider the possible charge and that they know the land."

"Plus it could be a setup. Doyle all but said he knew I was onto him. And then he invited me out deer hunting tomorrow night. He's not a stupid man. I can't believe he'd challenge us like this. We could come barrelling in and they'd be as clean and shiny as a butcher shop waiting on the state inspector."

"Erickson."

Reed recognized Gerald Doucet's voice on the telephone. "Doucet. What do you want?"

"I'm putting the chopper up and then everyone can zero in on the bull's-eye from all points of the compass."

"Keep your thumb up your ass where it belongs, Doucet. And keep that chopper on the ground. You can hear it twenty miles away. No one moves anywhere until I see hair. This guy knows we're after him. It could be a trap. And by barrelling from all points of the compass we're not going to stop a possum from crossing the road. First we see hair. Then we get their pattern. The second or third go around, if the layout looks right and we can get into position, we'll make our move. Until then you sit tight, Doucet. All stations respond to my command." Reed slammed down the telephone.

"Don't call us. We'll call you," Doug intoned. "I hate to see this operation end as much as you do, pardner. I was just getting used to the South. Finally met me a nice Southern belle. She wasn't Louisiana plantation soft like your'n as much as she was a Tennessee hillbilly. She said her and her ex moved down here to get work in the petrochemical plants there along the Mississippi."

"The German Ruhr." Reed related a common reference to the continuous stretch of industrial complexes between Baton Rouge and New Orleans. "The crap they put in the water, all in the name of progress."

"But then her ex got a job as a roustabout on one of the offshore rigs, doing seven and seven. She couldn't stand it when he was away and couldn't stand him when he came back."

"You sure she's divorced?" Reed's ardor had cooled.

Doug laughed as he protested. "Hey, that's what she said. I didn't go to her house. Who am I to doubt a woman's word? If she gives me her virtue that's good enough for me."

"It's always been good enough for you," Reed said. He bent low, concentrating on the map. "There's no way we can get close enough to these guys to even see through the starlight scope if they're loading deer or not."

"After the semi pulls out we could drive in and scan the area," Doug said. "If they're transferring fresh killed deer there has to be blood." He poked Reed's arm. "Maybe we can even find you a few tufts of hair, something you can put in a plastic bag and carry against your chest like a medicine man."

"And Doucet said you were as dumb as a rock," Reed said, by way of compliment.

"He just wanted to take control," Doug said. "You just wouldn't give him the reins. He's Cajun big shot. None of these boys down here like a fed."

By one o'clock in the morning, Reed had his evidence, pools of blood quickly scraped over with dirt and multiple patches of deer hair picked up at the spots the semi had stopped. He telephoned everyone to tell them the news and they quietly picked up the chase. The nearest vehicle remained two miles in back of the semi, one mile behind the violator's protective rear guard.

"We'll move in at the next stop," Reed said into the telephone. "If the layout is opportune. Otherwise we wait." Grimly he set about the task of directing his forces. He and Doug, trailed by the jeep with five men, sped at seventy miles an hour and circled some side roads that would hopefully bring them out in front of the semi. The one trailer continued to follow from two miles back, using the radio tracking device to get a fix on directional changes the semi might make.

"Not exactly the best procedure with a ring this big," Doug said. He referred to the fact that preferred procedure with larger conspiracies would be to gather sufficient evidence and then have teams of agents and U.S. Marshals show up at suspects' homes around dawn. That way suspects were isolated, confused, less likely to put up resistance and more likely to talk. "Well, at least we don't have to listen to any wives and kids scream and wail while we haul away the old man."

"I thought you like to listen to women scream," Reed said. He was bent over, studying and memorizing the various roads and trails on a detailed area map. At the moment they were approximately one mile over, driving parallel to the semi which was on a parish highway.

"But only when I make them," Doug said. Reed did not

respond. Doug glanced across at his partner. "You're still pissed, aren't you?"

"Of course. This is all premature. Especially as regards Wayne's murder. Doucet didn't want to believe Wayne had been murdered because it wouldn't look good for him or his department. The attitude is straight out of the military, always protecting the image no matter what the facts or the impact on people's lives."

Doug fell silent. He shouldn't have reopened the subject. For some reason Reed still hadn't cooled down.

For some time they drove in complete silence. What would he tell Marlis, Reed wondered. He was the case agent. And he couldn't control his own case. She'd already given him the look of the betrayed, as if it were part of her life, all consuming, as if there wasn't anything more. Could her father comprehend he'd ruined two lives that day, Sheila Jackson as well as his own daughter. They should have strapped him into the electric chair.

If they made the arrests, naturally they'd order him off the case. The murder wasn't department jurisdiction. P.U. had harped on that from the start. He'd have to go back to Washington, write up his report, and spend hours with some U.S. attorney putting together the case.

A brief sense of loneliness gripped Reed. There were times he craved, demanded, and needed the absolute solitude of the wilderness. But there were those other times, back with civilization, he needed the warm and soft touch of a woman, someone he loved, someone who loved him. Pam had been there once. And now there was Marlis—and he'd be the one to throw her hopes of finding Wayne's killer right back in her face.

The radio broke static. "Ten, this is five, they've stopped."

"Ten, roger." Reed spoke to the vehicle tracking the semi. "When you hear us move in, you move up and take that rear guard. Don't be premature, and be prepared to stop anyone that might run in your direction."

"Five here, roger that."

"They seem pretty professional," Doug said of the state wardens. "I guess they have their pressures also. Last year they cut out twenty percent of the force and people still expect the same results."

"Turn left at the dirt road right up here. Douse your lights before you complete the turn. They shine too high on the foliage." Reed radioed the jeep behind him to also kill their lights, to stay close and to have two men get ready to move in with him on foot. "If we go driving in, half of them will run off into the forest," Reed explained. "It's hard for them to hear with that refrigerator unit going. They've got a rear guard. They shouldn't expect us from the front. As soon as we get into position, I'll radio the word. You drive up. At the last second hit the lights and we'll take them from the opposite side. No siren."

"Sounds easy on paper," Doug said with knowledge born of experience. "If something can go wrong it will. I wonder if they'll be calling in on the same frequency."

"I doubt it, unless they want to get caught."

Doug doused his lights. He rolled his window down and thrust his head out into the warm evening, watching the black shadow of the roadside foliage as his guide.

Abruptly Reed seized the radio. "Five, ten here, get off the road and out of sight. No lights. They'll probably come in past that rear guard to ensure their tail is clear. They'll be coming down your road. Don't you move until their Boss One radioes that he's coming in."

"Five here, roger. We're already out of sight."

"Good man," Reed replied. "You should be a fed."

Doug grinned in the dark. Reed was on the job. Everyone was up and loose. "With all this manpower, we should be able to intimidate them," Reed said. "I don't think they'll take a shot."

"But they will run," Doug said.

"They always run."

When they were about a third of a mile away from what Reed judged to be a soybean or hayfield, Doug drifted to the side of the road and Reed, a state warden, and a U.S. Marshal climbed out of their vehicles and started trotting down the road in the wee hours of a cool Louisiana morning. They moved in unison, the others following Reed and watching his lead. He'd quietly and quickly briefed them on his plan and then headed down the gravel road, hand-held walkie-talkie in one hand, a 9mm pistol in the other. Standing orders: Don't fire unless fired upon. By then, of course, you could be dead. The public expected a lot for thirty-one thousand a year.

The air buzzed with crickets and frogs. The hum of the refrigerator unit on the trailer carried through the night. Reed cut down through the thickets and briars of the ditch line. The U.S. Marshal muttered at the scrapes across his face. Reed and his fellow warden smiled. They stepped out onto the stubble of a fresh-cut hayfield. The radio broke static. Reed held it to his ear.

"The first one's coming in," Doug said. "Same frequency. They just passed five's position. You were right on that one. They were covering their rear from way back."

"Roger," Reed whispered. "We're almost into position. As soon as these first boys clear their cab, I'll radio. We don't want anyone to call any warnings."

Reed pulled his two men around him. "The first pickup is coming in. When they get out of the cab, the Marshal here can take the rider, you can take the driver. We don't want them radioing a warning. I'll cover those in the semi. If your man runs, go with him. But only if he's not carrying a gun. Doug and the others will be there in seconds to help with the truck. Remember, these boys might have killed before, so be ready for anything."

The state warden squeezed Reed's forearm. "Nice job with Doucet back there. I wish I had your nerve. No matter what he said, I think you're right. Wayne wasn't the kind of guy who would ever run out on his wife."

Reed nodded his appreciation in the dark. He smelled sweat, felt the rush of adrenaline, of men pumped with excitement, set with purpose. If the truth be known, Reed thought, it was these moments in their jobs for which they all lived. At least this time he wasn't alone. "Let's go."

The three men swept in spread formation across the hayfield. They approached within thirty yards of the semi when a pickup truck turned into the access road and the hayfield. As the lights swept the field the agents dropped to the ground. Someone hollered and the lights were doused. The pickup swung around and backed tailgate to tailgate with the semi-trailer. A light from deep inside the trailer cast a dim glow onto the field. As the dark shape of the driver emerged from the pickup, Reed spoke softly into the walkie-talkie. "Ten here, go."

"Roger," Doug grunted.

Reed and his two men rose and started across the field. They'd closed to within twenty feet when a motor roared and headlights flashed on the roadway and a blinking red light bore down their direction. For a heartbeat the four violators froze, then turned as if to run.

"Federal agents, freeze," Reed roared as loud and as intimidatingly as he could. One man bolted but Reed stuck out a foot and casually tripped him. As a second man ran past, Reed viciously thrust his pistol into the man's face. "I said freeze." He whirled, and as the tripped man rose to his feet Reed grabbed him by the back of the hair, dragged him back into the light, and pushed him up against the back of the truck. "Hi, Ross. Bet you're glad to see me."

"You sonofabitch, you're dead," Ross hissed.

"You just bought a jail sentence," Reed said. "Threatening a federal agent. That's a no-no."

As Doug and the trailing jeep swung into the field, more U.S. Marshals and state conservation officers crowded the violators up against the back of the semi. They were bathed in the glare of headlights. Doug swung his spotlight to focus on one of the marshals chasing a violator across the hay stubble. The second jeep roared after the two and cut in front of the violator just before the woodline.

"Damn state wardens are pretty sharp," Reed remarked sufficiently loud for one of the wardens to hear. "Let's move it, guys. Put these guys inside the back of this nice warm trailer here and get these vehicles out of sight. If they give you any grief hang them from a meat hook."

With five men under arrest and seven agents, marshals, and state wardens to help handcuff and shuffle prisoners, the violators were quickly subdued and the excess vehicles moved down the hayfield where they could not be spotted from the roadway.

"You Cutter?" Reed spoke to a sweating, rotund man wearing a bloody white meatcutter's apron. The man stared in puzzlement at the sound of his name. His small, dark eyes glittered out of the puffs of his cheeks.

"That's Cutter," Doug said as he emerged from the jeep after parking it behind the semi. They pulled Cutter behind the semi, separating him from the others. Doug stepped close and seized Cutter's shirt. "We've got everything, joker, your truck registration, your outlets. We know you head this show. We'll take your truck, add on fifty thousand and maybe get you a couple of years in jail. What we'd like to add to that is you resisting arrest and failing to cooperate with federal agents. Now when that next truck pulls in here, we want you out by the tailgate, real nice and friendly just like normal."

Reed jumped in, bracketing Cutter from the opposite side. "And if you screw up, Doug and I will just have to tell about how you tried to run."

"And how you threw a punch at the both of us," Doug added. "We'll add enough. We'll take everything you've got. Understand? And perhaps a few years prison time besides."

Cutter's head bobbed in the dark like it was attached to a spring. "I understand. I'll cooperate. Please."

Reed and Doug looked at each other. The man was close to tears. And they'd thought he was the toughest of the lot, possibly the man who'd murdered Wayne. Nature's lesson had been learned anew, Reed thought, appearances often deceived.

Reed went to the four-wheel-drive pickup truck and picked up the CB radio on the violator's frequency. He tried to imitate Ross's thick-tongued voice. "Muskrat clear, eight in the bin."

"Boss one, roger. Rebel one, go."

"Rebel one in."

And then silence. Boss One definitely sounded like Doyle, Reed thought. A good man gone bad, or maybe he was like a lot of violators and didn't think of himself as bad at all. But then how did they explain Wayne? The mindset eluded him as something he could not grasp.

They stationed Cutter at the back of the semi. The second pickup pulled in and backed up. As the two men emerged from the cab two arresting officers seized each one.

"Easy as pie," Doug said. "Not exactly like Doucet envisioned. I think he wanted a statewide chase, something dramatic."

"I wouldn't doubt it," Reed replied. He walked to the truck to radio Rebel One as clear, this time attempting to imitate

Wyndal's reedy voice. Doyle radioed back, he was coming in. Reed went to the second radio and informed the trailing state wardens they should move up on the rear guard five minutes after Boss One had passed.

Reed emerged from the cab. "Is he coming?" Doug asked. "He's coming," Reed said. "But I think there was a bit of hesitation in his tone. Maybe they have a code. Or maybe he didn't recognize my voice. If we have a chase, Doug—you stay here and secure the scene. Jack," Reed spoke to a state warden, "you ride with me. In fact, get in that truck and be ready to roll. Everyone else stay here. I radioed for the outriders to move in so they'll be able to join in any chase. Stay low and be ready for anything. This guy knows what he's doing."

ELEVEN

Chuck was acting as rear guard, sitting three quarters of a mile back from the semi when Doyle and Billy Bob pulled up alongside. Billy Bob rolled down his window. "We got nine this time. Doyle shot four. I shot five."

"This is boring," Chuck replied. "Why don't you and I switch."

"You haven't seen or heard anything?" Doyle asked.

"Couple of opossum and a coon," Chuck said. "I got that one coon. Squished him good, both tires. Other than that I haven't seen a vehicle on any of the back roads since midnight."

"We haven't either," Doyle said. "It shows the feds are out here. They probably cleared the roads." Chuck and Billy Bob exchanged knowing glances. "That last call back, Wyndal sound all right to you?"

Chuck straightened in his cab. "Ah, well, for a second there I had a notion. But I wasn't listening clear. It had to be Wyndal. Who else could it be?"

Doyle drove ahead. "Who else could it be," he mimicked to Billy Bob. "I swear, Chuck's a good boy, but sometimes he's as thick-headed as an oak."

Billy Bob nodded. These days the best thing with Doyle was to keep quiet and agree. If the truth be known, he would have gladly switched from Doyle's truck to take Chuck's place as rear guard. At least he could listen to the radio and maybe have a drink, something to calm his nerves.

"The feds are out here," Doyle said grimly. "I can feel it. I can smell them, just like I could smell Charlie Cong. Taking our land, taking our game from the people. Just like they think it's theirs. You know when it's time, Billy Bob. Just like an old dog. They know when you're taking them on the last hike. They see your tears. They sense your remorse. But we're not dogs, are we, Billy Bob?"

"No sir," Billy Bob said as firmly as he could. He knew when Doyle demanded a response. Last hike! What the hell was Doyle thinking? Billy Bob glanced at the grim set to the block of granite behind the wheel. Suddenly he felt sick, the same way he'd felt the night Wayne Pog had died.

"No, of course not. We're men, God's creatures. Taking on an atheistic government. When it comes time to die, we die clean, fighting tooth and nail right down to our last breath. You never surrender, Billy Bob. Never. They'll hang you by your heels, slit your stomach, and then you just dangle while your guts slowly peel down until they're hanging past your face. And you scream and wonder why the hell you didn't die."

Billy Bob sat silently, as far across the seat and as tight to the door as he could get. His bowels roiled painfully. He'd have to move away from Magnolia. It was the only way to escape from Doyle. He'd try Baton Rouge. No, Baton Rouge wasn't far enough. He'd have to make it New Orleans. He made the decision then. He'd tell Debra Rittenhous in the morning. Debra had been nice, college girl and everything. Owned the mill and once or twice a month she'd invite him over to Sleidel for a little supper and bed at some fancy motel. And she paid for it all.

"There's the semi. Get that rifle ready."

Billy Bob stared without comprehension. Get the rifle ready for what?

Doyle wheeled the truck down into the field. Cutter stood at the back of the semi, framed in their headlights, waiting. Doyle stopped. Cutter stood motionless, a squat, short-legged man with a bloody apron hanging down to his knees and baggy brown pants hanging down off his ass. His eyes squinted into the headlights, tiny slits in a thick, puffed face. Doyle waited. And then Cutter glanced over his shoulder, back behind the semi in the dark.

"That fat, cowardly pig," Doyle hissed. He wheeled ahead, spinning the truck on the hayfield in a tight ground-chewing

[123]

turn. As they swung around in a spray of dirt their headlights picked up several vehicles parked down the field. "They couldn't have gotten in here if Cutter hadn't told," Doyle grunted as he horsed the truck back up onto the road. "Call Chuck."

As if ready and waiting, a vehicle roared out after them. A red light winked. Bright headlights glared in the rearview mirror. "Get that gun ready. Chamber a round," Doyle shouted. Spittle flew at the force of his words.

Billy Bob sat numb. A throbbing hammered at his temples. His hands lay uselessly on his thighs, thick sausages that had lost all mobility. He thought of his poor mother all alone in their tiny little home. What would she do if he died?

They raced down the dirt road at a fearsome pace. Billows of dust curled in their wake. Roadside foliage flew past in a blur. "This nation's going to hell, Billy Bob," Doyle shouted. "No spine. Used to be men would be men. Now they go on television and cry. Right in front of the camera. Charlie Cong was a better soldier than we were. He lived in a hole in the ground and took on artillery, jet planes, helicopters, tanks. He carried food and armament on his back. Our boys got screaming if they missed a meal."

"Doyle," Billy Bob pleaded. With great effort he raised his hand to point ahead to where headlights blocked the road beside Chuck's truck. A red light winked. They had the narrow dirt road covered ditch line to ditch line. There was no shoulder. The truck behind them closed onto their tailgate, red light winking, headlights on bright, blinding and seeming as if they were about to crawl into the cab.

Doyle laughed. He shouted. "You scared to die, Billy Bob?" Billy Bob whined. Doyle shook his head in disgust. At the last second he slammed on the brakes. The truck slewed sideways and then straightened, sliding in the dirt. They rocked to a stop in a choking cloud of dust.

A loud speaker blared and a spotlight glared into the cab. "Step out of the vehicle. Federal wardens here. You're under arrest."

Doyle seized Billy Bob's arm. "Not one word. Understand? You take your medicine and you take it clean. They'll tell you stories, but most of them will be lies. You know the government lies. If you talk, Billy Bob," Doyle increased his pressure until Billy Bob rose up in his seat, "there isn't a place on earth."

"I won't talk, Doyle. I won't. I promise." Billy Bob gingerly tried to pull free.

Doyle's hand rested on the .22 Hornet. "I don't know. Maybe I should just shoot you now."

"Jesus, Doyle, please."

Doyle jerked Billy Bob like he would a little boy. "You watch your tongue, boy, or I'll cut it out."

Billy Bob pleaded. "I won't tell. I won't tell. I promise. Swear to God."

The door on each side opened. Reed stood beside Doyle, pistol in hand. "Hands on the steering wheel, Doyle."

Doyle's right hand rested on the .22. Someone was pulling Billy Bob out from the opposite side. "Well, well, if it isn't the federal pimp and liar that moved in with the whore, Marlis," Doyle said as if making conversation. "You going to shoot me, Reed? If that's your name. You won't shoot drug dealers but you'll shoot a man for taking what the Lord has set down here as his."

With the speed of a striking snake, Reed jumped up, seized the back of Doyle's shirt and jerked him head first out of the cab. As Doyle came out, rifle in hand, Reed kicked hard at the back of his elbow and the .22 flew clear. Doyle sprawled in the dust, Reed on his back, the pistol pressed against the back of his head. "Pretty slick," Doyle said. And still, like a man with absolutely no fear of death, he started to rise. But then Reed clubbed him on top of the head.

The wardens and U.S. Marshals all understood it would be an all-nighter. Just keeping the prisoners separate and getting them and the vehicles back to the Federal Office Building created a logistical nightmare. Because Doucet already had the helicopter airborne, Reed radioed for the aircraft to ferry a semi-conscious Doyle and a state warden to the hospital. They then transferred the fresh deer carcasses into the back of the refrigerated semi and separated for the long drive into Baton Rouge. Reed rode with Cutter in the cab of the semi.

"How many years have you boys had this operation going?" Reed asked as they led the convoy of trucks onto the highway.

"It's not my operation," Cutter said. His thick arms wheeled the semi with a competence born from hours on the road. But as big and tough as he might seem, he was also terribly distraught.

"Then whose is it?" Cutter did not reply. "The way we see it you're the man in charge. You own and drive the big rig. You set up the outlets in Baton Rouge. You deliver the goods. No, when it comes fall guy time, we try to give the maximum to the guy at the top. Every one of those deer back there represents a separate charge. And I'm sure the guys on the outlet end want to cut their losses. They'll testify you brought in hundreds of carcasses over the last three years. When this is all done, Cutter, with you being the head guy and all, we'll take everything you've got."

"I ain't the head guy," Cutter muttered.

Reed shrugged in the sway of the big cab. "We have to go with what we've got. All the evidence says the big man is you."

"You've been onto us for a long time, haven't you?" Cutter asked.

"A long time," Reed agreed. "I thought you'd figured it out with the accident there the other night. I didn't think you'd be stupid enough to come out again right away. I'd have been covering tracks."

"I knew you were onto us." Cutter wheeled out onto the I-10 freeway heading east toward Baton Rouge. A convoy of trucks and jeeps followed behind. Several times in a row Cutter glanced at Reed. His lips were compressed, grim. "You the guy that went head to head with Doyle?"

"We had a difference of opinion."

"Yeah," Cutter sighed. "I guess the old days are gone anyhow. Doyle couldn't grow up to that." Cutter shook his head as if recalling good times. "We were a team. But somehow Doyle never left that time. He wanted it all to remain the same. Never change. Now he's lost his store. His wife walked out on him the other day. I never should have gone along—even if he is blood."

"Doyle's the main man?" Reed asked.

Cutter glared, one last show of defiance. "What do I get?"

"You get to keep your house. I'll see if I can limit the fines to twenty thousand. The truck here will cover a lot of that. And you won't spend time in jail."

"Twenty thousand! That'll break my savings."

"Listen, Cutter," Reed hissed, "if I go all out after you I'll break your goddamn nuts."

For a long time Cutter was silent. When he spoke he spoke quietly, with deep bitterness. "I told Doyle we shouldn't go out. I told him. He wouldn't listen."

The scene at the Federal Office Building on One America Place was a madhouse. Gerald Doucet had called in the press. This was top quality visual news, the convoy of trucks, lines of manacled men being led into the building, mounds of un-skinned and then skinned deer carcasses piled and hanging in the back of the refrigerated trailer. Even the most ardent hunters would blanch at this slaughter. And any cameraman worth his salt would gladly step on his rival's back just to get a clear shot of that. Except for thoughts of what he'd done to Marlis, Reed almost could have laughed.

"Follow me. Pretend you're one of us," Reed said. He opened the door to the glare of camera lights. Clutches of microphones and a chorus of questions were directed at him. He pushed through without comment, inside to the bright neon and linoleum of the Federal Office Building.

"I'm putting together a press release. Do you have anything to add," Doucet said before Reed even reached the command center.

Reed briefly read the sheet. "Only half of this is right. If you release that, I'll have to correct it in the morning. It would make the State of Louisiana look awfully bad. We've got U.S. Marshals going out at six in the morning to arrest the owners of the two outlet stores we've identified. There may be more. Everything's preliminary. We'll get a press release out in mid-morning. Tell those reporters there isn't anything more for them tonight. Tell them to go to bed."

"Are you kidding me?"

"You're the one who called them. You give them the news. But not this." Reed tore the release in half and walked away.

Reed quickly organized his various workers into teams to

isolate and question their suspects. As expected, most of the men were smart enough and refused to talk without an attorney. Only Cutter spoke freely. Nevertheless, Reed kept his men after all the suspects, trying to gather as much information as possible, especially as to if and where they were hunting the night Wayne Pog disappeared. And who was hunting with whom.

At one point Reed was forced to sit down with Gerald Doucet. The only federal charge might be Doyle resisting arrest and assaulting a federal officer. But because there had not been any known interstate transportation of game, the most serious violating charges would fall under state jurisdiction. Initially, Reed informed Doucet, they'd file with state authorities. Therefore they needed a state attorney as soon as possible.

"I'll get one out of bed," Doucet said. "It's about time one of those bastards did some real work." He'd expected a jurisdiction fight with Reed over the filing of charges, but there had been no fight at all. "My men said you really know your stuff. I thought these Louisiana boys would really give you a run. But except for that Monroe fellow, there wasn't much of a run at all. They didn't know what hit them."

"Thanks," Reed grunted with the knowledge of a man aware he is being stroked.

A state warden stuck his head into Reed's temporary office. "Just got word from the hospital, Reed, that Monroe fellow is conscious. Slight concussion. They'll probably release him after morning rounds and a cat scan."

"Thanks, Jack." Reed stood.

"I'll call for a state attorney," Doucet said. "He won't be happy though. There's a lot of paperwork with a case like this. Especially if we go after conspiracy. They don't care much for violating cases. They don't have the prestige of murder or rape."

"And then half of these good ole boys think the game laws and wardens are at fault."

"That's the other side," Doucet said. "Although it's not as bad as it used to be."

Reed walked to where some of the technicians were tagging and cataloging evidence. "Bring those rifles." They proceeded down to the janitor's room where Reed filled a five gallon bucket with water and dropped a one-half-inch thick piece of plywood on the bottom. With the door closed to the outside hallway, one by one Reed fired a round into the pail and tagged the bullet and put it into a plastic bag along with the ejected cartridge.

"Why are you doing this?" one of the technicians asked.

"Son, in this business there are some things you don't see. Other things you don't ask. This is a case where both pieces of advice appear to apply."

The young man smiled and nodded his understanding.

At five o'clock in the morning a single state attorney showed up.

Branden Wyss was not a happy man. He was dressed as if ready for court in a grey, three-piece suit. His grey moustache and the grey sidewalls on his black hair were neatly trimmed. Only his ruddy complexion, his bloodshot eyes, and the broken veins lining the sides of his nose gave him away.

"I hope he's as competent as he looks," Doug said, as he and Reed sat in the office while Doucet intercepted Branden.

"I've rarely met anyone who paid that much attention to being fashionable and looking right who had more than a real thimble full of reliability when it came to the crunch. Not unless they were British." Reed sipped at what seemed his tenth cup of bitter black coffee and grimaced. Doucet and Branden glanced in his direction. Reed rose, whatever they were scheming, he had to break it up.

Branden gave him a soft, fleshy handshake and then almost immediately began making his case. They'd file for everything they could and then plea bargain. He detailed his scenario and then concluded, "The government saves the expense of long and lengthy trials, these guys cut their fines in half, and we break up the ring. Everyone is happy."

"We're not out to make them happy, counselor. We're out to break their nuts."

"My, my, aren't you the tough guy. The only problem here Mr. Erickson, is that we're a nation of laws." Branden blew his fetid breath in Reed's direction. His bloodshot eyes focused on Reed with the disdain of a man who thought highly only of himself. "You represent those laws, as do I. If you can't respect the system, why should ordinary citizens?"

"You mean like these guys respected the law? The way they respected nature? These are exploiters of the worst kind. We have to make an example. I just want you to apply the full measure of the law. Not half. You're letting these bastards go, and relatively clean. What do you tell the widowed mother? Nothing. Her husband died working for the state. And no one gives a damn. I'll go tell her the news."

"We went over that, and you have no evidence, none." Branden waved as if in dismissal. "You've done your job, Mr. Erickson. A fine, fine job," he said with patronizing exaggeration. "Now you can go back to Washington. With a little luck you won't even have to come back and testify. I'll take care of that for you." Branden's eyes bulged with the effort of his speech.

Reed turned away. One more word and he knew he'd be ramming a flask down Branden's throat. What did people think? Doucet knew about Marlis. He'd stopped the search for Wayne. He'd blocked the declaration Wayne had been killed in the line of duty. And now what could he say? In truth he didn't have a single hard piece of evidence to tie these guys to Wayne. He swallowed at the bitter bile building in his mouth. Blood throbbed at his temples. A heavy weight pressed at his shoulders and he knew it was not from a long night without sleep.

In early morning Reed telephoned Marlis. There was no answer. He tried at mid-morning. Again no reply. He called the Rittenhous place but Blaine answered and then as quickly hung up the telephone. He reached Debra at the feed mill. She thought Marlis was home.

Around noon, still without sleep, he received a call back from Hank and briefly told him the story of the arrests. The general story had already been broadcast.

"Hank, I'm going to be tied up here until I don't know when. And then they want me back in Washington to write up my report. I've got to reach Marlis. Why don't you drive past and see that she's all right."

"Sure thing," Hank said.

"And then go to your boss. Tell him some weeks ago you heard a rumor about a couple of trucks on Strait's Levee the night Wayne disappeared. Tell him you've been going out there on your days off and poking around. Tell him you found a vehicle under water and would like to get the county rescue team to dive down and check it out."

"He's going to kick my shit," Hank said.

"I'm sorry, Hank. I can't think of any other way. You have to push it. When they see it's Wayne's truck, all will be forgiven. A widespread search of that area might turn up the body. Try to tell the sheriff in front of other deputies. That way he can't take full credit."

"Yeah, thanks. After he gets done with me I won't have credit anywhere in Louisiana."

"You can always go to work for Uncle Sam, Hank. I know a couple of guys in the custodial department."

"I'm going to tell Sheila you said that. She doesn't take kindly to racial jokes."

"That was no joke," Reed said and quietly hung up. He smiled but then looked up into a two-headed nightmare, Gerald Doucet and Branden Wyss. God—he hated this job. It was, he thought, going to be one hell of a long day.

And still he and Marlis had not talked.

It was late the next morning before Reed could make the two hour drive to Magnolia. He drove the I-10 freeway in order to save time, racing down the four lane highway that cut off travelers from the graceful lanes and tiny, aging communities dotting the countryside. They'd managed to get the violators, those out in the field as well as the owners of two supermarkets that provided outlets for the meat, arraigned before a magistrate. Reed had encouraged Doucet to take as much to the press as possible. Doucet had been more than pleased. The increased coverage seemed to act as a prod to Branden Wyss to file as many charges as possible. After all, the more severe the case, the more the reporters and cameras solicited Branden for information on the case.

"Times have changed," Doucet informed the press. "People understand the need for conservation laws, for game management, and for sharing the resources. No longer is there automatic derision for conservation officers who are out to enforce game laws and protect resources for the public good. These violators put themselves above the law." And then, without really understanding, he added Reed's statement as well. "And they tried to put themselves above nature, as if they were kings. But they're not."

Yes, times have changed, Reed thought. It wasn't everything, but at least they'd broken up this one ring. They'd made a public point, resources in abundance had to be shared, resources that were scarce had to be protected. It wasn't much but he couldn't deny a small feeling of satisfaction. For the brief period they'd been together, he, Doug, and the state wardens had become a team united with a single goal in mind. They'd worked surprisingly well. Even Doucet had come around, the leader following his men. If only he hadn't failed Marlis.

He pulled his brown U.S. government issue car off the freeway. He drove past the busy strip mall on the highway bypass just outside Magnolia. He turned off onto the quiet, tree-lined streets. The green of palm and banana and black oak contrasted harshly with the brown, dusty, and noisy industrial excesses of Baton Rouge. The reaching limbs of the oaks formed a shaded corridor down the road. Small, stucco bungalows sat side by side, two and three generation dwellings, where the working class and the elderly lived out their final years. And one home in particular where a pretty little widow, without job experience and without her husband's death benefits, lived with her two children and waited on her life.

Reed slowly walked up the cracked sidewalk. The grass needed cutting. The flower garden hadn't been touched all summer. The scent of jasmine filled the air. A dead limb lay beneath the grey trunk of a Royal Palm, a dead warden's one claim to a life of wealth. The few weeks Reed had lived here blended together as if they were a lifetime. There'd been too much emotion, from that first day in P.U.'s office.

And still it wasn't resolved.

Reed hesitated at the doorway. Yesterday, he'd have opened the door and walked right in as if this were his home, his family. But of course that was all pretend. And yesterday was past. Reed closed his eyes against the ache in his chest. He could not bear the image of other people in pain, especially knowing that, at least in part, he was the cause.

He knocked on the door.

"Come in," Marlis said. She looked up as Reed entered.

Her eyes were wide, clear, and direct as those of an innocent child. Her voice was even, with perfect pitch, without a hint of emotion. "I washed your things and packed them. They're in the closet there beside the door."

The attitude, the words, the look struck Reed as if some beefer had ripped a hard shot to his solar plexus. The good mother, Reed thought, sitting there so nice and clean and pretty, her tiny and pretty children seated tight on either side while she read them a story from the book perched on her lap. The good mother—it was all Marlis had.

"Everyone's been arraigned. They're free on bail."

"What did you expect?"

Reed nodded toward Jody and Patty. "Can we talk?"

"Only what's fit for my children. They hear stories, rumors. They have to survive."

"It's not over, Marlis. I promise you that. I have to fly back to Washington, help put together the case, write up a report. As soon as I wrap that up I'll apply for vacation or a leave of absence and return."

"Why would you do that?"

"To help you, Marlis. To continue the search."

"Unofficially, of course."

"Not entirely. When Hank tells people about the truck, the county should reopen the case. Who knows where that will lead."

"Yes, who knows," Marlis agreed with a toneless refrain. Jody sat tight at her side, watching Reed, absorbing every word, working out the nuances in his mind, fitting it with who knew what he possibly knew. The boy was following his mother, Reed thought. If her life had gone on hold from the moment she witnessed the horror of her father raping Sheila Jackson, Jody's life had been on hold since the disappearance of his father.

If he could only get Marlis alone, Reed thought, out from behind the protective shield of her children. He glanced down at his worn leather boots, at his veined hands. For a few days there Marlis had loosened up. There'd been a closeness, he liked to believe. It had not simply been sex. But now a gulf as wide as the Mississippi Delta brought to them a strain as painful as that between himself and Pam. He raised his hand

[133]

without purpose, like a man sinking under the brown waters of the swamp, seeing nothing, knowing only the cold and the blackness that lay in the mud at the bottom of the hole.

Somehow he managed to speak. "I'll call you from Washington. Maybe when I get back we can have dinner."

Marlis waved a hand as if in protest, then weakly let it drop. "I don't see that there's any point."

Reed licked at dried lips. He sought to keep his pride in line. He silently picked up his things while Marlis read to the children.

"I'll just make a quick check of the closet and bathroom."

"I've got everything right there." The voice was sharp, like a command.

Reed nodded, feeling like a puppet jerking at the end of a string. A violent rage abruptly coursed through his body and brought a series of knots to the muscles across his shoulders. The problem was he did not know against whom to vent his rage. He stood, waiting in silence until Marlis finally looked up. "I'll call."

"Whatever you like."

It was a long, lonely, and frustrating drive back to Baton Rouge. The next day's flight to Washington was just as bad. Reed got in at night. He took a taxi to his basement apartment. It was cold, dark, musty, and as empty as a high mountain cave. Time marched on. He was crowding forty and here he sat in the dark in a dingy little apartment in Washington DC. He thought of calling Pam, but did not.

TWELVE

Hank Jackson looked for the most opportune moment to commit career suicide, or at least, that was the way Sheila put it. And right now it was the way he felt. Sheriff John LeBitche, known behind his back simply as "The Bitch," was a dark, swarthy Cajun with black eyes and thick mats of black hair coating his arms and chest. As the tall, stout sheriff crossed the squad room, Hank nervously got to his feet so he could meet his adversary eye to eye and in front of witnesses as Reed had suggested.

"Sheriff."

"What is it, Hank?" LeBitche had erased much of his Cajun accent, although he still spoke Cajun French fluently, a major factor in his re-election campaigns. Hank had once been one of his boys, an up and comer, a model black, Hank had once overheard the sheriff say. It was then Hank had quit the inner circle, the sheriff's game. He'd become a little political. Sheriff John LeBitche was not pleased. If you did not eat LeBitche manure, you shoveled it. All the deputies knew that.

"I think I might have located Wayne Pog's truck." Conversation ceased. Fifteen deputies and administrative assistants turned their heads. The Wayne Pog disappearance had been one of their biggest cases of the year. Hank tried not to swallow or lick at his lips. He could see the fury in the sheriff's black eyes. The Bitch knew why he'd brought this up in the open squad room. In gravity's grasp, Hank boldly plunged ahead, speaking much too loud. "A couple of weeks ago some old guy mentioned that the night Wayne disappeared a couple of vehicles drove down Strait's Levee at about five in the morning. Only one came back off." Hank waited, giving the sheriff the next move.

"You didn't file a report."

"It didn't seem like much to go on. The case was closed." Again Hank paused.

"So what do you have?"

"I've been going out after hours and on my days off in a canoe and poking down in the water beside the levee. I found a truck underwater beside the levee."

"It's probably an old piece of junk, Hank. There're hundreds of cars and trucks sunk in those swamps."

"I snorkled down to the roof," Hank said. "It's brown like Wayne's. It's a newer model. It had a CB antenna. I'd like your permission to get a parish rescue scuba team and check it out." Hank boldly held The Bitch's gaze. If he'd been on the down slide before, he'd just fallen over the edge.

"You've been working this case behind my back?"

"No sir, just this one lead. It didn't seem like much for a closed case."

"Rumor is you've been hanging with some feds."

"There was a guy over in Magnolia that got into a street fight. Nothing came of it. I didn't know until later he was an undercover Fish and Wildlife agent after that violating ring."

"You think you've got this figured up one side and then the other, don't you?" Sheriff LeBitche gave a tight little smile. He glared at the room. "Don't any of you convenient witnesses have any work?" Everyone turned and shuffled as if going to work. "Jackson," he snarled, and jerked his thick head across the room. "Into my office."

"Yes suh," Hank said, in his best imitation of a plantation slave. Sheriff LeBitche stiffened. Hank shook his head as if questioning his own judgment. That damn Yankee agent had moved him off center just like Sheila said. He'd never been suicidal in his life.

Once under water it took less than ten minutes for the dive team to confirm the truck was indeed Wayne Pog's. Hank radioed the sheriff who said to hold tight, that he was coming out with a wrecker and some men from the state crime lab. And of course the press, Hank thought.

He was correct, of course. But before the press was allowed close enough to film the dramatic shots of the mud and weed-covered truck being hauled from the black depths, Hank was conveniently assigned elsewhere so he wouldn't accidently walk in front of a camera.

Sheriff LeBitche stood close, trying to intimidate with his size and presence. Hank stood his ground until The Bitch had his face less than six inches away. "First get over and tell Marlis Pog before she hears it on the radio. Second, go over to the bank in Magnolia. They have a court order to foreclose on Doyle Monroe's grocery store. You can serve the order and make sure Monroe doesn't interfere."

"Sir, Doyle Monroe's a friend of mine. I had to serve the replevin papers on his inventory."

Sheriff John LeBitche smiled and turned away. Did the deputy actually think he didn't know that?

Hank's heart sank. In medieval times, how often did the peasants overthrow the king. Not often, he supposed. And probably never when it was one peasant all alone.

Despite her misgivings, Hank talked Sheila into going with him to inform Marlis that the truck had officially been located, that they'd be conducting a widespread drag and search operation, and that undoubtedly the press would be around asking questions. He did not inform Sheila that Marlis already knew about the truck. This would just make it official, bring it into the public light.

Despite Marlis's prior knowledge that Wayne's truck had been found, relaying the official news proved more difficult than Hank had imagined. First he had to make sure the children weren't present. And then Sheila went stiff on him, tightening up like a steel rod and refusing to move from just inside the front door and take a seat in the living room. So Hank left her and went and sat with Marlis while Sheila stood across the room.

"So what do you have now that you didn't have before?" Marlis asked after Hank relayed the news. The smooth, pink, triangular lines of her cheekbones and jawline were evenly set, delicate lines along which a man would love to run the back of his hand. She was, Hank would say later, surprisingly calm, deadly calm.

"We've got it in the public eye. The investigation will reopen. We'll be conducting a massive search of the area. Maybe, ah, something further will turn up."

"Maybe, maybe, maybe. They were supposed to go after that violating ring, find out who murdered Wayne. Instead they just arrested them and now they're free on bail. Debra even bailed out Billy Bob. Because he works for her she said. Because he doesn't have anything except his poor elderly mother he lives with at home."

"Reed didn't want that. They forced his hand. He's been calling, says you don't answer. This isn't all his fault. He'll be back."

Marlis closed her eyes and laughed as if in disbelief. "For what? More unkept promises?"

Hank sat quietly, uncertain how to proceed. Something about Marlis had changed. There was a gulf, a wall he could not seem to penetrate.

"Hank, you have to get to the bank," Sheila said from her post at the door.

Hank shot her a dark glance. He stood, awkwardly waving to and fro. Marlis leaned forward with her elbows on her knees. The thin bones of her shoulder blades stuck out like fragile lines of glass beneath her cotton print dress. Marlis always wore a dress, Hank thought, just like Sheila almost always wore slacks. He thought of patting Marlis's shoulders, something to give her his touch and lend a small measure of human comfort. But of course Sheila stood across the room.

Hank cleared his throat. "Perhaps you'd like to come over to supper with us one night." He motioned toward Sheila but did not meet her eyes.

Marlis looked up and smiled her wonderful angelic smile. She was truly amused. "Sheila doesn't want me over for supper, Hank. You should know that."

"What are you talking about?" Hank protested. "Because Sheila worked for you as a maid? She was a young girl."

"Marlis!" Sheila spat the word as if giving a command. But the dark features of her face were twisted, her dark eyes teary-eyed and pleading.

"I'm sorry, Sheila." Marlis spoke as if from the depths of her soul. "I'm sorry. I should have said something. I should have killed him. I just didn't have the nerve. I'm sorry."

"What's going on here?" Hank demanded.

Marlis took Hank's elbow and led him toward the door. And he was supposed to lend comfort, be in charge. Her voice again took on it's pure but flat tone. "Thanks for coming, Hank. You've been a friend. But no one has found Wayne's body. And his killer is still walking around as free as a wild animal." Marlis opened the door. She glanced at Sheila once and closed her eyes as if in apology.

"We'll find the body. We'll get the killer," Hank said. He felt pushed aside, outside looking in. He saw Sheila squeeze Marlis's hand as if in comfort. Sheila! And then he thought she was going to cry. Sheila? His Sheila!

"No," Marlis said. She looked Hank in the face. Her eyes were dry and clear. "You won't get him. I'll have to get him myself. Just like I should have done months ago." She gently pushed Hank outside and closed the door.

That afternoon Marlis cleaned out her refrigerator. Even though garbage pickup was not for two days, she threw all perishable food into a garbage bag and set it out by the street. Then she packed two suitcases, one for herself, one for Jody and Patty. She put the suitcases and children in the car and drove to the Rittenhous mill.

As Marlis stepped from the car she saw Billy Bob on the loading dock. His stomach thrust out over his belt and from under his dusty tee shirt. Marlis stared, but Billy Bob turned away and went back into the grey, galvanized metal warehouse. Marlis carried the children's suitcase as the two of them dutifully trailed her into Debra's small, cluttered office, adjacent to the small display area and the sales counter. A thin film of grain dust seemed to cover everything. Kathy, the black sales girl, said hi and smiled at Jody and Patty. Marlis nodded, then stepped into Debra's office and closed the door.

"I need you to take care of Jody and Patty for a few days," Marlis said. The two children backed against the wall, their suitcase at their feet. They stood silently, eyes wide and staring, still as little dolls. Jody watched his mother, then his aunt, listening to every word.

Debra's dark hair was pulled back and pinned at the back of her head. Numerous stray hairs had worked free and a thin film of grain dust coated her hair as well as her blue jeans and shirt. "What's going on here? I know you need to get out of here. But where are you going?"

Marlis shrugged. "Who can say right now."

Debra went to her sister. She towered over her. How many times had men joked that she didn't look at all like Marlis; and there'd be that wistful catch in their voice. "You need some counseling. Someone who can help you."

"You mean like Doctor LeFleur who always made me get undressed and who always squeezed my breasts and squeezed my stomach right down to my crotch, just for a cold or the flu?"

Debra glanced to Jody and Patty. "Marlis, please!"

"The children should know," Marlis said. Her voice rose, becoming almost shrill. "They should know everything. Otherwise they find out and don't trust us at all. I told them about Doyle."

"Doyle? What does he have to do with this?"

"He probably killed their father."

Debra stepped back as if she'd somehow lost her balance. If she tried to subdue Marlis, an easy task, she thought, would Marlis ever forgive her? She knew Marlis. Once Marlis carried a grudge, she carried it the rest of her life. Debra tried to ridicule her sister back to sanity. "What are you talking about? That's absurd."

"Doyle's the head of that group. He's the one that leads the way. He's the one that's forcing everyone to remain silent and face the maximum charges."

Debra glanced at Jody and Patty to see how they were absorbing the accusation.

"They already know," Marlis said. "I told them everything, including about Daddy. You keep them away from him. Don't ever let them be alone with him. Never. I told mother. She knows."

Debra glanced at the children. They were like two peas in a pod, almost as dry-eyed as their mother. She glanced at the telephone, wondering who she could possibly call. "Mother knows what? Why is it always you and Daddy? You and Daddy? What did Daddy ever do to you? You were always his favorite, his little girl."

"It wasn't me, Debra. It was Sheila."

"Sheila Jackson?"

"When she was our maid. She was fourteen. So was I. Daddy raped her. I saw them. I never said a word. Not a word, Debra. Sheila saw me close the door. And then I just walked away and left her in there with him." Marlis shook her head. Tears briefly materialized. "I just walked away, told myself it was Sheila's fault. Even though she was terrified. I see that fear on her face in my dreams to this day."

Debra sat back. A terrible burning tightened her stomach almost beyond endurance. Jody and Patty stood silently, two little soldiers listening to their commander speak. Children could be resilient beyond belief, but they were also malleable and easily abused. Debra shook her head as if to clear her thoughts. Her voice was hoarse, barely coherent, her thoughts clouding her brain. "Yes, of course. That explains so much." She saw her sister's dead expression and felt a terrible fear. "And you never let it out."

"That wouldn't be the Rittenhous way. Mother taught us that."

"Where are you going?" Debra asked. If she was more physically powerful than Marlis, she'd been defeated by her psychology. Wayne's death, Sheila's rape, how could she make all this go away, she thought numbly?

"Not far."

Marlis knelt in front of Jody and Patty. In turn she hugged each one close. "Remember, Jody, never let Patty alone with Grandpa. And do as Debra tells you. She'll take you to school and then you can walk over here afterwards. I'll be gone a few days. Until then Debra's your mother."

Debra trailed Marlis out to her car. "Where are you going? What are you going to do? I have to be able to reach you if one of the children get sick."

Marlis took her sister's hand. "You know what needs to be done. You've always known what needs to be done. I can trust you, Debra. I could always trust you. I've just never given you any reason to trust me." Marlis climbed into her car.

"Are you going to Washington like you did last time? Are you going to contact Reed? He called and said you won't answer the telephone or else you just hang up. He cares, Marlis. If you can trust anyone you can trust him."

"No. He betrayed me before."

"He did the best he could. He has other responsibilities. Not just you, Marlis. The world is wider than that." Debra had recovered from her shock. She spoke with some anger. "You're being selfish, just like always."

"I trust you, Debra," Marlis said and then she backed away. She did not notice Patty and Jody standing side by side peering out the office window.

Doyle had various items laid out on the floor as if preparing for a camping trip. He wore an olive drab tee shirt, camouflage pants, and leather and nylon jungle boots. A large hunting knife hung from one hip, a pair of needle-nose pliers from the other. He'd cut his blond hair down to a rough stubble. He wore his old Marine Corps dog tags taped together on a chain around his neck. Along with the items of clothing lay camping gear, fishing gear, and a rifle and a shotgun. He looked up at the light tapping on the door—a woman, he could tell.

"My doors are never locked. Just turn the knob."

Marlis walked in. She wore a maroon and flowered cotton dress that gently caressed the curved outlines of her slender figure. Her hip bones stuck out through the cloth. Her calves were firm, perfectly shaped. She set a suitcase just inside the door and then stood there with her purse clutched across her stomach like a nervous schoolgirl on a first date.

Doyle bounded to his feet. "Marlis!" He took the suitcase into the living room. "You came. I never dreamed." He shook his head and smiled. "The Lord has His ways."

"Are you going camping?" Marlis asked. Only a slight flutter of nervousness betrayed the pure, firm tones of her voice.

"Moving," Doyle said. "Rachel and Lisa want their house back." His pleasured grin disappeared. He scowled darkly. "Can you imagine, their house? I built it with my own hands.

I spent twenty years down at the store paying the mortgage. The bank wanted a second mortgage on it as collateral for the store loan. Rachel wouldn't sign. Smart. If she'd consented the bank would have our home as well as the store. Women know how to get what they want."

"Where are you going to go?"

"Out into the swamp. Right in the middle of the Atchafalaya Basin."

"I thought people weren't allowed to live there."

"Government rules. That's why they picked me up for violating, you know. Government rules. Men out harvesting the Lord's bounty and the government comes along and places them under arrest. Can you imagine?"

Marlis said nothing.

"Of course they used you also," Doyle said. "Brought that Reed guy in to pretend to be your lover. And then he just ups and walks away, goes back to Washington to wait for some other poor citizen to attack."

"They said they'd find Wayne's killer," Marlis said. Her grey eyes were direct on Doyle. "Of course they didn't."

Doyle motioned at Marlis's suitcase with his thick, muscled hands, hands that could be strong, hands that could be gentle, hands that could take a fragile flower such as Marlis and caress it with infinite care. The carnal notion stirred within his groin. His voice became husky with anticipation. "Were you coming to me, Marlis? You and me like I talked about? As the Lord intended? Were you coming to be with me?"

Marlis nodded yes. That she trembled with a terrible fear, Doyle misinterpreted.

He dropped to his knees, his arms upraised. Tears welled in his eyes. "I've been a forsaken man. Betrayed. My wife, my family, business associates, people I called my friends. I gave my life to Magnolia. And today, when they came to take my store, there wasn't a single soul around. Not one man stood at my side. Not one.

"And do you know who served the papers? Hank. Hank Jackson. I gave Hank his first job. I helped get him into the sheriff's office." Doyle laughed as if at a ridiculous joke. "And then Hank comes and takes away my store. Is that justice? Is that what a man deserves for a lifetime of work? I ask you."

Doyle suddenly jumped to his feet. "Orders, Hank said like a snivelling coward. Orders!" Doyle bellowed with a force that rocked Marlis on her heels and reminded her she had as much force against Doyle as a leaf trembling before a storm. Doyle's face turned beet red. Cords stood out on his neck. "Orders! Orders, hell. Illegitimate orders are supposed to be ignored. Hank knew that. I told him. He just didn't have the guts. And after all I've done."

Doyle sighed. He carefully unclenched his fists. "Hank's a weak man. He goes along. He doesn't have the courage to stand alone. Not many men do. That Reed, that agent, he was a different breed. At least so I thought. I just can't understand what a man like that would be doing working for the government." Doyle squinted as if looking into the distance. "Of course he was a liberal. He as much as said we had to change, that we couldn't hunt like the old days, that we had to pay attention to how man impacts nature. Like we were God." Doyle snorted. "Can you imagine. He lectured me in jail. One of those humanists, I guess you'd call him. I just don't know where those people get their ideas."

Doyle bent to his knapsack and began stuffing items into the bottom. "It'll be a tough life, Marlis. You can bring your children if you want. I'd be a good husband. I don't drink. I don't smoke. Other than an occasional use of a willow switch on Lisa, I've never struck a woman in my life. A man never hits a woman. Never."

Doyle glanced up. Marlis stood mute, a tiny angel waiting on his call. "Like I said, it won't be an easy life. I do have a small houseboat. But mostly we'll be living off the land. I don't believe in material things. If we need money I'll trap a few muskrat and nutria. Dredge up crawdads during the season. We can catch catfish in the canals. Maybe an occasional gator, if you don't mind gator tail. It's the only way to live, Marlis, the only way. It'd give me great pleasure if you'd be at my side."

Marlis felt the thinness of her dress, the weak construction of her low, flat shoes. She hadn't dressed or packed to live in the swamp. She did not have the clothes. She did not have the strength. But she had nothing else. "Sure, Doyle. When were you going to go?"

Doyle grinned widely, like a schoolboy. "Tonight. I have to finish packing and then take care of Saul, my dog. He can't live in the swamp. He's too old. I can't leave him for Rachel and Lisa. They don't care."

"I don't have the right clothes," Marlis said. "All I brought were dresses."

"That's all a woman should wear," Doyle said. "That's one thing I always admired about you. I never once saw you in any of those damn slacks, those ugly blue jeans women wear. It's like they're trying to be men. You just bring what you've got. You'll be just fine. I give you my promise on that."

"Jody and Patty are with Debra. I'm going to leave them there until they finish school."

"As you wish," Doyle said as he busily packed. "I think it's a mistake. School's an abomination. They destroy our young. They alienate children from their parents. They teach lies. When I was a youth I used to spend weeks on end in the swamp. That's where I learned about life. The community of the swamp, all one big whole. The community of man." Doyle's face twisted bitterly. "And they all threw it back in my face."

Doyle picked up his pack and, as he passed, Marlis's suitcase as well. He gazed down into her clear, grey eyes, the whore now reformed. She'd come to him for forgiveness, he thought. It was up to him to lead her straight.

Marlis trailed him outside while Doyle tossed the suitcase and pack in the back of the truck which was already laden with groceries. "I wasn't about to let the damn bank steal it all," Doyle explained. He pulled an old military issue .45 out of the back of the truck. Marlis moved back a step. Doyle laughed. "I wouldn't harm you. You're too pure, a doll with a porcelain neck. I have to take care of Saul."

Marlis nodded as if in mute understanding.

Doyle walked stiff-legged across his front yard. The grass was long, laying over, and in desperate need of cutting. No more. He gazed at his house, lights ablaze in every room. Stick by stick, nail by nail. Twenty years, sucking the blood out of his veins. Gone, just like the store, just like Magnolia, his home town. He shook his head as if amused. It was the way the world had changed. If a man gave, people would gladly take, and they'd take, and they'd take. But they'd never give an ounce in return. It was the one positive thing about the hippies of the sixties, he thought. They weren't as selfish as most—at least not then. Later, of course, they'd changed, and their children were the worst of the lot.

Saul whined his pleasure and sat at attention. He knew better than to jump. Doyle opened the kennel door. Saul still sat, poised, waiting on his master's command. "Come," Doyle said. Saul bounded out and as he was given no contrary command, began running in a wild circle as if to stretch his legs. "Run, Saul, run," Doyle shouted as if to egg him on. Saul ran faster. But he quickly tired and took to sniffing the yard. After several minutes Doyle called and Saul made a direct line toward his master and sat obediently at his side. If only people could be as obedient as a well-trained dog, Doyle thought.

Doyle knelt, the .45 in hand. He hugged Saul close and buried his face in the furry neck. Saul wriggled in the joy of his master's seldom expressed love and licked at Doyle's neck as if to return the affection. Doyle cocked the hammer on the .45. The damn government had seized his .22 Hornet. That was the gun for the job. It wouldn't leave such a mess.

"You were a good dog, Saul. A good dog." Tears streamed down Doyle's cheeks. He stood. Saul sat obediently at his side, looking straight ahead as he waited for his master's command. Doyle held the muzzle less than an inch from Saul's head. He squeezed. A thunderous roar split the night. Saul sprawled, his brains splattered over the yard.

Doyle tucked the pistol in his belt. He brought his heels together as if standing at attention. He snapped a military salute over his fallen friend, executed a crisp about-face and marched across the yard to where Marlis stood clutching her purse. Doyle opened the door on the passenger side and Marlis climbed in. Doyle walked around the front and climbed in behind the wheel. Neither person looked at the other.

Doyle stared at his house, at Saul's sprawled form. The muscles and cartilage lines of his jaw snapped and popped as if under tremendous strain. Abruptly he started the engine and backed carefully into the street. Then he and Marlis drove out of town and into the night.

THIRTEEN

"You better wear a suit to work," Doug had said in warning. But Reed didn't own a suit. Once Pam had bought one for Christmas, but other than one funeral, he refused to put it on. Another one of his mistakes, he realized now.

Trying to keep enough money for two apartments and also Stacy and Trish put a strain on the pocketbook. Nevertheless, Reed opted to purchase three–piece jobs, tailored to a near perfect fit; one conservative blue, one conservative brown. Seven hundred dollar suits. Who would have believed it? Of course he only paid fifty dollars each. Georgetown specials.

He'd called some ads in the newspaper. Some woman was selling her attorney husband's clothes. The fit wasn't bad. A more expensive cut than he'd ever worn, Reed thought. The cleaning bill would be more than he'd normally spend new. "Did your husband die?" He asked the woman. She was thin, haunted, once wealthy but now with hard eyes.

"Don't I wish. At least then I'd have life insurance, something. He took off with his secretary. Went to Los Angeles. I hope he rots in hell."

I'm supposed to be getting divorced too, Reed thought to say by way of conversation, but he could not feel the humor. The lawyer owned twenty-five suits or so. Reed took two. The next morning, his third back in Washington, he trimmed his beard and hair and wore the dark blue one, vest and all, into work.

On the streets he looked just like everyone else in Washington, a government worker, an attorney, a politician. They all wore suits, conservative blue, grey, brown, something that made everyone from twenty feet away look exactly the same, clones drinking from the public trough.

As soon as he entered the rows of desks and computer terminals in the main office, Reed felt like a fool. It wasn't that people in the office didn't wear suits. It was that the famous Reed Erickson, the most reknowned undercover agent of all, had put on a suit. Everyone turned to stare. Big Doug, his thick jowls quivering with mirth, met him halfway across the floor and spoke loud enough for the entire room to hear. "Good morning, sir. Can I help you? Are you lost? This is the department of Fish and Wildlife."

Reed raised a clenched fish. "This is the department of knuckle sandwiches."

Doug backed away in mock fear. "Oh, I see. That's a disguise, you're not really civilized." Everybody laughed. Reed diplomatically gave everyone in the room the bird.

"Guess where you're going today?" Doug said. "Your good buddy, Mr. Doucet talked to his higher-ups in the state who then talked to the distinguished senator from Louisiana who then talked to the distinguished Secretary of the Interior who has then instructed some sixty-five-thousand-dollar-a-year assistant under secretary, some political appointee no doubt, to guillotine some fine agent and thereby placate the ruffled sensibilities of the distinguished senator from the great State of Louisiana."

Reed winked. "You missed your calling, Douglas. Why do you think I wore this used suit."

"Used. Phew. You had us all worried there for a minute. We thought you were going to pretend to be civilized. In any case, Peter's going along. He wasn't invited, but he's going anyhow. It's the only way he'd let you go. It's a good thing he has his twenty-year shield. Otherwise they'd chew him up as well."

Judging by office size and the quality of the furniture, Assistant Under Secretary of the Interior Joel Bingington, of the Virginia Bingington's, should have been a governor. Judging by his attitude, Joel should have been a king. He was Napoleon short, and as loud as he was fat.

Reed had learned from Peter that Bingington was the

Administration's nominal head of the program to use caterpillars to drop on South American jungles in order to eradicate cocoa plants. Of course, being an informed environmentalist, he'd have no idea what else the caterpillars might eat when they ran out of cocoa plants. It was like when the government imported the West Indian mongoose into the Antilles so the mongoose could exterminate the deadly fer-de-lance, which it did. Needing to eat, the mongoose turned to rats who, being somewhat more intelligent and adaptable than man, took to tree-dwelling and nocturnal habits. With no snakes, and being able to avoid the mongoose, the rats proliferated. The mongoose turned to domestic poultry. Experiment complete. Man's hand.

Bingington frowned at Peter's presence. "This meeting was with Agent Erickson."

"Reed Erickson is one of my most trusted agents," Peter said in his hushed, bureaucratic voice. "As Director of Special Agents I'm responsible for initiating operations and for what takes place in the field. As I informed your secretary, if any action is initiated against my men it comes through me or it doesn't come at all."

Bingington's plucked and shaped eyebrows rose at the hint of insolence. He filed the name Peter Ulysses Waldheim in his memory bank.

Reed nodded his thanks to his boss. Peter knew he'd reached his top in rank. Too many of the higher paid positions in the upper echelons were political, reserved for those who know how to play the game or for expensive political patronage payoffs. In fact Reed had read that the sum total of wages from high paid patronage jobs without real function represented the budget of a medium-size country. And of course, the best paying jobs seldom accrued to the scut workers actually doing the work. But Peter had been around. He knew his position, he knew his rights. When Peter Ulysses Waldheim sent agents on an operation, he never left them out to dry.

Bingington focused on Reed. He thrust a thick, pink finger in Reed's face. "You're going to have to learn to get along with people or you're going to be looking for work. I can guarantee you that."

Reed stood silently. His eyes were clear, unblinking, focused directly on Bingington, the predator stare. It wasn't a staring contest exactly, for in that the prey stood no chance. It was more a stare of judging, the more dominant judging the capabilities of the other. Of course Bingington knew better than to get into childish staring contests. He held the gaze an appropriate amount of time and then looked away. The practised projection of his voice droned on, cataloging Reed's transgressions in dealing with employees of the great State of Louisiana. But each time he looked back, Reed still stared. And each time he met Reed's gaze the time he held it grew a little shorter.

"You represent the United States of America. The American people. Do you understand that?"

Reed leaned back and sighed impatiently. Peter shot him a glance. He knew when Reed was on edge.

"I asked you a question," Bingington roared.

"Well you aren't the American people," Reed said thinly. "You're just one fat little demagogue all by himself. You don't know what I do out in the field. You don't know what agents face, and they do and risk one hell of a lot more than some suckup like you."

"Reed," Peter snapped.

"I apologize," Reed said. He stood as if the meeting were concluded. He addressed Peter as if Bingington did not exist. "There aren't many men like you who will stand up for his men. You don't shirk responsibility, not like some."

"Sit, Erickson," Bingington commanded in his most forceful voice.

"If you were capable, I'd tell you to do the obvious," Reed said bitterly.

"Are you going to turn in your badge and resign, or do we have to go through the motions?" Bingington said. His face blazed a mottled purple.

"It won't be going through the motions, Bingington. It'll be a fight. Doucet, the jerk-off in Louisiana, was just as useless as you. All the state wardens know that. They know who put the operation at risk. The distinguished senator from Louisiana will know that shortly. I don't risk my life and then take this kind of crap from anyone." Reed turned and easily glided across the embroidered Persian carpet.

"You get him the hell out of government," Joel snarled at Peter.

"You'll have to do it by the numbers, Mr. Bingington," Peter calmly replied. Peter never got loud. "But you should know that Reed Erickson is the most decorated agent in the department. There are half a dozen senators from half a dozen states who know what he's done for their constituents. Every time he goes out there he puts his life on the line. Heck, the FBI have fewer than a dozen agents who have the nerve to conduct deep undercover operations. No sir, Mr. Bingington, Reed Erickson's one of our finest. He may not have been diplomatic about it, but I'm certain he was correct and that Mr. Doucet was wrong. Reed knows his job. As Reed would put it out in the field, he's just one little red ant. If you stomp him, others will explode from directions you never imagined. Good day, sir." And Peter Ulysses, known as P.U. to his men out in the field, politely took his leave.

Peter stepped out into the long linoleum hallway. Bureaucrats wandered back and forth. Even with computers, entire forests of paper shuffled back and forth. He breathed deeply as if standing in the great outdoors. He'd actually felt a surge of anger in there. Perhaps that was the good of being around Reed. The Bingingtons did not understand their only function was to support the people in the field, the people actually facing the dangers. I'd be out there myself, Peter thought, if only I had the guts.

"What is this, a joke?" Pam said of Reed's new suit. She fingered the cloth. "Pretty fancy. Looks expensive to me. And you'll wear it what, once?"

"I bought it used," Reed said. "Supposedly it cost seven hundred dollars. I paid fifty."

"But why?" Pam asked.

For you, Reed thought, but the words sat unsaid, like a thick lump in his throat. Trish walked into the room. She wore bright green pants and a white turtleneck. "Daddy!" She laughed and hugged Reed. "Why are you wearing a suit?" Abruptly she got serious and looked to her mother. "Did someone die?"

Pam laughed much too loud. "No. Remember your father's

lectures, that fashion is just a cover. It doesn't change a person's character one iota. Well, see, now your father is trying to change his cover."

Reed could not help but hear the hard edge at the end of Pam's explanation. It wasn't just his exterior he was trying to change, Reed argued. But again only to himself. The suit was just a symbol, a symbol of what he could be if it meant holding onto his family. Either Pam saw that or she did not. He wasn't going to tell her the obvious.

Stacy, not quite sixteen yet, walked into the tiny kitchen. At least in the country they'd had room, and light, Reed thought. Here in Washington they were packed in on each other like a bunch of rats. Well, whatever people were used to, he thought.

"Hi, Stacy," Reed said brightly.

"Hello," she said, as if doing him a favor. Her brown hair was frizzed into a flaring rat's nest. She wore a terribly tight black skirt and a white blouse. A half a dozen bracelets jangled at each wrist and she had a series of half a dozen tiny pin earrings covering the exterior of her ears. "You look ridiculous," she said of Reed's suit.

"Thanks," Reed said. "Might I say the same about you, but then that's always true." And he heard in his voice the spite he'd promised he would avoid.

"What are you doing?" Pam asked Reed.

"Making a fool of myself, all right?" Reed snapped with mock anger. He smiled. Everyone laughed, except for Stacy. Ever since they'd announced their divorce she'd been as spiteful as could be, even after Pam graciously admitted she was the one who initiated the proceedings.

"Let's go to dinner," Reed said. "Whatever you want. My treat. Tomorrow I have to go up before the Administrative Board."

"Why is that?" Trish asked. She stood affectionately at her father's side. "First they want to give me a medal. And then they want to bawl me out because, as they put it, I have the same respect for authority as your sister there."

"Cute," Stacy said. "You're always looking for a way to dig at me, aren't you?"

"No. I'm just looking for a way to make contact," Reed said with obvious strain.

"Enough," Pam intervened. "You two can't go ten seconds and you're at each other's throats. Now let's go."

In actuality the dinner did not go too badly, Reed thought. As much as he could he followed Pam's advice with Stacy: don't force conversation and don't crack any jokes at Stacy's expense. She couldn't take a joke. Unfortunately she couldn't take her father either, Reed thought with macabre humor. Make do with what you can.

Reed told them about Louisiana, about the operation and apprehension of the violating ring. He told them about Marlis and Jody and Patty and the fact they had been unable to locate her missing husband or the killer, even though they did locate the truck. He wanted to impress on them that there was always someone in more dire straits than they could ever be.

"I promised to resolve what happened with her husband," Reed said later, as they walked the halls of the Smithsonian. "I couldn't. The woman's not in good shape." He spoke with obvious sadness. "When she was a young girl, Stacy's age, she witnessed her father raping one of their young black maids. She didn't say anything. It's been with her ever since."

"That's horrible," Pam said.

"Do you love her?" Stacy asked.

"Stacy!" Pam snapped.

"No," Reed replied. "But I do feel sorry for her. And I do feel I let her down."

Trish put her arm around her father's waist as if to lend him comfort. "Why did you come home then, Daddy?"

"I don't know," Reed said. "Orders, I suppose. But mainly I wanted to see you guys. I was feeling a little lonely out there."

"It's getting late," Pam interrupted. "We better get home."

He'd gone too far, Reed understood. Pam was not the sentimental kind, at least not to where she ever let it show. They climbed into the car, a five-year-old Oldsmobile, and Pam swung by his seedy little basement apartment. With the prices in Washington, they could not afford two cars. Besides, Reed took the bright and safe Metro, it was cheaper than paying insurance and having his automobile ripped to shreds on the streets.

"I'll walk you to the door," Pam said.

"You'll walk me?" Reed asked. "In this neighborhood?" He turned to his daughters. "Lock the doors. Good night now."

"Good luck at the hearing," Trish said.

"Stacy," Reed said, looking for a response.

She spoke with exaggerated politeness. "Good night. It was a very O.K. evening."

"Thanks," Reed said. She never called him daddy, not any more.

Pam escorted Reed just a few feet to the old brick building. For the most part the neighborhood was comprised of blacks. Those still out at this time of night seemed to move in groups as if for safety. Pam warily eyed the streets and quickly handed Reed a thick envelope. "This is the divorce decree. I'd like you to read it over and see if you want to make any changes. Maybe we can get it signed and notarized and filed with the court."

Reed's fingers were numb as if unable to grip the envelope. A strange tightness squeezed his chest and made it difficult to breathe. "I thought, ah, maybe you'd think about giving it another chance. I'll change." He unconsciously fingered the lapel of his suit. A group of half-a-dozen young toughs passed. When he wore his work clothes they seldom paid any attention. But now, him wearing this suit, Pam wearing a nice dress, their curiosity was aroused. "Don't even think about it," Reed snapped and gave them the stare. If they were going to try something it wouldn't be easy. He wanted them to know that.

"No," Pam said after the group had passed. The group stopped fifty yards down, looking back, debating any moves. "That suit's not you, Reed. You know that. If you don't, you should. This is hard enough, why make it harder. We're just not the same. Why pretend we are? No, absolutely no. I'm not going back." Pam turned, a steel rod, straight and firm. She climbed into the car and drove away. Only Trish turned and waved.

The six young toughs returned. Reed stood in the middle of the sidewalk and faced them directly. They stopped and gathered around. "What's in the envelope, man?" one asked.

"Divorce papers," Reed snarled. "You want to read them?" His tone was vicious, inviting. If there was one thing he'd welcome now, it'd be a damn good fight.

The young tough grinned as if in doubt. "Yeah." He glanced at Reed's level predator stare and then away. Reed stood quietly, giving the man one avenue of escape. "Yeah," he grunted again and the young toughs went on their way.

Ten minutes after he entered his apartment the telephone rang. "Where you been, Yankee?" a voice with a heavy Southern accent said. "I've been trying to call you all night."

"Hank, how're you doing?" Reed managed to say.

Hank hesitated as if digesting Reed's tone. "I've got bad news. Can you bear it?"

"Sure, give me a shot," Reed said with false enthusiasm. He kicked off his new vinyl dress shoes. Already he'd worked up a blister. And he stripped off his tie and tossed his suit coat onto an old rocking chair. The floor was cold, a blue threadbare carpet laid without a pad on top of raw cement. A hole in the ground. A cave had more character, more sense of being. At least you could commune with the earth. Here there were nothing but rats.

"Marlis ran off with Doyle."

The ceiling wasn't much over seven feet high, closing in, pressing down. He could reach up and touch the asbestos tiles with his hand, something good to breathe. At least something for the poor. "Oh, Pam," Reed whispered. And now Marlis as well.

"Reed," Hank called. "You with me, buddy?"

"Why would she run off with Doyle?"

"She left the youngsters with her sister, Debra. I think Marlis thinks Doyle knows who killed Wayne."

"Anything new on that?"

"Not a thing. The sheriff is still on my case. Now that I reopened the issue, he wants me to close it down. Reporters have been asking questions. Someone put out the rumor Wayne was investigating the violating ring."

"I wonder who did that?" Reed asked.

"Yeah, I wondered, too."

"You questioned all the participants?"

"As hard as I legally could. I'm pretty sure Doyle and Billy Bob were hunting together that night. And Cutter said they got back to the last rendezvous awfully late and only had a couple of deer. If they did it I don't think the other boys were informed. I moved on Billy Bob as hard as I could. He was frightened, but it wasn't of me."

"Doyle," Reed said. "Well I can be just as badass as Doyle."

"You coming down?"

"Tomorrow afternoon. I have an administrative hearing in the morning. If I work it like I want, I might get off for a week or two."

"You mean suspended?"

"Time without pay."

"State wardens I talked with said you did one hell of a job. As smooth and professional as they've ever seen. They said you weren't exactly kind to a Mr. Doucet. Said he had connections. I guess he called them in. I'll have to have a talk with some of those boys. Get them to organize and stand up and tell their legislators who really did what. Doucet's a little weak since we located Wayne's truck. But if we don't find the body pretty quick he's going to walk and preen."

"If I can work it I'll catch an airplane tomorrow afternoon."

"Maybe you want to meet Sheriff LeBitche," Hank said hopefully.

"In actuality I was thinking of taking Billy Bob out gator hunting, maybe tying him out as bait. That is legal down there, isn't it?"

"As long as the boy's white," Hank said as if Reed was kidding.

But Reed's lips were compressed, grim. A tear rolled down his cheek. "Thanks for the call, Hank. You've been a friend."

Hank hesitated. "The old lady serve the papers?"

Reed nodded.

"That's tough, man. See you tomorrow."

Reed could not speak. He nodded again and gently hung up the telephone. He looked around the small, dark basement apartment. The reek of sewage carried from behind the walls. The floor creaked overhead and voices carried through the walls. Pam was right. Pam was always right. This was not him. This was not his home. It was why she'd set him free. "So why," he said in a choked voice, "do I feel so goddamned bad?"

FOURTEEN

Reed rented a car in Baton Rouge then drove down toward
Magnolia where he met Hank at the freeway wayside. Sheila
drove Hank. She walked with Hank as they crossed the Bermuda grass to where Reed sat on a picnic table. She was tall,
angular like Hank, lean, athletic, and distinctively dark in
contrast to Hank.

"I couldn't leave my car," Hank explained. "The highway
patrol watches if a car has been sitting here unattended."

"Hank can't afford one more incident," Sheila said with
some venom. "If he does he'll be out of a job. As it is he's
forfeiting his promotion opportunities."

"Sheila, please. There's no guarantee LeBitche will be re-
elected."

"Hah," Sheila spat beside Reed's feet. She was tough. If it
came down to a predator stare, Reed had no doubt he would be
the prey. "You're lucky. When this is all over you can leave and
go back to some other life. This is our home, family. Why do
you care?"

"Sheila, please," Hank pleaded as if embarrassed.

"That's all right," Reed said. "Sheila's right. When this is
all over I just leave. Meanwhile there's a responsibility here.
Someone killed Wayne Pog. Now Marlis is in deep trouble. We
can't just all turn our backs." He stared deep into the ebony
brown of Sheila's eyes. "You can't blame a child for turning
away, especially when it's a parent in whom they've given their
trust. As you know better than I, something like that costs the
rest of your life. In this case we're adults. We should know
better. We have to lend a hand."

[157]

"What are you talking about?" Hank said.

"He's talking about Marlis," Sheila said. "Reed said she needs help. I guess you guys better help." Sheila's face twisted as if she was about to cry, but then she turned and walked swiftly to her car.

"Sheila!" Hank called.

"That's O.K., Hank," Reed said. "Maybe when you get home and get in bed, cloaked by the night. Maybe then Sheila will talk."

"Talk about what?"

"It was a long time ago. It's up to Sheila if she wants to talk. You have to respect that."

"How the hell would you know?"

Reed stood. "Let's go. We've got a job. The first thing we want to do is get hold of Billy Bob."

"And do what?" Hank asked.

They jumped Billy Bob at a familiar haunt, the darkened parking lot of the Blue Moon Tavern and Dance Hall. As he stepped from the raised cab of his four-wheel-drive truck, Hank and Reed crept up from behind. Reed put a quick full nelson on Billy Bob while Hank jerked a pillow down over Billy Bob's head.

The big boy lurched to one side, taking Reed with him. Reed struggled for purchase in the loose limestone gravel, but Billy Bob had too much weight and momentum. They slammed sideways and Billy Bob smacked his head against the side of his truck. He moaned.

Hank jumped in. He cocked his pistol, a metallic clink in the night. He held the muzzle to Billy Bob's temple. "Settle down or you're dead, fatso," Reed hissed in a whisper in Billy Bob's ear. Billy Bob went rigid. Hank anxiously glanced back toward the tavern to make sure no one was coming out the door. His hand shook. At the last minute he'd tried to back away. Kidnapping. A major felony. No way. "Fine," Reed had said. "It wasn't nice of me to ask you in the first place."

But Hank had relented. He'd come along. But now he shook with the fear of getting caught.

Reed quickly looped a rope around Billy Bob's wrists and they each seized an arm and herded and dragged their victim across the parking lot to where the rental car, it's license tags smeared with mud, sat in the dark. They stuffed Billy Bob face down in the back seat and then, without using headlights until they were well down the highway, drove into the night.

As previously agreed, they did not talk. Billy Bob's heavy breathing carried from the back seat. Several times he whimpered. "What do you guys want?"

"Shut-up," Hank said in a hoarse whisper.

"Hit him next time," Reed admonished in his phony whisper. "This isn't a game."

Hank thought to argue but glanced at Billy Bob and remained silent.

Except for the occasional sound of Billy Bob's tears, they drove in silence out to Strait's Levee. Billy Bob sobbed louder as he felt the automobile bounce down off the road and up on the narrow ridge of the levee. As a result of the search for Wayne and dragging his pickup out of the swamp, the levee had been beaten down and the reaching foliage knocked back. They passed the beaten swath where the truck had been located and entered thicker foliage.

"What'd I do? Where are we going?" Billy Bob asked. He'd gained a small measure of self-control.

"Gator hole," Reed grunted. "You're our bait."

Billy Bob, his head still buried in the pillowcase, lay silent, digesting the news.

Hank understood then Reed was right. When it came to torture, Billy Bob would not be a man to stand firm. Cutter had given them the break. Billy Bob had been hunting with Doyle the night Wayne disappeared. The two had been late arriving at the last rendezvous. That they could establish in court. But beyond that they had no link, nothing that tied Wayne to Doyle or Billy Bob.

From time to time Reed slowed and shone a bright flashlight down onto the bog covering sections of the swamp. Eventually he found what he was looking for, a scattering of fish, bird and raccoon parts, evidence of a feeding station for a good size alligator. He stopped the car and turned off the lights. A sense of guilt sat heavy on his shoulders. He loathed the old tradition of Southern justice. As he and Hank had discussed, too often the motivation was not justice as much as simple ego, wanting credit for resolving a case, using an innocent man's life to put a feather in your cap. Hank firmly believed there were hundreds of innocent blacks in Southern jails. Once a lawman makes up his mind, he closes off other avenues, he looks for evidence to fit his perception. It usually wasn't hard to find.

No, you take some black man into the back room and beat him until he confesses. And then you put him in the hanging cell, Hank had said. Justice, Reed thought. Only this time he was right and he was doing it for a just cause. He laughed and shook his head.

"You all right?" Hank asked.

"Yeah." Reed grunted with exaggerated hoarseness and punched Hank in the arm. The hollow pain of guilt in the pit of his stomach would not ease. But he simply had no choice.

Abruptly Reed jumped from the car. He roughly jerked Billy Bob out of the back seat. If they were going to do this, they would do it all the way. Billy Bob, his hands still tied behind his back and the hood still covering his face, tumbled on his nose. Reed jerked him upright. Hank rushed around the car and gently took Billy Bob's opposite arm. He shot Reed a questioning look.

Reed manhandled Billy Bob forward until his feet were at the edge of the steep bank. They then made him lean forward until only their grip kept him from tumbling down the slope and into the black swamp water below. Reed jerked off the hood and flicked the flashlight beam to where the alligator feeding station was located. He whispered viciously into Billy Bob's ear. "Big bull alligator lives out there. We're going out on that bog, cut a hole and stuff you in."

Billy Bob trembled from head to foot as if racked by convulsions. "Why? What?" He tried to turn his head but Reed flashed the light directly into his eyes. "What did I do?"

Reed hissed in his ear. "You murdered Wayne Pog."

"No, no. I had nothing to do with that. Nothing. I swear."

"Wrong answer, gator bait," Reed said and pushed. The move took Hank by surprise. Billy Bob flopped in ungainly fashion down the slope and rolled into the water.

"What are you doing?" Hank snarled at Reed and rushed to the rescue. He quickly hauled a coughing Billy Bob from the water. In spite of his anger, Hank thought enough to pick up his phony whisper. "The man means business. I'd advise you to talk, or it's not going to be good."

"I can't," Billy Bob blubbered. He'd already lost control. "I can't. Please!"

Hank looked at Reed, pleading. He wasn't cut out for this torturing stuff.

"C'mon gator bait," Reed said brusquely and pulled the hood over Billy Bob's head and jerked him to his feet.

They worked down the shoreline and out onto the bog. It seemed like every other step Billy Bob broke through and flopped awkwardly forward burying his face in the bog and water. After a few feet Reed stopped and returned for a shovel and a small pole he located beside the road. To the sound of Billy Bob's sobs he peeled back a chunk of bog. Even Hank looked frightened, as if forgetting that they were well down from the alligator feeding station and that it was extremely unlikely that even a big alligator would try to attack an object as large as Billy Bob.

"O.K., boy, time for a swim," Reed said. They each seized an arm. But then Billy Bob exploded with all the fury of a cornered rat fighting for its life. He kicked and flailed and bucked and heaved, one direction and then the other, kicking and pushing back from the direction they wanted him to go. They rolled in bog and water, all three men thoroughly mud-covered and soaked. But finally Billy Bob was out of breath and out of strength. He gasped for air, sucking in the pillowcase, almost gagging on the cloth until Hank raised it up enough so he could drag in clear air.

They stood, waiting until Billy Bob's heart slowed and he gained enough air so as not to hyperventilate. Hank jerked his head toward the car, he'd had enough. Reed did not blink or say a word. His lips were compressed, grim. After a minute or so they dragged Billy Bob over to the hole. He was sobbing and his muscles had turned to Jell-o.

"Please, no. Please. I beg you."

The cries were pitiful, not even human, Reed thought. He jerked Billy Bob's arm. "Who killed Wayne?"

"No. No. I can't. He'll kill me. He promised. He promised, no matter what."

"Was it Doyle?"

"No. No. I can't say. Please. My mother's all alone."

"Tell us. Show us where the body is located." Reed pushed so Billy Bob dropped waist deep in the water, held up only by Reed's grip under one arm. Hank, standing on the opposite side of the hole, moved the pole under water until it gently brushed Billy Bob's leg.

Billy Bob screamed. He thrashed and rolled and clung to Reed. "Please, no. Doyle killed him. I didn't know. Wayne stopped us with a couple of deer and Doyle shot him in the head. Twice. He shot him twice." Like a drowning man clutching a life preserver, Billy Bob clung to Reed's leg. The sour odor of urine and feces rose from their victim.

Hank stood across the pond, his head lowered in shame and disgust. Him, a peace officer sworn to uphold the law. He'd never felt so ashamed in his life. He spat as if trying to clear the copper taste from his mouth. The taste would not go away. He'd never imagined Reed could be that cruel.

"Where's the body?"

"Just down the levee a little further. Doyle buried it under the bog."

"Show us."

"Sure," Billy Bob said weakly. Anything they wanted. Anything at all.

They kept Billy Bob positioned so he could not even venture a guess at their height and weight. He walked down the levee in the glare of the headlights and pointed out the bog where Doyle had concealed Wayne beneath the bog. They replaced his hood and they drove him back to town. He was an accomplice, they informed him. Other members of the group were on record saying he'd been hunting with Doyle the night Wayne disappeared. Whether he fired the shot or not, he was party to the murder. He could get the death penalty just like Doyle Monroe. The best thing he could do would be to go to the police in the morning and turn himself in, turn State's evidence.

"Doyle will kill me," Billy Bob argued. He'd lost all sense of dignity when he'd been immersed in the water. The knowledge of his cowardice now angered him and he spoke with some defiance.

"I'll stick you back in the damn gator hole," Reed hissed.
Hank tried for a sympathetic whisper. "If we pick up Doyle and you at the same time, the charge will be the same, murder in the first degree. That's death. If you come in you'll get a limited jail term. And in jail you'll be protected. Think about it."

"Ma will die," Billy Bob said. "I'm all she's got. I didn't want to kill Wayne. I had no idea what Doyle was doing. None. I just wanted to kill deer."

They loosened Billy Bob's ropes and, while still wearing his hood, dumped him off beside the road just down from the Blue Moon.

"Yankee, you are a sonofabitch," Hank said as soon as they were out of sight. "One cold, unfeeling S.O.B. First class. And I went along."

"I wasn't proud," Reed said. "But it had to be done. If he does come in tomorrow, make sure you intercept him. If he doesn't I'll call in shortly after noon and tell the dispatcher where the body is located. Then we'll have to take it from there."

They rode in silence. A block away from Hank's house Reed pulled the car over to the side of the street to where thickets of foliage blocked them from neighboring houses. "Good night," Reed said. Hank did not reply.

Reed sighed and slowly pulled away. He drove out to the freeway wayside, rape alley for a woman after midnight. But all was quiet. At the back of the lot a couple of truckers were pulled over catching a few winks. Reed crawled into the back seat and tried to fall to sleep. In the morning he'd head out and try to locate Marlis, and Doyle Monroe.

The fat blubber of Billy Bob stood out a hundred yards across the swamp. He was surrounded by police. Half-a-dozen marked and unmarked cars sat one behind the other on top of the levee, Strait's Levee, directly out from where he'd concealed Wayne. Oh, they'd found something all right, Doyle could see. It couldn't be much, not after all these months. He'd warned the boys over and over, loyalty above all else, be true to your fellow man.

And then Cutter let him down, his own blood. What could

he expect after that. Doyle clicked his teeth. He should have brought the rifle. It would be an easy shot. He'd warned the tubby lad, talk and you're as good as dead.

Doyle faded into the swamp. Of course no one could see him anyhow. He wore Marine camouflage fatigues and had grease painted his face. Besides, he knew how to move, slowly, like a branch moving with the breeze, a brief illusion, there and then gone. He crossed the high ground of a hammock and stepped into a brown, hollow log pirogue concealed on the opposite side. He poled easily and methodically through the stands of towering cypress and willows. He took turns through the thickets of foliage with the same knowledge as a city boy walking the streets. This was home, Doyle thought. He'd never been happier. But now he had to leave, just for a while, until Billy Bob lay dead.

Marlis waited in the small twenty-foot-long house boat Doyle had managed to work back into the depths of the swamp. She wore a tan skirt, white blouse, and shower clogs. The sight of her hair tied up in a knot behind her head irritated Doyle but he held his peace. He liked her hair long, hanging down. But he did not like to nag. He nodded. As usual they did not speak. It had become a routine, say only the necessary. Point out a bird, a gator, a snake. Ask what was for supper. Surprisingly Marlis never complained. She made do with what was available. Doyle hunted and fished, Marlis cooked and cleaned. At night they went to bed and made love. But mostly they were silent, each living their own life and having very little to say.

Doyle went to the tiny bedroom and brought out his rifle and began to clean it.

"Is something wrong?" Marlis asked.

Doyle stared and then he shrugged. "They found your husband's body."

"Wayne?"

"Did you have another one?"

Marlis shook her head. "How? Where?"

"Billy Bob showed them. Over on Strait's Levee, down from where they found the truck."

"Billy Bob killed Wayne?"

"No. Billy Bob wouldn't have the nerve for something like that. I killed Wayne."

Marlis swallowed. This was the news she'd come to hear. Her eyes locked with Doyle's. "Why? Wayne was just out after violators. I just could never understand why."

"It was betrayal," Doyle said. "After all I'd done for Magnolia, your husband was going to run me in for shooting a few deer, for harvesting the Lord's bounty. I tried to tell him. I tried." Doyle's eyes became twisted with the memory. Slowly, as if talking more to himself, he told Marlis the entire story.

He'd been hunting with Billy Bob. It was their third trip out that night. Billy Bob was having a hot night and as usual he had been running at the mouth.

They'd met Cutter and the semi for the second time, dropped their load and headed out.

Even before Doyle left the straight stretch he noticed the semi lights come on as the truck pulled onto the highway. Inside the refrigerated back they would hang the deer, slit the bellies, drop the entrails into a washtub and then move onto the next. Livers and hearts would be saved. They'd next slit the hide all the way up to the neck, cut around the base of the head, cut off the forelegs at the knee and then slit each foreleg down to the chest. A few inches of neck hair would be peeled back, a cable wrapped around a tennis ball nestled in the hair and then the cable wound around a power winch which pulled the entire hide down over the back, the hind legs, and as smooth as silk right off the tail. The hide was tossed on a steadily growing pile and the deer was slid on a ceiling track to the front of the trailer. In less than an hour Cutter and his crew had the twenty-eight deer gutted and skinned. At four o'clock in the morning they stopped on a bridge and dumped the entrails into the river below, then drove on. The men in back began to bone out the carcasses, packing the meat in plastic lined boxes so it could be frozen. In an hour they'd receive another load.

Meanwhile Doyle and Billy Bob headed in toward Magnolia. They'd hit this area two months before. On occasion they reached as far out as eighty miles from home. Doyle and Cutter had both agreed, it wouldn't be good to leave an obvious gap and avoid their hometown.

The first two deer happened on Doyle's side. He took the

Hornet and snapped them down. One had been standing right on the shoulder of the road. On a levee near the outer reaches of the Atchafalaya Swamp a row of red eyes glinted. As Billy Bob swung the spotlight the black leather of some four foot long alligators waddled down and slid into a canal. "No orders for gators tonight?" Billy Bob asked a question to which he already knew the answer. "I haven't shot me a gator in three weeks. Remember that six footer I thought was dead? Whew," he laughed and wiped his brow as if it had just happened. "That tail caught my leg and I thought I was dead. I still get swelling on my knee."

"A gator's like a cottonmouth. They're never dead. Never," Doyle lectured. It had been a long night. Billy Bob was getting on his nerves. It'd do the fat boy good to pull some guts. Next time he'd take Chuck. Chuck was slow, but at least he didn't run at the mouth.

"Shit, there's six of them." Billy Bob spun the spotlight on six deer out in the stubble of Carlson's recently harvested okra field.

"You watch your language son or I'll give you the back of my hand. There's always deer here. We got two out of here last time." Doyle hesitated. He didn't like patterns, it had always been his margin of safety. But then again it had been two months. And Billy Bob already had the rifle pointed out the window. He fired. A deer dropped. The others ran. One stopped not far away. Billy Bob fired again. The deer staggered then picked up and ran. "Damnit!" Billy Bob exclaimed. It was the only swear word he could think of that Doyle did not mind.

"That's the second one you wounded tonight."

"I'm sorry, Doyle. I . . ."

"Git out there and git the one," Doyle hissed.

Billy Bob started as if he'd been touched by a whip. He bolted from the cab and picked up his lumbering run across the field. As soon as he got the deer, Doyle doused the spotlight and stepped out into the night. A chill had begun to descend and touches of fog had gathered in some low areas. The stars had begun to fade, and the dark had become more pronounced. The straight stretch ahead appeared to be clean. They'd just rounded a corner before the field but there'd been no evidence of life for miles around. The nearest house was some coon-ass shack set on stilts at the edge of the swamp. And that was more than a mile behind.

As Billy Bob came grunting back dragging a medium-size doe by her front leg, Doyle trotted down the field to assist. They crunched through some brush and splashed through some water of the ditch as they climbed back up to the truck. Even with his own truck still running, Doyle sensed a second noise. As he tensed to run, the headlights hit him and Billy Bob and the dead deer directly in their glare. Doyle started around to the front of the truck.

"Doyle, Billy Bob."

The shout stopped the two men in mid-stride. A truck pulled to a halt just a few feet away. "It's been a few years, but I finally caught you guys."

Doggone, doggone, doggone, Doyle chanted in his mind. He peered into the glare of the lights. They'd muddied over their license plate in case there ever was a chase. But this. A short, slender man stepped around the front of the truck. "That you, Wayne?"

"I thought you were one of 'em, Doyle. I hoped I was wrong." Wayne Pog walked up to converse with the two men. He stood five feet five inches and weighed one-thirty-five. He was one of fourteen kids, Doyle knew. Wayne and two of his sisters were the only ones to finish high school. Then Wayne joined the army paratroopers and after that went to college. Became a naturalist, and then joined the Department of Conservation as a game warden. A game warden living amongst relatives and friends in the town of Magnolia. Once he'd even arrested his uncle. For that Wayne's father took a shotgun and peppered his son's new state truck. The old man had even put a couple of pellets in his own son.

"I've been staking out this field off and on for the last two months," Wayne said. He wasn't bragging, just stating a fact. He peered into the back of the truck. "Three deer. And how many others tonight? Three thousand dollars, your rifles, the truck. We know you're part of the ring that's been operating this area, Doyle. I've got authorization. If you boys talk, give us the whole works, we'll go easy on you."

"You were born and raised here, Wayne. You know better than that. Billy Bob and I were out here alone. This is the first time we ever violated, and you can rest assured it will be the last."

"I told my boss," Wayne said. "He wouldn't listen. If it had been up to me, I would have tried to follow and see where you dumped the deer. We don't have that end yet."

"What are you talking about?" Doyle said softly. "You state boys forget, nature's bounty belongs to the people. Man doesn't make the laws. God makes the laws. You reap what you sow."

"This would be a case in point. Billy Bob, how you doing? Did you get your quota of killing tonight, or were you way behind like normal?"

"I got . . . Ah," Billy Bob sighed deeply and looked to Doyle for direction. "We were just taking a ride. Ah, I shot all these. Doyle didn't do any."

"It doesn't matter who fired, Billy Bob," Wayne pointed out. "The two of you were together." He paused, considering. "I hate this Doyle. I tell you."

"I'll tell you once and I'll tell you clear, I can't take an arrest just now, Wayne." Doyle kept his voice low, even, hard, a tone Billy Bob recognized only too well. "I've got too much at stake. A lot of people depend on me. You know that. I don't exploit things and I don't kill for fun. Everything I take I use."

"I know that, Doyle. But there's the matter of the law. If everyone did what you do, there wouldn't be game enough to go around."

"Everyone does do what I do," Doyle roared. His shout split the night. He was pleased to note, Wayne had jumped. He immediately caught himself and picked up his hard, even tone. "Now I'm asking you as a friend, as a deacon in Marlis and your children's church, as a neighbor, turn around and walk away."

"You know I can't do that," Wayne said. He did not want a fight. For a moment he considered reaching for his pistol, but stopped. Pulling down on Doyle would represent the final affront.

"Wayne, please," Billy Bob pleaded.

Billy Bob was frightened, Wayne thought, but misunderstood the cause. "It's just a fine. You're not going to jail," Wayne pointed out.

[168]

"You're taking us in?" Doyle asked.

"I have no choice," Wayne said. "I'll get your rifles, then you can ride with me, Doyle. Billy Bob can follow us in."

"Billy Bob, you come around here and drive," Doyle said. "I'll go around and get my things. I tried. The warden here doesn't know a thing." Doyle passed behind the truck and walked up to the open door on the rider's side.

Wayne moved down the road to the truck cab. He opened the door on the driver's side. The right side of his face was illuminated from the headlights of his own truck. He looked at Doyle standing on the opposite side of the seat. Doyle had a short rifle in his hands. The muzzle raised toward Wayne's suddenly intense face. "No! Christ!"

The rifle cracked. Wayne dropped on the blacktop just at Billy Bob's feet.

"Jesus Christ, Doyle, you killed him!" Billy Bob shouted. One of Wayne's legs kicked in reflex back and forth. A loud gurgling sound carried from the blacktop.

"Watch your language, boy," Doyle said as he passed around the front of the truck.

"He ain't dead," Billy Bob wailed as Wayne continued to thrash. Unconsciously Billy Bob backed up as if he could somehow escape.

Doyle moved Wayne's head so the lights shone on his blood-covered face. The bullet had entered just beside the nose. "He's dead. It'll just take a minute or two for the reflex to stop. You know how a head shot is. A deer can kick like the dickens, but he's no longer there."

The gurgling continued. "He's breathing." Billy Bob's wail rose to near panic.

Doyle seized the big kid and slammed him against the truck. "Stop it. Understand. Stop it. He's dead." He turned, placed the muzzle to Wayne's eye and squeezed. The body jerked and the gurgling stopped. Without losing his grip on Billy Bob's shirt, Doyle turned back. "We'll get rid of the truck and we'll get rid of the body and no one will know a thing. Wayne didn't radio anybody and tell them who he'd stopped. Not at this time of the morning."

Billy Bob nodded. He didn't trust himself to speak. Whatever Doyle said.

With considerable trepidation, Billy Bob grabbed Wayne's legs. The flesh was still supple. The body was warm. The sour taste of vomit rose into his throat. He'd tried to warn Wayne. He'd tried. He knew Doyle's voice.

They lifted Wayne into the back of the truck and set him down. They did not toss him like they would the carcass of a deer.

"What about that doe?" Billy Bob asked. His throat was parched and it was all he could do to move his tongue.

"Might as well get it. We're going to have to meet the others just like normal."

Billy Bob nodded. Just like normal? Somehow his mind had lost a connection. Just like normal?

"Drive Wayne's truck. Follow me." The words echoed as if inside a huge chamber. Because he could think of nothing else, Billy Bob complied.

They drove five miles, almost back over to Strait's Corner, before Doyle turned down a narrow, dusty road. Roadside foliage, completely caked with dust, gleamed in their head-lights and raked the sides of the truck.

Eventually they rattled through a ditch and up on top of a levee. A few yards along Doyle stopped. He climbed out of his truck and walked back. "We'll push the truck over the edge here. It's deep enough."

"Yessir," Billy Bob said.

"You going to stay in there and go down with the truck, or are you going to get out and help me push it in?"

"Oh," Billy Bob laughed. "Should I leave the motor on or turn it off?"

"Turn it off. Also turn off the lights. Leave the gearshift in neutral."

"Yessir."

With the windows rolled down and the topper back open, the truck sank in less than five minutes. While Billy Bob watched the truck, Doyle broke off a pine limb and brushed away the tracks leading down the levee.

"Let's go," Doyle said.

"What about Wayne?" Billy Bob asked as if Wayne was still alive.

"Not here."

[170]

"Oh, right."

A quarter-mile down the levee Doyle turned down a narrow side road that bordered on a marsh that comprised a part of the endless depths of the Atchafalaya Swamp. With Billy Bob's assistance, he tossed Wayne over his shoulder. The first signs of rigor mortis were stiffening the body. Billy Bob seized a shovel and the two of them waded into the swamp. After a few feet of muck they climbed up on top of the matted wiregrass that formed a floating bog. On several occasions they broke through and Wayne fell off to the side. It seemed Billy Bob broke through at ever other step.

"Keep your knees flexed and go to your knees if you break through," Doyle advised. His throat was dry and he was rasping for air. "Don't forget those big bull alligators make their homes under here."

Billy Bob whined. "Aren't we out far enough?"

"I suppose," Doyle said. "Start shoveling a hole in this bog. We'll stuff him underneath. It won't take long with the critters around here and he should be gone."

Billy Bob tried to nod. He pried ineffectually at the bog. After watching him for several seconds, Doyle gave up. He spoke with quiet force. "Give me the shovel."

"Yessir."

"We don't want to mention this to anyone, Billy Bob. Not your girlfriend. Not even one of the boys. I asked Wayne to drop the issue. I asked him real polite."

"Yessir," Billy Bob said. His jowls quivered and his voice took on the high-pitched tone of a sixteen-year-old. He looked up and realized Doyle was staring. His Adam's apple bobbed. He felt a desperate need to spit but could not find the strength to gather the cotton coating his mouth.

"Wayne didn't listen to me, did he?"

"No sir," Billy Bob gave it more force. He recognized that tone.

"But you hear me don't you, Billy Bob? You won't mention this to anyone. Never."

"Oh, no sir. No sir."

Doyle patted Billy Bob's arm. "Good. Now get back up to the truck. Check the door on the driver's side. Wash it off if need be."

"Yessir." Billy Bob scrambled away, grunting and splashing and half-crying in frustration each time he punched through the bog.

With easy thrusts of the shovel Doyle peeled back a section of grass. Eventually he worked a small rectangular hole five feet long. He paid no heed to mosquitoes feasting on his flesh. He rolled Wayne into the black brine beneath. He lay the carpet of grass back on Wayne's face. He said a quiet prayer and then crossed the bog back to the mainland.

Doyle paused to collect himself. The first rays of morning light framed a nearby line of live oaks covered with Spanish moss. The water of the marsh gleamed as still as glass. Doyle sighed as if he carried the weight of the world. A deep sorrow would not let him be.

"I tried. Why couldn't Wayne be reasonable? Why couldn't he listen?" he asked Marlis. "He should have known better. He gave me no choice, no out."

"That was Wayne," Marlis said. Her voice broke. She turned to where she had some okra steaming on the small gas stove.

"Are you angry?" Doyle asked.

Marlis laughed. She couldn't help it, she laughed. Are you angry? And then she dropped to the floor and cried. It had been years since she had cried. For in the midst of her tears she saw a truth. She'd loved Wayne. Not at first, but after some time. It had been like an arranged marriage, one she'd arranged herself. In all those years Wayne had been trustworthy, considerate, attentive to her needs. At first she'd submitted, the dutiful wife. And then she'd turned him away, using Jody and Patty as her shields. And still he'd tried to understand her, like the brother she'd never had. A brother. All those years together. Jody and Patty. And now he lay dead.

When she looked up Doyle was still cleaning his rifle. "I should have known," he said. "That's what you wanted to hear." He stood, rifle in hand. "I have business, Marlis. I'm sorry it didn't work out. You've been a good wife. You can stay, or you can go. If you want to tell the authorities, that's fine. Billy Bob's already spilled his guts. The decision is yours. I don't have an extra boat, but you can have one of the life

[172]

preservers. Go straight north and you'll hit the freeway in a couple of miles. You'll have to swim parts and it's pretty muddy at times. Don't worry about snakes or alligators, they're not really a danger to a fully grown human being. It's mostly a state of mind. If you make enough noise like most Americans, they'll get out of your way."

And then he was gone and Marlis was alone, sitting on the floor of Doyle Monroe's houseboat in the middle of a swamp.

FIFTEEN

As quietly as the gathering of an evening fog, Reed slipped through the depths of the Atchafalaya Swamp. He balanced easily on his knees in the bottom of an old wooden, olive drab-colored canoe. His paddle angled in point first at the same speed as the canoe. He swept back through the black water without sound or splash, leaving only a tiny, silent whirlpool behind. At the end of each stroke he gave a slight, rudder straightening J-stroke. He'd purchased the canoe from Story for a hundred dollars cash. Story had been pleased.

Once they'd found the mushy skeleton of Wayne's body the news had broken fast. Although there wasn't much of a body. The lower extremities had disappeared. The upper torso had all but been picked clean and consisted of the spine, rib cage, and skull, all held aloft and entangled in the root growth of the bog. Dust to dust, Reed the nonreligious thought, the elements returned home.

The state crime investigators had yet to obtain dental records and confirm the identification, but Billy Bob's word was good enough. Reporters were hawking the scene before the body had been extracted from the bog. After all, it was just down a quarter-mile from where they'd located Wayne's truck. You didn't have to be much of an investigative reporter to add those two together.

Hank had been watching and had snared Billy Bob even as he walked into police headquarters to confess. He'd read Billy Bob his rights and then strongly urged the lad to obtain an attorney, to work out a deal before he confessed, not after. Sheriff LeBitche hadn't been happy about that. To the sheriff's way of thinking if a guy decided to be a crook, he also decided to forfeit his rights. But not to worry, even after Billy Bob had been set up with an attorney and struck a deal limiting him to five years in jail for aiding and abetting a felony, he'd sung, freely and completely. If he had any suspicions Hank had been one of the two men that jumped him, he gave no sign.

"He's a broken man," Hank informed Reed over the telephone. "No spine left at all. His mother came down, wailing, crying, wondering how she was supposed to live if we took away her son. She wouldn't shut up and she wouldn't leave. LeBitche wanted to throw her in jail as well. You should have been here."

"I'd rather have been with Wayne the night Doyle shot him in the face," Reed snapped angrily. He'd had enough of this guilt. "Look, I'm sorry that we did Billy Bob the way we did. That isn't me. And sure it isn't you either. But you were there the same as Billy Bob was with Doyle. You knew the score. Or if you didn't you damn well should have."

Hank signed, faced with the reality of what really bothered him all along. He did know the score, and that was what hurt.

Hank relented. "They found a bullet imbedded in the back of the skull. It looks like a .22 Hornet. I had my guy compare it to the one you fired out of Doyle's gun. It looks like a match. I called down to Baton Rouge to get a properly documented bullet from the rifle they're holding. The sheriff has put out an all points bulletin. I tried to tell him Marlis was traveling with Doyle and that she may be in danger. But he didn't even mention her. Just said Doyle was armed and dangerous."

"You think he took to the swamp?"

"Possibly. That was one rumor. I mentioned it. But Le-Bitche just snarled and said why don't you go take a look. And then he gave me all the paperwork to put together on the case. And then I have the pleasure of going out to question Rachel and Lisa Monroe."

"Maybe I'll go talk to Story," Reed said. "Some of the guys mentioned Doyle owned an old houseboat at one time. Said they used it during duck season back in some of the bayous."

"Let me know if you find anything."

"Sure. Talk to you later, Hank."

Hank hesitated. "I'm, ah, sorry if I flew off the handle the other day. You're right, I'm just as guilty as you. We were wrong. I could have stopped it. If we hang, we should hang side by side."

"The hell with that," Reed said. "I'm copping a plea. Giving you full credit. With LeBitche's attitude toward his glory hound department, I'll be walking the streets and you'll be in jail for life."

"You sonofabitch," Hank said.

So Reed had talked to Story. The quiet Indian knew of Doyle's houseboat, knew where he usually parked it spring, summer, and fall. Reed showed him a large pictomap of the swamp, something Story had never seen. Reed indicated where they were located and pointed out the lines of the surrounding dikes. Story grinned. He'd never seen anything like this in his life. With remarkable ease he gained his orientation and pointed out the possible locations of the houseboat. When Reed rolled up the map he could sense Story's disappointment.

"I'll get you one," Reed said. That had made Story grin.

And so Reed paddled on, a long shot, but what else did he have?

He broke out of a dark, emerald canopy into a relative opening of grey and tangled cypress. The area could have been a bomb site, where one-thousand-year-old cypresses lay fallen and half submerged in filmy black water, covered with birdnest fern and moss. A blue heron dropped out of the grey dead limbs and glided through the tangled branches and down a brown ribbon of water surrounded by green. The pure white of an egret stood out sharply against a far shore. Mud turtles dropped one by one off dead logs and into the brine. A water snake cut a shallow V on the brown surface. A few visible flat-cut trunks stood up like gravestones, markers to the days during the twenties and thirties when logging companies had pushed barges into the swamps and casually taken down a thousand years of the past. The loss was enough to make Reed cry.

Man had gotten better, but only marginally so and in the high demand areas of the third world not at all.

The tree stumps, as did any lumbering operation, made him think of his father, Guy, seventy plus years old and still living alone in the wilds of northern Wisconsin. And still cutting pulp and skidding it out with a work horse. Four to five cords a day. For all his simplicity and lack of education, Guy had been a conservationist. He knew the big lumber companies that restored what they took. And he knew of the operators who cared little for how they scarred the earth. And he knew when a cut or drag line would wash and he knew when it wouldn't. In the harsh January days of a deep snow winter he'd cut browse for deer, and only occasionally would he take one for a meal.

Old Guy. It had been quite the life growing up alone with Guy Erickson. He hadn't called him in two months, Reed thought. After all he'd paid for and installed the telephone just so he could talk to his dad. But of course Guy would ask about Pam and the girls and Reed would have to tell him about the divorce.

Reed paddled on, pausing frequently to check the sun and consult his compass and map. After a time the bayous and sloughs and hammocks of hardwood and secondary growth blended together until one spot looked like another. Gnats swam before his eyes. A deer poked its head between two trees and stared as he glided past. And always the thick, sweet smell of decaying leaves, trees, and organic waste filled him with a sense of being.

And to think how people were so terrified of the unknown, of myths, of unfounded stories of terror in the swamp. It was the way of the world, people were losing touch. Stories meant more than reality.

A small blue heron, crumpled, decaying and buzzing with flies ruined Reed's sense of communing. Was the death natural, or man's impact? Perhaps pesticides or the buildup of toxic waste, PCBs as they worked up the food chain and eventually, and hopefully Reed thought, back into the bodies of man. Now that would be justice. Was that justice they'd practised with Billy Bob? Reed closed his eyes as if against a black cloud. Even out in nature he could not escape.

In time he slowed, working through the thick lily pads surrounding the outside of small willow hammock. Sun glinted off a window. Reed paused. His canoe drifted and quickly snarled in the weeds. It was a houseboat all right, painted a duck green and broken up with slashes of black. A man would really have to know the waters to work something as big as a houseboat back in here like this.

Reed backed off and worked into the willow hammock. He concealed his canoe under the overhanging branches and worked up on the island. The footing was dried mud. It had been some years since the area had been flooded. Once past the exterior thickets the ground foliage was sparse, washed out by previous floods and cut off from sunlight by the canopy overhead. He skirted the rust brown of a moccasin, an aggressive, territorial snake. A bite now could put him in the hospital for days.

Because of the thick screen of shoreline brush, he almost passed the houseboat. If his approach was difficult, it was also concealed. As if Doyle or whomever, had no fear of approach from the island. If anyone was on board.

With steadied movements, knowing the movement of brush itself would reveal his presence, Reed twisted down through a patch of brilliant green swamp grass and maiden cane. By the time he reached the bow of the boat he stood waist deep in water. He peeked over the edge and at the front door less than two feet away. Still no sign of life, no movement inside. But if they were there, once his weight touched the boat, they'd feel the movement inside. And Doyle was no fool.

Reed set his pistol on the dark, indoor/outdoor carpeting of the deck. Then slowly, slowly, he brought his weight onto the bow. But then, as he brought his buttocks up out of the floatation of the water, the boat gave a tiny lurch. Reed lay motionless, vulnerable if anyone looked out or opened the door. But there was no movement inside.

Eventually he rose to his knees, picked up his pistol and, keeping his silhouette low, cupped a hand and peered inside. No life. But it had been lived in, and recently. His heart lurched as he spotted a flowered dress draped over a battered wooden chair. Marlis's. She'd been here all right.

The browned leather of his hands slowly turned the knob. They could be in there. Around the corner. In the tiny bedroom. In the absolute silence of the swamp the door creaked.

"Doyle!" Marlis said as if in alarm. She peeked out of the bedroom. "No," she recoiled at the sight of Reed and his gun.

"Reed!" She sounded relieved. "You painted your face. I. . . .
What are you doing here?" And then she sounded angry.

Reed quickly peeked past Marlis into the rest of the boat.
Then he turned and faced those large, grey eyes. She'd been
crying. Marlis hardly ever cried. "I'm looking for Doyle. We
found Wayne's body, or at least what was left. Billy Bob confessed. Doyle killed Wayne."

"I know," Marlis said simply.

"You know?"

"Doyle told me. He told me the whole story. He saw the
police and Billy Bob looking for the body."

"Where's Doyle now?"

"He cleaned his rifle and left. Said he had business."

"Business?" Reed surveyed outside, watching in every direction. If Doyle approached, he'd approach unheard.

"Billy Bob, I think," Marlis said without emotion. "He's
probably going to kill him."

"Billy Bob's in jail."

Marlis laughed. "Do you think that'll stop Doyle? He said
he gave his word."

A sense of alarm swept through Reed like a flood. Of
course. He should have seen it coming. Who knew what Doyle
would do. Doyle was a man of principle, proud of that fact.
Once an action had been set it could not be stopped.

Reed glanced at the tiny houseboat. A person could barely
turn around without bumping into something or someone.
The paneling was warped and buckled. Holes were worn in the
linoleum floor and green mold had gathered at the corners of
the windows. And Marlis stood in the middle, pale, haunted,
eyes wide and staring like those of a woman too long in prison.
He spoke gently, with great compassion. "What are you doing
here?"

"I had to find out who killed Wayne."

"And now what?"

Marlis hesitated, considering. "I don't know."

"I have a canoe. We have to get back and warn Hank about
Billy Bob." Again Marlis hesitated. "They'll get Doyle now.
You can try to get on with your life."

Marlis laughed. "Get on with my life? What is that? I've

[179]

never had a life of my own. Never. It's all been pretend. One big game."

"We had a relationship, of sorts," Reed said.

"We had sex," Marlis snapped as if to a child.

"We better go," a red-faced Reed said softly.

Marlis turned into the tiny bedroom and began to put some of her dresses into a suitcase. Reed poked around the main part of the houseboat. A chewed sofa stood against one wall and a few books, including a worn Bible, were stacked on a shelf. An overhead light was battery-powered. They didn't have much for provisions, a sack of rice, potatoes, dried beans, a can of lard, and a rack of spices.

"Where does Doyle keep his guns?" Reed asked. He lay his nine millimeter on the formica counter so it would be in easy reach. As always he kept glancing outside, watching the approaches from every direction.

"He has a rifle and a pistol that he took with him. The others he hid in the swamp, along with some other supplies."

"I don't suppose you know where."

Marlis exited the bedroom and shook her head. "I'm completely lost."

Reed turned to peer out the window. When he turned back he faced Marlis pointing his pistol at his chest. She thumbed the safety off. "You've held that gun before," Reed casually observed. But his heart throbbed like a woodpecker attacking a dry tree. Why hadn't he anticipated something from her?

"Wayne taught me to shoot, for safety reasons he said."

Thinking of suicide, Reed wondered. He gauged the four foot distance between them. He didn't think Marlis would shoot, but you never knew for certain. A reflex jerk, too much pressure on the trigger. A bullet gone cannot be recalled. How many times have people held their finger over a trigger and then the gun went off in surprise?

"Go. Please. They won't get Doyle. I know. If they do, you can come and get me. I'll go home."

Should he risk the shot? Grab her, tie her up and throw her into the canoe? Why had he set the gun on the counter? A test? It wasn't him. It had been an invitation, giving her a chance. He looked into the pale grey of Marlis's eyes. They were wide, void of emotion. She felt nothing for him, nothing at all. Her mind was set, like Doyle's. If he moved she'd try to shoot. That much was clear.

He'd go call Hank. If they missed Doyle, Doyle would return. Reed would be here, waiting. He'd intercept Doyle before he could get to Marlis.

"There are nine shots in there," Reed said. He backed to the front door. "I'll go warn Hank." He tried for eye contact, it wasn't there. He turned and dropped over the bow and into the brown water.

"Where are you at?" Hank asked into the telephone. He half stood as if getting ready to run. "What do you mean I don't know who this is? I'm done lying, Reed. I. . . . Damn." Hank slammed the receiver. He vaulted into the squad room.

"Karis, could you do me a favor and get in back and make sure they have a vest on Billy Bob before they take out him outside?"

Karis, a stocky white cop who'd long had a dislike of Hank and other blacks, sneered. "You've got legs."

"I just got an anonymous telephone call. They said Doyle's after Billy Bob. I'm going outside and look around."

"You get that work done like I said," Sheriff LeBitche said from across the room. "Doyle Monroe is on the run with the Rittenhous dame. She's a city girl, an aristocrat if you will. By now they're probably down in New Orleans or Miami. We'll take care of Billy Bob. I think we can get a prisoner over to court without help from you. You take care of your work."

If he told them it was Reed would it make any difference, Hank wondered. Or would it just sink Reed's ship as well? He started for the door.

"Jackson," LeBitche bellowed with the lungs of a drill sergeant. "Get the hell back here, boy, or your career is dead."

Hank turned back. He looked to Karis who was thoroughly enjoying the show. "Please," Hank said evenly. "Do the vest. The threat is real. Why take a chance?" And then he was gone.

"Gun and badge," LeBitche screamed.

The shout died behind the closing door. Hank squinted around the area. The sheriff's office was located on the edge of town, in a valley of sorts. The area across the road was a gently sloping hill covered with small oaks, a potential housing area some developer had bought ten years before. He hadn't sold a lot. Doyle had a rifle, Reed had said. Or Marlis had said, but Reed wouldn't say where she was at.

Hank squinted against the bright, warm sun and looked back at the pale green stucco of the office. Once the deceit starts it never stops, he thought. They didn't know it was Reed who'd given the suggestion that located the truck, or Reed who'd worked the confession out of Billy Bob. No, Hank, the kidnapper, the felon, just took credit.

Hank climbed into his brown squad car and drove out of the blacktopped parking lot and down the highway. But once around the corner he turned down a side street and doubled back and parked. He took the twelve gauge pump shotgun and stepped into the cool shade of the forest, working from the side, parallel to the office building. Doyle was a hunter, a woodsman; if he was going to shoot it would be from here. Hank smiled, it was what he'd learned from Reed, know your quarry, know how he thinks.

But could Doyle be here right now? Would he know Billy Bob had a court appearance scheduled? It was common knowledge on the streets.

A heaviness sat with Hank like the shadows in the trees. Small patches of briars and underbrush filled everything in so a man could hide almost anywhere. LeBitche's shout rang in his ears. He could apply for the U.S. Marshals or maybe even the FBI, Hank thought morosely. Reed knew people at decision-making levels in both departments. If he qualified, he'd be in, Reed had said. But would Sheila consent to leave her home?

Focus, Hank thought. What if Doyle was around?

He stepped forward, his low-cut, black leather policeman's shoes crunching on the leaves. Spit polish, clean and strake, but he knew his work, he knew procedure, he knew the law, even when he broke it.

He could fight LeBitche, but he'd lose. The sheriff would manufacture something that might ruin his life as well as his career. There were too many stories of how LeBitche had manufactured evidence in the past against his enemies. The man had no morals, no scruples, you had to be aware of that.

Hank peered out at the wall of foliage. It all blended

together. A man could hide anywhere. How did Reed do it, moving out here with armed men. And usually alone.

"Drop it, Hank," Doyle said. He materialized out of a screen of brush just down the hill. With his camouflage fatigues and lying perfectly still, Hank would have had to step on him. Or maybe been just directly behind, as he would have been in just a few more yards.

Hank's eyes shifted at the movement in front of the office. They were bringing Billy Bob out to a squad car. Doyle followed Hank's stare down between an opening in the trees. "Now," Doyle hissed, and raised the rifle.

Hank wanted to be brave, keep Doyle occupied until Billy Bob made it safely to the squad car. But the grim expression on Doyle's face and the twisted intensity in his blue eyes slammed home the pure knowledge that if he stood he was dead. Even as Hank dropped and twisted he saw the rifle buck in Doyle's hand. A sledge hammer thumped him high in the chest and he crashed down in a pile of leaves. He was conscious he could not breathe.

Be brave, he thought, lift the gun and fire. But there was no gun in his hands. Someone was shouting. A rifle exploded nearby. A second shot from Doyle? At Billy Bob? Leaves crunched and a pair of combat boots with nylon sides for quick drying, went past Hank's face. There were more shots, these from further away. The images clicked. A fifty pound anchor sat on his chest. He could not breathe. He strained against the incredible pressure in his chest and tried to cough. Flecks of blood splattered on the crisp, brown oak leaves before his eyes. That was not good, he knew and wondered then if he would die. Sheila would be sad.

Leaves crunched. Doyle? Back to finish him off? And then more footfalls, these running. "Over here," someone yelled. "Call for an ambulance."

Big Karis dropped at Hank's side. He looked concerned, Karis? It didn't make sense. Hank tried to move. Karis gently held him down. "Easy now, Hank. Help's on the way. Get me a first aid kit," he snapped over his shoulder. "As usual you were right. LeBitche was wrong. We'll leak word to the press about who did what. You can bet your spit-shined shoes on that."

"Billy Bob?" Hank grunted. Frothy lung blood bubbled at his lips.

"Why do you worry about him? After you drew Doyle's fire we were on the move. Doyle still got one that clipped Billy Bob's vest. He must be one hell of a shot. That's a hundred yards and we were on the move. Billy Bob shit his pants. Why you risked your life for that murdering tub of lard is beyond me."

"He was just killing deer. Doyle shot Wayne. Billy Bob didn't know what to do." Hank coughed more blood.

"Easy, easy."

"Tell Sheila I love her."

Karis spoke gruffly. "Tell her yourself. You may be the best man on this force. And maybe someday you'll be sheriff. And I may vote for you. But I still ain't your messenger boy."

Hank closed his eyes. He felt Karis squeezing his hand. All those years. All that work. Now he'd been shot in the chest by the man who had given him his first job, his first chance in life. He wanted to cry as if taking pity on himself. But he felt Karis's hand in his and he'd never felt so good.

He heard a siren. The ambulance.

Karis bent close. "You're going to make it, Hank. The ambulance is here. Your pulse is strong."

Hank thought he nodded. The ambulance. A chance. That was all he'd ever asked from life.

SIXTEEN

The concerned tone in Hank's voice informed Reed that Hank would do whatever he could to protect Billy Bob. Of course he should have informed the police about Marlis and the location of the houseboat. At least give the police a chance. But they were town and roadway cops. They were not experienced in the forest. Who knew what they might come rumbling in there with.

Reed beached his canoe so it was concealed under the thick willow brush on the edge of the island hammock where he had beached the first time. The question loomed, had Doyle returned? Would he return? Was he truly after Billy Bob? If so, he would return, Reed thought. But then would he come by land or by water? One lantern or two. Reed smiled. He was feeling all right.

The thickets along the shore were so heavy he couldn't begin to see the houseboat from more than ten or twelve feet away. Water would be the most likely approach if Doyle wasn't suspicious. But he could not cover the water from shore and he could not cover the shore from the water. The houseboat would be the best location, but if he approached the boat, Marlis just might shoot.

He decided the best bet would be to cover the approach by the water. He returned to the canoe, stepping carefully so he did not leave telltale tracks in the mud. He pulled the canoe through the thickets and onto shore, restored the damage to bent limbs the best he could and then hoisted the heavy canvas and wood canoe onto his shoulders. He staggered momentarily, managed to catch his balance, then slowly moved ahead.

Without the benefit of a portage yoke the canoe bore down on his shoulders and the top of his head. He walked bow-legged, quick little steps as he tried to maintain his direction and balance. He could see but scant feet ahead. He rammed an unseen tree and staggered sideways. Low hanging limbs abruptly stopped his forward motion and all but forced him to the ground. He grunted as needles of pain flared across his shoulders. If Doyle was on this island, Reed was one dead man.

Fortunately he only had to move fifty yards. But by then he was sweating freely. Mosquitoes and gnats homed in for a feast. Reed bent down on hands and knees to set the canoe on the ground and then he crawled out from underneath. He found an opening and worked the canoe through the soft mud and into the water beneath overhanging limbs. Just outside the limbs the water was covered with thick duckweed. If he'd come by water he would have been visible from the houseboat, and he would have opened a path in the weeds, left an obvious trail.

Reed covered the scuff marks made on shore the best he could, sprinkled some dried willow leaves to cover the stirred marks in the mud, picked up his pack, waded through mud and water, and quietly climbed into the canoe. He doused himself with mosquito repellent, carefully sawed a couple of limbs so he could glimpse the houseboat twenty feet away and then settled back. It was not the most comfortable place to wait, but it was the only place where he had a reasonable glimpse of the front and back of the houseboat. Of course Doyle could approach from the opposite side of the boat and Reed wouldn't see him until he was inside the boat.

Reed checked the lever action 30-30 he'd borrowed from Story. It was a mobile and accurate little brush gun, but he wouldn't mind having his familiar nine millimeter for backup. The problem was, of course, he couldn't just kill Doyle in cold blood like Doyle could kill him.

For a few moments Reed leaned back, resting, listening closely until he became intimate with the sounds of the swamp. A hawk keened in the distance. Insects buzzed. Something splashed. A frog slipped across the algae and weed covered surface just beside the canoe. Reed gazed down at the tunnel over the canoe, at his wet and muddy boots that were taking another beating. From the swamps of Louisiana to the halls of Washington DC, they were one good pair of boots.

Of course he was using Marlis as bait, some might say. Especially if he failed. Or then there might be those, like LeBitche, Hank had said, who asserted that Marlis ran off with Doyle because the two of them were long-time lovers. Indeed some people might assert Marlis knew Doyle had killed Wayne from the start. Whatever fit their narrow visions and preconceived notions. People were supposed to be getting smarter, more educated, more civilized. Somehow it didn't seem to be going that way.

Hank said he'd almost hit LeBitche for his speculating. Almost. The notion made Reed smile. Hank was a good man, until they'd forced Billy Bob to confess. One more friendship gone sour, which naturally brought him to thoughts of Pam, Stacy, and Trish. People were like cement, once cast they seldom changed. He'd tried. It had been a joke. Bile coated his mouth and he sipped from a flask of water. He'd always been a positive man, looked for the light. But these days life hung as heavy as that canoe had upon his neck.

Reed chastized his wandering attention. He sat up and peered out into the emerald and black atmosphere of the swamp. Redwing black birds trilled in the cane across a pool of water. The deep bluish-purple of a male indigo briefly flashed in nearby limbs. The air whistled as a flock of wood ducks wheeled overhead. Jumped by someone making an approach? Reed tensed. Mosquitoes droned. Gnats whirled like little black dots before his eyes. Something splashed in the lily pads across the way, a bass taking a meal? A green caterpillar moved on a leaf six inches from his face. A woodpecker drummed its mealtime song. The acrid odor of the distant burning of pine slash drifted through the air. The swamp teemed with life. Reed sat motionless, an integral part of the whole.

In time the isometric tension of sitting straight and motionless took its toll. His back ached. He leaned back, listening to the normal pattern of forest noises. He momentarily closed his eyes. A jet droned high overhead, the impact of man changing all that lay below. In a cosmic sense human beings were but an eyeblink. In all the universe the earth represented but one grain of sand in all the deserts of the world. Only the blind and unseeing would presume they were alone and unique. And yet he had his life, the here and now, a world to taste, experience, and enjoy.

He opened his eyes. The gloom of dusk invaded the swamp, smudging in the shadows and the enclaves back in the brush. Carefully, so he did not disturb the water, Reed sat forward and peered out at the pure black water populated with the thick grey trunks of cypress and overhung with tangles of Spanish moss. The pure white of an egret stood out against the dark of the opposite shore. A bream popped in the lily pads. Evening feeding time. It would take but a few minutes to go out and round up a meal. Fish were like people, whatever seemed easiest at the time.

Reed looked to the houseboat. There was no light, no movement. But he knew Marlis sat inside. What a life. There'd been promise once, but that had been taken away. People got off track, they got out of their natural element and then they were lost.

He felt the movement in his buttocks more than he saw the ripples. Something bumped the houseboat and Doyle materialized on the back of the boat. The stocky, square-jawed figure turned to tie up his pirogue. With considered stealth Reed raised the rifle and quietly cocked the hammer as he poked the muzzle through a tiny opening. He could shoot and kill Doyle, he knew, but he was never going to get him alive. So why had he sat out to the side?

"Don't move, Doyle," Reed shouted, angry that he'd been reduced to playing mind games like Marlis. Doyle turned and stared at the brush. If he was armed the weapon was not visible. And he did not bolt as Reed had expected. Because then he would have shot. "Federal warden. You're under arrest. Put your hands on top of your head."

Doyle, still half crouched, stared. In the gloom Reed could have sworn he smiled. "Well, well. You do get around."

"Move forward and come down this side of the boat," Reed ordered. Again Doyle refused to move. The best thing would be to shoot him in the leg, Reed thought. At least then he could not run away.

Abruptly, as if turning toward movement and noise inside, Doyle turned his head toward the interior of the houseboat. A shadow passed the window. Marlis. Doyle started to whirl and turn even as a pistol discharged and glass splintered over the back of the houseboat. Reed hesitated but a heartbeat, thrown by the shadow and Doyle's sudden move. The blur of Doyle disappeared with a huge splash into the dark water at the back of the houseboat.

Reed jumped from the canoe and clawed through the thick brush reaching out over the shoreline. The time to move was now, while Doyle was wounded, dead, or disoriented. He slashed in toward the front of the houseboat and vaulted onto the bow. "Marlis, it's me, Reed. Don't shoot." he called inside. He worked along the narrow side to the back of the boat. Ripples still stirred the black water but there was no sign of Doyle.

Reed crouched, eyes racing over the water and foliage that hung out over the water all the way along the shore. Was Doyle wounded? Dead? Was he armed? The pirogue had broken free and drifted fifteen feet away to the center of the small pond. A pack or something lay inside but Reed could not see a gun. He pressed lower on the deck and snorted as if in irony at the fact he'd just swapped positions, given Doyle the concealment of the brush and placed himself out here exposed in the open.

He whirled at the movement beside him. Marlis, pistol in hand, stood framed in the front doorway. "Get down," Reed hissed.

Marlis did not move. "Did I hit him?" she asked in a flat voice.

"I don't know. There's a spot of blood. It could have been flying glass. Now get down, Marlis. Doyle's armed. If you can't think of yourself, at least think of Jody and Patty."

"So then I missed," Marlis said and turned back inside and sat down on the floor.

Reed lay on the back of the houseboat and surveyed the water and the shoreline. The darkness deepened. If something moved, he would fire. It seemed to be his best chance. Although he hadn't seen a weapon and Doyle had yet to fire on him.

Ten minutes passed without a sign of life. Swamp life all but returned to normal. Something heavy splashed across the way. A swamp otter playing? A gator taking a raccoon or egret for a meal? A wounded man escaping the water? The pirogue had drifted even further away. A quarter moon provided wane light over the water. But the shadows were absolutely black.

Reed spoke softly. "Marlis, we have to get off the boat. It might be best if we get off into the water and swim."

"I can't swim," Marlis said. She giggled at Reed's silence.

"Could you tell if Doyle was carrying a gun?"

"I don't know. I do know that he used to have other guns that he took off the houseboat and hid somewhere."

"Damn," Reed muttered. "We have to move, and now while he might not be armed. Do you have a transistor radio on the boat?"

"Yes," Marlis said with some doubt.

"Crawl over here and bring it with you."

"Crawl?"

"If you show a silhouette at a window, you might just die."

Reed found one of those interminable AM talk shows and turned the radio on low, something that might make just enough noise to confuse or distract. He pulled Marlis to his side. "We're exposed here. We have to move. He could be on shore. We have to go into the water."

"I can't swim," Marlis said with a trembling voice.

"There's no choice," Reed said with a tone that left her no out. He took the nine millimeter pistol from her, checked the safety and stuck it securely in his belt. If he had to carry Marlis, he might not be able to carry the rifle as well. But for now he used the homemade rawhide sling Story had provided and slung the rifle across his back. With as much stealth as possible, Reed slid off the back of the pontoon and into the water where Marlis grimly clung to the low-cut transom beside the motor.

"We'll hang onto the boat and work around the side to where we can touch bottom," Reed whispered.

In the dark Marlis seemed to nod. The entry into an element with which she could not cope had destroyed her resolve. Her only thoughts now were to escape.

Reed spoke as soothingly as he could. "Don't kick with your legs or splash. Just move slow and look for a new hand hold. I have hold of one arm here so you know you can't fall."

"He was right there," Marlis said. "I moved forward a step in order to get a better shot. But then he saw me."

Something flashed in the night. The air moved. Instinctively Reed ducked beneath the surface and dragged Marlis with him. A tremendous explosion and spurt of flame ripped the black night air. A mild concussion rocked Reed under the water. He felt Marlis writhe in panic. As he kicked out and surfaced he faced a towering inferno of what had once been the houseboat. Some kind of rocket? A shoulder-held LAW?

But then Marlis surfaced, gasping, clawing to climb on top of something for support. Reed was there. He pushed out, trying to keep her clawing hands away, trying to move out of the circle of light. They were perfectly framed.

Huge water spurts erupted in front of him and the sharp cracking of a fully automatic rifle, an AK-47 he could have sworn, thundered from across the water. Reed dragged Marlis beneath the surface, manhandling her now, seizing her by the hair and viciously kicking and stroking toward the overhanging brush just down from the boat. Marlis clawed and thrashed in his wake, but he paid her no heed. Long tentacles reached out for his arms, shoulders, and head, closing around, gripping him so he could barely move. What? Reed surfaced. He was thick into the duckweed and could touch the soft muck bottom.

He hauled Marlis out of the depths. She was coughing, and frantically flailing for something solid to hang onto. They were still bathed in light. But fortunately they'd circled enough so the boat lay between them and where Reed had observed the spurt of light from the rocket. The crackle, snap, and roar of flames from the houseboat covered Marlis's desperate efforts to clear water from her lungs.

With one arm wrapped down across one shoulder and ribs, Reed dragged Marlis through the tangles of duckweed and in behind the covering foliage of thick, overhanging limbs. He glanced back, looking from inside a cone of light out into pure black. Doyle had an arsenal all right, an arsenal fit for a war.

They moved quickly into the foliage, working away from the roaring flames and scalding heat until they reached the canoe. Doyle had been across the pond. The time to move was now, before he reached this side.

Reed touched Marlis's thin, trembling shoulders. By nature she had never been a physical woman. Her fight and resolve of the last few days had taken its toll physically as well as mentally. The water, the explosion had taken her to the brink of death. She turned into his chest. "I want Jody, Patty. I want to go home," she whispered. She was coherent and she still had some strength in her. But it was a single-minded strength pointed only toward survival.

If they tried to drag the canoe across the island in the night it would take some time and make a tremendous amount of noise. Doyle would never expect them to emerge back into the light. They'd surfaced behind the boat. Doyle may have thought them dead. He could be on the island this minute, working down toward where some of the scalding flames had jumped up in the hot rising air and consumed some dried moss high up in a dead cypress.

"We're taking the canoe. We'll have to go out into the light. We'll work to the left through those weeds. Hang onto the side rail there and keep your head below the canoe. If we move down a few feet we'll be into the shadows and be able to climb into the canoe and paddle out of here. Have you ever been in a canoe?"

"Wayne took us once. He took Jody a lot. Jody used to like the outdoors. Like his father." Marlis fell silent, sagging against Reed as if for strength.

"We have to move," Reed said. He unslung the rifle and put it in the canoe within easy reach. They carefully pushed the canoe out from under the limbs and into the duckweed, staying low so the limbs provided a screen against their back and the canoe provided a screen against anyone across the water. They moved out into the orange light of the flames. An explosion from one of the gas tanks scalded them with heat and rolled a billow of flames into the sky. Black smoke rolled out over the swamp. A sharp hissing sound carried as pieces of the burning boat fell into the water. If he'd delayed ten or fifteen seconds they'd probably be dead, Reed realized.

Marlis grimly clung to the front of the canoe. Her movements were firm, controlled, as they pushed on through the weeds. They rounded the corner and moved into dark shadows. The water had risen to Reed's chest. "Climb into the canoe and lie flat," he quietly instructed.

He stabilized the canoe while Marlis crawled inside and they moved on. Twenty yards later, in more complete dark, Reed climbed inside himself and gave a couple of hard strokes in order to propel them away from shore. He glanced back. The flames were concealed by a black wall of foliage. But the orange light flickered out over the water and on the underside of foliage higher up. By morning the flames would be dead, and there might not even be a lingering sign of smoke.

When word got out they'd send in an army, an untrained army like the early days of Vietnam. It was what Doyle wanted. Men would be killed. He could die a man.

But why should Reed remain? He'd gotten Marlis out. Doyle wasn't his responsibility. Why risk his life?

Reed silently paddled on. His eyes were growing accustomed to the wane light provided by the quarter moon. He guided between a wall of cypress, pushed through some thickets of cane and drifted to a stop. Marlis, sitting on the front seat now, looked back. "Do you think you can make it on your own?" Reed whispered. He knew how voices carried over water.

"The police will get him," Marlis replied. "We don't have to. Not any more." She sounded concerned, for him, or for herself moving through the night?

"They're not trained or equipped. Doyle will get some of them before they get him. You just have to go north. Follow the North Star off the front lip of the Big Dipper. As much as possible stay with open water. When dawn comes keep the sun on your hard right."

Marlis considered the matter. "Why? What will you prove?"

"It's my job. It's what I need. Can you try?"

"I'll get lost," Marlis insisted. "But I'll try. If that's what you want."

"Good. There's mosquito repellent in the knapsack. I don't think they'll be too thick until it gets warmer. I'll leave you the rifle. You just have to cock the hammer with your thumb for the first shot. Flip the lever for the rest." Reed guided the canoe over to the spread roots of a dead cypress and stepped out onto a log. He grabbed extra clips for the nine millimeter from the knapsack and a string to tie the pistol to his waist while he swam. He stabilized the canoe while Marlis worked back to the stern and took the paddle and her seat.

Reed felt her breath warm on his cheek. Her hand briefly rested on the back of his. But as quickly as he turned his palm to show affection she pulled away. Even now. He was not Marlis's level any more than Wayne had been. Surely his divorce from Pam should have taught him something. People sought their own level, their own comfort zone. No matter how she might pretend otherwise, Marlis was gentility, born to crystal and sterling silver, used to smooth silk and pure pearls. Some New Orleans doctor, lawyer, or industrialist would take her in their homes. There'd be a thousand men who'd want Marlis for a charm, a trinket. Only Marlis was no trinket. Out of all that had transpired, he was sure she'd learned at least that.

"You're going to swim back across the swamp?" Marlis asked in wonderment. No, she did not understand a man like Reed, no more than she understood Wayne.

"It's only a couple of hundred yards."

"But. . . ." Marlis trailed off. She looked up to where Reed had showed her how to locate the North Star. "If I used you, and I did, I'm sorry. For years I didn't care who I used, just like Daddy. That was why I had to find Wayne's killer."

"Well that you did. Keep north. Stay to open water. You'll run across the freeway sooner or later. Then work back west. The seat cushion will serve as a life preserver if you need it. Good luck." Reed gave the canoe a firm shove out into the open and away from the line of trees. He watched until the dark silhouette disappeared and he heard only the gentle splashing of her paddle. But soon even the noise of splashing was swallowed by the night.

Reed checked his equipment to see the clips were safe and the pistol tucked securely and then tied. He checked the alignment of stars, the outlines of trees, and plotted a course back to the island hammock where Doyle, fully armed with automatic rifles and rockets, could still easily lie in wait.

He felt the rush of adrenaline, the old familiar excitement, the old Hemingway quote that once you'd hunted man, nothing thereafter would satisfy. Hemingway was right, Reed knew, and he'd never gone one-on-one deep within a swamp.

He slid off the log into black water and was immediately over his head. He took up an easy, careful breast stroke keeping his head and eyes above water so he would not splash. He set out across the swamp, gliding as quietly as an alligator.

SEVENTEEN

It took almost an hour to breast stroke and crawl and occasionally walk through the cane, weeds, between trees, and across the open pond. Already the telltale glow from the fire on the opposite side of the swamp hammock had almost died.

As Reed reached the outer line of duckweed and could touch in the soft muck of the bottom, he perceptibly slowed his pace. He'd quartered to one side so the dark shadows of a wall of cypress blocked the feeble light from the moon. Now a series of thickening cumulus clouds at times completely blackened the night. With great care he parted the weeds with his hands, then tip-toed ahead through the mud keeping just his head above the surface.

In time he was on hands and knees, and then crawling, inching along like some huge prehistoric worm slithering out of the mud. He reached dry land, crawled silently through the underbrush until he felt the trunk of a tree. He carefully rose to his feet, untied his pistol and turned it to drain water the best he could. In truth it should be cleaned, but normally it would work even after being submerged. A suspect pistol against an AK-47 Doyle must have snuck home from Vietnam. If Reed saw Doyle he'd simply have to shoot, just like in a war. After all, Doyle had fired at him. He had the cause. And he had the desire, and that made Reed sad.

Hank would have given Doyle a chance. And Hank would end up dead.

Reed shivered from the long time in the water and the cold night air. He dropped to one knee, took off his soft cotton and fleece shirt and carefully wrung out what water he could. If he'd been up north he would be wearing wool, something that, even wet, retained a measure of body warmth.

For a time Reed listened, drinking in the pure black of the night. He breathed gently, tasting the moist swamp air on his tongue, taking it into his lungs. He stepped gingerly ahead, touching his heel and then slowly rolling his weight forward onto the ball of his foot. The method gave him an opportunity to feel the earth for any dry twigs and to roll back or roll up over the twig before it snapped. He picked up a very slow, but steady rhythm, a ghost slipping through the night toward the faint glow of the burning houseboat.

The continuous trilling of bullfrogs, cicadas, and crickets had greatly ebbed from the early evening symphony. In the distance a barred owl gave notice of its presence with its cry of "who-cooks-for-you." Sometime later a cat screamed, bobcat, Reed figured. For all practical purposes swamp panthers around Louisiana were extinct. Reports were there might be fifty or sixty panthers left in the Everglades, but for the most part the encroachment of man's developments and the ravages of men such as Doyle and his gang had depleted numbers beyond redemption. Just another varmint to be eliminated had too often been the ignorant attitude. He knew of the old timers and their panther dogs. Once the female panther had been killed the dogs would eat the screaming cubs while their grizzled masters casually blasted their trophy out of the tree. For every hunter who was a conservationist there had to be two who simply did not give a damn.

As always such thoughts burned as a distraction at a time when Reed could ill-afford to let his attention wander. But the theme, as it always did, stayed with him. For all his acuity at moving in the woods, Doyle Monroe was as ignorant as a rock. God's Majesty set here to be harvested by man. Beyond that singular thought, Doyle had no need to justify his action. He was man, God's creation. Or was it the other way around?

A billowing whistle exploded to Reed's right and something crashed in the night. Reed whirled, pistol ready, heart thrashing even though he instantly understood he'd walked face to face with a deer. Several more times the deer whistled in the night, a loud warning to all something evil was afoot.

"Damn," Reed muttered. Unless Doyle was so close he

thought the deer winded him, the element of surprise had effectively been destroyed.

For fifteen minutes that seemed like an hour, Reed did not move. Patience, patience, the mark of the true hunter.

The thought struck Reed that if Doyle had sent home military paraphernalia such as a LAW and an AK-47 he could have other devices such as a claymore mine or grenades. Doyle believed in the good old American way, the populace armed to the teeth.

Reed quietly picked up his movement, angling away from the dim flames. He'd squat in the foliage and hide, wait until dawn. He walked into some tangles of thorn vines and backed and stepped just a little too quickly to his left. Something popped and the brilliant light from a trip flare bathed him in its glow.

Fortunately he'd been in this situation before, on both ends. At the pop he started to move, turning away, vaulting one direction and then another. He'd taken three long strides before the AK thundered in the night, a continuous burst, a thirty shot clip on full automatic. At the first zing of lead past his head Reed changed directions and dove into the weeds of a mudhole. Huge spurts of dirt exploded into the air. Bark slapped like shrapnel out of trees. Leaves fluttered to the ground.

Doyle wasn't so smart after all, sending the full thirty shots, a premature ejaculation out of which Reed again scrambled to his feet, running, dodging back and forth behind foliage and trees. He'd dropped down into a second depression before a second burst came his way.

Once in the shadow, Reed did not pause to look out or look back and give Doyle a target. On hands and knees he quickly backed down a slight slope, then rose and at a quick trot began to circle, moving on the outer limits of the circle of hissing flare light, changing his location while Doyle was concentrating on where he'd last been seen. It was easier here than in Vietnam. Here you only had to worry about one man.

Reed made half his circle when the flare finally fizzled, spurted a few times, and then died. Before the last light flickered dead, Reed glanced ahead, judging the hardness of the ground so he wouldn't leave tracks, picking out a thicket in which he could comfortably hide until dawn. He slipped between some branches and quietly settled down with his back against the truck of a tree. He was sweating and covered with mud. The dried cotton of his mouth moved slowly as if searching for water. The flow of adrenaline still kept him on high. He'd seen even experienced soldiers momentarily freeze in the raw white light of a surprise flare. Too often they had died. Who said going to Vietnam had been a waste? It had just saved his life.

Reed sat quietly, looking into pure black and listening to the night. In time his breathing returned to normal. His heartbeat slowed. He mentally settled in for the night, for the duration. If anyone moved it would be Doyle coming for him.

Time passed. His sweat dried. He began to shiver from the dampness and the cold. The way Doyle was armed he should get out of here. It'd be easy to do. Smart. A pistol was not something a reasonably intelligent man used to take on an automatic weapon.

But who said he was reasonably intelligent, Reed thought with some anger. He'd lost Pam, Stacy, Trish, his home base, the place to which he could always return for sustenance and rejuvenation. He'd failed with Marlis from the start. And then he'd ruined his friendship with Hank. Why the hell not take on an automatic rifle with a pistol? What did he have to lose?

No more than Doyle.

The thought startled him. The raw truth of the notion burned. He'd tried to be a good citizen, considerate, responsible, a leader in times of need. And he'd ended up like this, chasing himself like a dog chasing its own tail.

His shoulders slumped. He thought to curl on his side, tucking his legs up for warmth, get a little sleep. Sure he'd been hard on Billy Bob. But he wasn't Doyle Monroe casually shooting a game warden in the face. He'd been after the truth, justice, the fact of the law had simply stood in his way. For if the law pointed people toward civilized behavior, it too often stood in the path of justice and truth. Reed shook his head, the inane ramblings of a crazy man in the dark. He thought to laugh at how ridiculous he must appear, and then to cry at the anguish of his plight. He knew these nights. Too often he'd had a drink. You just had to get through them; wait until the light of a new day and then he'd feel all right. Usually the best thing was to sleep.

But not tonight.

Concentrate, get back to the swamp, back to the night. Be a part.

A single mosquito droned nearby. It stopped. Tiny legs touched his cheek. He gently crushed it with the palm of his hand. One large bullfrog croaked, over and then again. No other frogs replied and the big frog went silent, a hidden life in the night. A tremendous splash carried from out in the water. A deer? An alligator seizing a meal? A branch made a scraping sound like scratching across the stiff canvas of starched Marine fatigues.

Reed ceased to breathe. He cocked his head, nose raised, straining at the night. One leaf brushed another. Something scuffled softly, like a boot scraping the ground. Then silence reigned. It became so quiet he even feared that if he flipped off his safety the click would echo in the night.

In the corner of his eye a dark form loomed. A man stood poised, looking into the brush, pointing a rifle directly at him. Reed's chest ached from lack of air. He had not one drop of moisture left in his mouth. He sat motionless, waiting, ready to react. Although he should fire first.

With steadied stealth he moved his left hand, using thumb and forefinger to slide the safety down so it would not click. He slowly brought the pistol to bear on the looming form. And then off to his left, even further away, another branch seemed to slide across fatigues.

Reed slowly drew in air. He lowered his head in shame. Fear triumphed logic and he'd been fooled by a bush. But there had been movement. Of that he was certain. Doyle had passed some scant feet away. But going where? It didn't make any sense unless he was simply trying to escape.

He had to follow along, Reed knew. If Doyle wanted to hide in the swamp, it could take weeks, or maybe forever. Stealthily he rose to his feet in the pitch black of night and stepped out of his enclave. Slow and steady, step by step, he moved off in the direction he'd last heard noise.

Don't rush, he repeatedly reminded himself. Move slow and steady, like a tortoise creeping through the night. Other than splashing off a log, when did a turtle ever make a sound? The notion made him smile, a narcotic high like a runner's, a grim reminder of how much he'd used of his precious reserves. He wasn't getting younger. That was for sure.

He moved a few mincing steps, one arm feeling ahead, rolling his weight on muscles taut with isometric tension least he stumble in the dark and make a mistake. Then he stopped and listened. Nothing.

He moved half-a-dozen times and then increased his pace. A half-dozen more moves and he wondered if he'd moved too fast. Was Doyle now tracking him? Had Doyle heard him? Did he now lie in wait? And all Reed could see was the pure black of night. He shivered. His teeth rattled. He drew a deep breath to calm his nerves. He moaned, soft and low. No, he didn't moan. The moan had come out of the night.

And then the wind blew, the first time it had blown all night, a rippling puff rustling like sleet on glass as the wayward breeze passed on into the night. Reed tried to swallow the dried and caked mucus coating his throat. He smelled cordite, gunpowder he thought. And then again, this time to the left, but further away, the quiet, dragging moan of a creature badly hurt.

Every muscle went taut. Reed was acutely conscious of his heartbeat, his breathing, every rustle of his soft clothes, the squish of mud beneath his feet. In his mind he became a rogue elephant bashing through the trees. So much passion over the killing of a man.

He stepped forward, stopping, listening, the agitation of his mind churning like a madman. He wanted to kill, to stamp out this abomination who so casually destroyed the wilderness. For what was one human being?

So why should he become so hyper at the prospect of killing one man, a man who'd murdered in cold blood?

Doyle moaned softly. His fatigues rustled. He couldn't be more than ten feet away.

Reed stepped forward. Blood tingled in his fingertips. He could not see a thing, not even a shadow or a shape. If he closed to five feet he could shoot and still might not score a direct hit. Doyle could fire a clip, four hundred rounds per second, thirty shots and then level the forest.

A solitary bull alligator groaned from somewhere in the

swamp. Another puff of wind moved some distance away, a reminder of clean sunny days on Reed's Laser sailboat, seeing the puffs, knowing soon the wind would fill. Thunder rumbled from somewhere south, out over the Gulf. Could lightning be far behind? One shot of light and Doyle would be framed. If Reed could shoot as fast as a surprise flicker of light he could shoot him in cold blood. Yeah, right.

Reed paused. A sickness still roiled in his guts. He had all the justification required. And he'd killed men before. He'd felt a little bad. He saw the images clear, even several years after the fact. But he did not lose sleep. The kills were all just, combat, his life or theirs. But Doyle . . . it seemed like he'd be shooting himself. All those years, the community man, and now this.

Reed listened to the night. No breathing, no movement. What the hell? He gritted his teeth. How often had he lectured his young troops that a moments lack of concentration was all it took to die. An eyeblink.

The wan light of distant lightning flickered too high in the sky to penetrate the swamp. Almost a minute later thunder rumbled. The storm was a good ten miles away and moving who knew in what direction and how fast.

Something loud and metallic clanged in the night. Doyle moaned loud and long. Water splashed. Somehow Doyle had moved thirty feet away. More water splashed and Reed quickly set off in that direction. If Doyle had been a picture of stealth before, he made no efforts to conceal his movements now. Something thumped in the night. Brush moved like cane raking the sides of a boat. The pirogue! Reed moved faster, now making tiny hints of noise. An unseen limb smacked his mouth, splitting his lip and drawing the warm, salty taste of blood, liquid for his parched throat. His foot dropped down on water and made a significant splash. He froze.

The night air blew, rustling the trees. Distant lightning flashed, a wan light just enough to reveal a man standing in a pirogue and slowly poling out across the pond. Fifty feet, Reed estimated. No way he could hit that, not with a pistol and a dim flash of light.

He checked to make certain his safety was on and pushed the pistol deep into the front of his pants. He grimly waded ahead, through the cane and out into the tunnel of water extending down through what the lightning had revealed was a majestic cathedral of fully mature cypress.

Crazy, Reed thought. Did he want a kill that bad? Of course he could just as easily be killed himself. Besides, he could never swim and keep up with a pirogue.

He reached chest deep and began his quiet breast stroke, a muskrat crawl so his hands or feet never broke surface and made a splash. Lightning flashed. The pirogue was further away. But Doyle was on hands and knees, gripping the sides, head hung down between his shoulders. The man was clearly in pain.

So let him go. Let him stiffen, like a wounded deer. Doyle might just die on his own. But then he might not. Or keep after him while he was hurt, before he had time to recover? When you got them down and reeling, move in for the kill. Like bayoneting the wounded. What kind of man did something like that?

Reed swam on. From time to time he took water into his mouth, sloshed it around and then spit it out. Once or twice he let a little trickle down his throat, taking relief now with the faintly denied knowledge the bitter tanic acid and swamp bacteria would reap havoc tomorrow. He was, he thought as he took the water into his parched throat, a weak man.

He swam on. His movements became repetitive, numbing like the dull throbbing that hammered in his temples. What the hell did it all mean?

Doyle had risen and poled away, a hundred feet or more. The storm had moved closer. The lightning flashed more frequently. Tree limbs tossed in a rising wind. Bass jumped back in the lily pads. Alligators were on the move. Several smaller ones splashed nearby. Reed could only hope they were not so ambitious as to try to bite off more than they could chew. Nature's power, nature's glory, it filled his spirit with life. Come a storm and he took it inside himself and went into a frenzy of his own.

And then Doyle turned off from the thirty-foot corridor of water and, bent over as if he could barely stand, pushed the pirogue into the cane and disappeared.

Reed swam on. A larger black log glided across his path.

There weren't many gators deep in the swamp, but those about were active tonight. Lightning and thunder blended into a continuous symphony and tree limbs waved like giant arms and hands grappling in death throes with the wind. A freight train rumbled in the distance then rapidly moved closer, approaching rain, a solid wall drumming up from the side. And then Reed was engulfed.

He could not breathe. The deluge splashed so thick and hard he could scarcely draw a breath but for water spraying into his nose, mouth, and eyes. Lightning flashed like a laser searing his brain. Thunder exploded like a mortar round. Reed thrashed wildly through grey pounding rain and quickly struck for shore some feet short of where he thought Doyle had cut in.

He gasped for air. Thick lily pads and weeds encased his head, arms, and shoulders. He could not pull free. He reeled, thrashing in momentary panic before he found the calm within. He held his breath, thinking clearly. He pulled the weeds free with one hand and slowly gained his freedom. He moved on. Closer to shore hanging vines tried for a hold around his arms and throat. He wheeled in confusion, bent only on surviving. He found higher, albeit muddy land and groped for protection tight against the smooth bark of a tree. He was soaked, worn, exhausted beyond reason. He only wanted a nice warm bed in a nice cozy home and Pam feeding him hot soup. But for the rain streaming down his face he would have thought he cried.

How long he lay there he could not discern, eons, a lifetime. Somehow the storm passed. He barely moved. Mosquitoes came behind the passing of the rain. He doggedly covered his face and hands with mud. Then, sopping wet, he huddled with his arms covering his ribs, knees pulled up to his chest, chin buried toward his knees. The night dragged. His mind refused to work.

And then he realized he could see. Dawn had come unnoticed, filtered in by a covering fog that hung over water and land. From what he could see, twenty or thirty feet, Reed looked out over a jungle garden, a sea of ferns interspersed by the thick, grey trunks of mature cypress. Beautiful, he thought, a picture here and then gone, a portrait solely for him.

And for Doyle.

Without moving a body muscle or even turning his head, his eyes surveyed the forest. Thigh to waist-high ferns covered the landscape, blending together to form a continuous carpet that lost itself somewhere in the white shroud. The space above was relatively open, covered above the fog by a canopy of connecting limbs that formed a ceiling so complete that on a sunny day it could blot out the sun. The ground seemed to rise, a slight slope, as much of a hill as you'd find anywhere in the swamp. In the center, barely discernable with the fog, was a large rock outcropping. If he was back in Vietnam he'd look for a bunker up there, Reed thought; it was a natural.

Very slowly he turned his head, one way and then the other. The key was to keep movement slow and steady, not quick and abrupt. He slowly uncoiled his cold, stiff, and sore body. His muscles screamed in tearing agony. His lower back burned as if on fire, the old injuries reminding him of his fragile flesh. But he'd survived the night.

He should crawl, keep his head below the ferns. But he did not have the strength. He stepped ahead. His feet had been continuously wet for two days and the prune-wrinkled skin was beginning to peel. He moved without a sound. With the cloak of fog, soft mud, and gentle ferns it was relatively easy to do. He moved down toward where he thought Doyle had beached the pirogue. Every step was a deliberate progression and every few steps he stopped.

And then he saw the wire, lying like a coiled serpent across his knee. He backed off and carefully knelt and peered in under the graceful symmetrical tops of the ferns. In the world of dark shadows and long green stems the wire led to a trip flare, and just beyond that to the tiny curved green of a claymore mine. Reed slowly released his breath. He'd been that close and there would have gone the trip flare and then the claymore, thousands of tiny steel balls impressed in front of the marshmallow substance of C-4 explosive, benignly waiting to rip off his legs and then to penetrate the bodies of anyone who followed behind.

The knowledge seemed clear. It would be the way Doyle would think; reacting to his training in a time of crisis, to the only thing that seemed rational in his fallen world. The rocks on top of the small rise were indeed a bunker—Doyle's fortress, his last defense where he'd take on an army of men. If the water level wasn't so low he would probably have tunnels and spider holes all over the hill.

Keeping his head below the ferns, Reed carefully disarmed the trip flare and claymore. And then, staying on hands and knees and below the top of the ferns, he slowly crawled toward the water. Even if you knew booby traps were set you could not spot all of them, not in foliage as thick as this.

An hour later he'd covered twenty yards and located the pirogue; and a squashed spot where Doyle had lain in the ferns. Water-diluted spots of blood dotted the light green of flattened ferns. Tracks stood clearly in the mud. Reed bent close. The edges of the tracks were settling. Water in the boot grooves had soaked in. They were after the hardest part of the rain had passed, and at least two or three hours old.

Reed drew his pistol and set off crawling in the tracks. Dow low, beneath the ferns, the torturous trail led him on a distinct and twisting path. Standing up, peering down on a covering of ferns, the tracks were all but invisible. So he crawled, hoping the trail avoided the mines and tripwires. Of course, Doyle could have set one behind him after he passed.

In two hours Reed crawled up to the rocks. He was so caked with mud he'd gained ten pounds. As he neared the edge of the ferns he spotted what he was certain were firing ports. If he crawled out into the open and Doyle was looking out he'd die. But was Doyle looking out? It was pretty difficult for one man to watch 360 degrees out of a few tiny holes.

In cover—move slow. In the open—quick. Reed gathered himself then suddenly sprinted forward to one side of the rocks. Doyle's staggered tracks showed the man was hurt. Reed had no doubts of that. The entrance loomed, a trap door normally covered with a rock. But Doyle had been unable to pull the rock in place over the trap door. Reed gently touched the wooden handle and gently pulled. The damn thing moved. He gently set it in place and sat down to think.

When he opened that door he'd flood the interior with light. He'd be blind. And then how did he enter, head first, feet first? No, in Vietnam you went into these things behind a couple of grenades.

No, he did not want to die. To miss the quiet beauty of a fog-shrouded scene of dripping wet ferns and huge towering cypress. To miss the raging beauty of a storm as he'd experienced it last night. To miss the flash of a flock of wood ducks as they banked against a pure blue sky. To miss the graceful flight of a Great Blue Heron down a corridor of green. To miss the warmth and laughter of his friends, the feeling of togetherness, the warmth, like that of a family. A family. A part of the whole had died. An emptiness that could never be replaced. But at least he had the rest. He had to focus on that.

Reed sat patiently. He'd wait until Doyle showed himself and then he'd club him in the head—just like clubbing a baby seal. Yes, he was feeling all right.

Time passed. The fog burned away. The sun rose, a warm day steaming down through the canopy above. In part his clothes had dried and now he began to sweat. He became bored and plucked at chunks of mud as they dried. Two hours passed and he heard not a sound from inside the bunker. In time he crept back to the trap door and flung it wide. He peered inside, pistol ready. Nothing moved.

He waited another hour. He backed from the door and closed his eyes and buried his face in his arms, listening closely while he gained some night vision. With his eyes still closed he crawled to the door. His stomach sucked in as if touching the inside of his spine. The sandpaper of his tongue attempted to moisten cracked and dried lips. Do it, he thought. Abruptly, leading the way with his pistol, he dropped his head and shoulders inside the bunker. He jerked one way and then the other. Nothing, just a tiny room with a muddy floor. An M-60 machine gun sat off to one side. An M-60 for crissake.

But no Doyle.

As quietly as possible Reed dropped inside. There were a couple of different openings, mostly leading to firing ports. But through one low door was a plank floor. The only light flooded through the trap door and the small firing ports. Reed backed to one side and patiently stood, giving his eyes a few more minutes to adjust to the interior gloom. In time, with pistol off safety and leading the way, he stealthily crossed the planks, keeping his shadow so it did not fall across the opening of the low door. Dried, dark blotches of blood were splattered on the floor.

He poked gun, arm, and head inside. Doyle! He turned, finger squeezing. But then he stopped. The big, blond-haired man lay still, his head turned to one side, an AK-47 clutched and ready for use across his chest. Dead or sleeping? Reed quietly reached forward and then tried to jerk the rifle away. Abruptly the gun exploded, a hammering burst that flashed in Reed's face and slammed a line of bullets into the walls.

Before he knew it Reed had dropped to his knees. The acrid smell of gunpowder burned his nostrils. All those hours of stealth and silence and now his ears rang. How was he to know rigor mortis had tightened Doyle's grip? He'd been smart enough to jerk so the barrel pointed away, but if he hadn't? Hank and the boys would have had a time figuring out how he got killed by a dead man.

Reed sagged against the wall. He had no strength. In time he dragged to his feet and lit a lantern. He examined Doyle. "You poor, dumb Marine." The bullet Marlis had fired had entered just under the left front collar bone and exited out of the opposite shoulder blade, a quartering shot as Doyle turned away. He looked relaxed, a man in repose. Had he asked for forgiveness, a coming together with the Lord in his final minutes of life?

He'd spent a long time building this fortress, more than just the days since he'd lost his marriage and store. His mind had been pointed in this direction for a long time. The world had changed and Doyle did not want to be a part.

Reed found water, and dried provisions. He sat on the edge of the bunk beside the dead man and drank and nibbled at some dried fruit. Doyle had a narrow ideological view. What he saw he saw clearly. But like a teenager, what he saw was not all there was to see. A good man, and yet he could justify killing Wayne Pog.

For a moment Reed considered pushing Doyle aside and getting a little sleep. But no, he did not want to spend the night with a dead man and his thoughts.

Reed left things in place and crawled from the bunker. He closed the trap door and then slowly walked the trail down to the pirogue. He marked his passing well so the police could not mistake the way. With great effort he climbed into the tippy pirogue and slowly poled down the corridor. If he poled steady and didn't tip he might make the highway by dark. Tomorrow he could return with Hank.

He took off his shirt, giving his lean, wiry body to the healing balm of the sun. It gave him strength. Mud turtles dropped off logs as he passed. A bass surfaced out of a glass smooth pool. The black of an eight foot gator lay sunning on a sandbar. Doyle died and life went on. If Reed had died it would have been the same. He was tired, very, very tired. He wanted to go home. But of course he had no home. He'd wanted to kill. He knew he'd wanted to kill. But he had not. And somehow that made him glad.

A Southern Loon called its joyous and haunting cry, a wilderness cry, the cry of Reed's home, the cry of where he belonged. It sang within his heart.

Look for these other
Walker thrillers and adventure novels
you'll enjoy:

CABOT STATION, *William S. Schaill*—In the tradition of *The Hunt for Red October,* and *The Cruel Sea,* a vigorously authentic high-tech naval thriller. Cabot Station lies 3,000 feet below the surface—an undersea listening station and solitary, neglected outpost against surprise attack. Despite warming relations with the Soviets, the crew and captain find themselves called upon to investigate a mystery submarine that is quickly guarded from prying US eyes by two Soviet killer subs. Where has it come from? And how did it get past the navy's underwater detection network?

THE VESPERS TAPES, *Albert DiBartolomeo*—It all begins when Philadelphia schoolteacher Vincent Vespers gets a late night call from his brother, Frank. Arriving at a local bar, Frank, long connected with local hoods, introduces Vinnie to his Mafia boss. The Don is dying, and coerces Vinnie into helping write the Don's memoirs. So he and Vinnie make a series of tapes. Vinnie expects a few unhappy people, but he is not prepared for old ghosts that rise to haunt him, and the imminent danger his life is plunged into.

THE DEADFALL TRAP, *Barry Taylor*—Set in 1971 against a backdrop of President Nixon's ping-pong diplomacy to Communist China, a CIA rescue mission to Chinese occupied Tibet goes treacherously wrong. Taylor's first novel, SHADOW TIGER (Walker; 1988) won the National Writer's Contest Award. An exciting new author who picks up where Alastair Maclean left off.

"For sheer narrative punch, for intriguing non-stop action, Barry Taylor with *THE DEADFALL TRAP,* has proven himself a master of suspense adventure," *Clive Cussler* (Author of *TREASURE, CYCLOPS, RAISE THE TITANIC).*

"Taylor's second thriller is another bonanza for adventure buffs. Thronged with incident and diverse characters . . . tension mounts as [we] head into a final confrontation . . . Taylor builds an irresistible thriller." *Publishers Weekly*

"The political intrigue[s] are expertly woven into this taut and crisply written novel." *Booklist*

SNAKES IN THE GARDEN, *L. S. Whiteley*—A sardonic thriller in the *Presumed Innocent* class, about a rich, 30-something Florida real estate agent accused of murdering his grandfather. But if narrator Tom Clay didn't do it, who, out of his weird family and friends, did?

"Nice brittle characters . . . perceptive asides . . . more than a touch of acid in the clinches . . . and a plot that works. Who could ask for more?" *Robert Campbell*, (Author of the *"LALA LAND"* Series and *THE JUNK YARD DOG*).

"Here's a tangy cocktail of a novel; it generates a pleasant high and leaves a satisfying aftertaste. . . . a murder mystery reminiscent of Erskine Caldwell. . . . In short, this author has written an amusing, unusual and absorbing novel. I enjoyed it," *Joseph Hayes* (Author of *THE DESPERATE HOURS, ACT OF RAGE*).

"Whiteley's wonderfully captivating hard-cover debut . . . focuses on a southern family so quirky that they seem to be the by-blows of Holly Golightly and William S. Burroughs. . . . Brash, outlandish, unusual fare—with surprises for the reader throughout, especially in the confession. This time, Whiteley serves up a rococo, endearingly eccentric southern Florida winner." *Kirkus Reviews*

THE GREY PILGRIM, *J. M. Hayes*—A striking and original thriller (based on a true incident) set in Arizona on the eve of World War II, about the last armed Indian uprising protesting conscription registration. In 1940, a half-American half-Japanese *agent provocateur* is sent secretly to the US by the Kempeeitai to exacerbate the insurrection. Spanish Civil War veteran, now Deputy US Marshal, J. D. Fitzpatrick must deal swiftly with the consequences before someone gets killed.

"Wow! Here's one you shouldn't miss. J. M. Hayes is my kind of writer. *The Grey Pilgrim* is a clever plot, peopled with great characters," Edgar Award winning Author *Tony Hillerman* (*TALKING GOD, A THIEF OF TIME*).

LAIR OF THE FOX, *Daniel Pollock*—Islamic Kurdish terrorists steal poison gas from the Russians and take an American film crew hostage in the mediterranean. Then left wing actress Amanda Morgan becomes their hostage in exchange for the lives of the crew, and US Diplomat Paul Cyrus has to work with the KGB to set her free.

"The pace, the tension, the sheer intrigue are spellbinding. Great action. Dan Pollock is a bright new force in adventure writing," *Clive Cussler* (Author of *TREASURE, CYCLOPS, RAISE THE TITANIC*).

"Written with authority, this is a classic can't-put-it-down thriller," *Publishers Weekly*.

"Mr. Pollock knows all the tricks and has put together a can't-put-it-down book," *New York Times Book Review*.

WHITE ROOK, *J. Madison Davis*—A PI goes undercover in a white supremacist group to track down contract killers. The new novel from the author of THE MURDER OF FRAU SCHUTZ, Edgar nominee for Best Novel of 1988.

"J. Madison Davis has a knack for choosing fascinating milieus and creating compelling characters. He is a welcome new voice in the world of mystery fiction," *Gerald Petievich* (Author of TO LIVE AND DIE IN LA, and SHAKEDOWN).

"A spellbinding thriller," *Publishers Weekly*.

SPRING THAW, *S. L. Stebel* (with an afterword by Ray Bradbury)—A troubled young sea captain, anxious to prove his manhood, takes command of his father's sealing ship and sails to the far north where he is forced to confront his own ghosts and sins and those of his father, in a novel as refreshing and insightful as any by Camus or Hesse.

"Magical and mysterious," *Ray Bradbury* (from his afterword);

"Electrifying adventure-fantasy . . . impossible to put down," *Publishers Weekly;*

"SPRING THAW has a vigorous moral relevance, and its fablelike tale of love, betrayal, and redemption echoes with conviction." *Lawrence Thornton* (Author, IMAGINING ARGENTINA, winner PEN Faulkner Award);

"Whirls into a magical morality tale about brutality of the flesh and the spirit," *Digby Diehl, Playboy.*

"SPRING THAW is immensely enjoyable, a book with considerably more going for it than its evocation of ice-bound wonder," *Judith Freeman, Los Angeles Times Book Review.*

THE MURDER OF FRAU SCHUTZ, *J. Madison Davis* (Edgar Award nominee for Best First Novel, 1988)—a murder mystery set in a Nazi labor camp on the Russian Front at the end of World War II.

"Give it four stars and start reading," *The New York Daily News;*

"Exceptionally intelligent," *Kirkus Reviews;*

"Tautly-written, multi-layered fiction debut," *Publishers Weekly;*

"A damn good read . . . engrossing," *Parnell Hall* (Author of DETECTIVE and FAVOR).

"A first-rate novel," *John Casey* (Author of TESTIMONY AND DEMEANOR, AN AMERICAN ROMANCE, Winner of the 1989 National Book Award.)

IN THE MINDS OF MEN, *Max Owen*—A female Russian GRU officer has to go undercover in the US to track down a stolen American nuclear missile before detente is deliberately shattered by Hawks on both sides.

"Grandson of editor Maxwell Perkins, Owen has written a first novel that is refreshing and compelling," *Library Journal;*

"Owen's deft plotting evokes admiration," *Kirkus Reviews;*

"A solid debut," *Publishers Weekly.*

TROY, *Richard Matturro*—In an age when romance was unknown and heroes clothed in myth, this is the story of the carnage that surrounded one woman—Helen of Troy. Classical scholar Richard Matturro retells the tale of the ten-year Trojan war with a reimagining of this desperate struggle of heroes.

"TROY offers insights on the first and greatest Western epic . . . a new and refreshing perspective," *Publishers Weekly;*

"Lucid, thorough synthesis of legendary material with some contemporary perspective," *Kirkus Reviews;*

"For fans of mythology . . . TROY is a rare treat. Fans of good terse writing should enjoy it as well," *Daily Record, Troy NY.*

If you have enjoyed this book and would like to receive details of other Walker Thriller and Adventure titles, please write to:

The Thriller and Adventure Editor
Walker and Company
720 Fifth Avenue
New York, NY 10019